The Big F

JANE WENHAM-JONES

A division of HarperCollins Publishers
www.harpercollins.co.uk

Harper*Impulse* an imprint of
HarperCollinsPublishers
1 London Bridge Street
London SE1 9GF

www.harpercollins.co.uk

This paperback edition 2019

First published in Great Britain in ebook format by
HarperImpulse 2019

A catalogue record for this book is
available from the British Library

ISBN: 978-0-00-827869-4

This novel is entirely a work of fiction.
The names, characters and incidents portrayed in it are
the work of the author's imagination. Any resemblance to
actual persons, living or dead, events or localities is
entirely coincidental.

Set in Birka by Palimpsest Book Production Ltd,
Falkirk, Stirlingshire

Printed and bound by CPI Group (UK) Ltd, Croydon, CR0 4YY

MIX
Paper from
responsible sources
FSC
www.fsc.org   FSC® C007454

For all those in their fabulous fifties. And beyond ...

Chapter 1

Facing Fifty
Fighting Fifty
Nifty at Fifty
Shifty at Fifty
Fat at Fifty
Fit and Fifty
Fed up and fifty
Fucking Fifty!

*T*hey were all laughing like drains when we were writing the invite. So I tried to laugh too. Come to our Joint 50th Birthday …
Charlotte and Fay and Sherie and Roz. All four of us are hitting the half century this year, so it's going to be a ball. We've been planning it for weeks. A big venue, lots of friends, banners, balloons, fizz and strictly no Oh-God-I'm-Fifty tears …
That's what they tell me.
I am crying because that party is going to happen without me. I don't know how this nightmare is going to unfold but I know in my heart it won't end well.
I'm so afraid but I can't bring myself to tell them. Sometimes I take a deep breath and my mouth opens but I always close it again. As if the very act of saying it out loud will make it

real and I won't be able to pretend any more that things might still be OK.

So each time we add to the arrangements, I have to keep smiling. I have to nod and look pleased and thrilled at the thought of every last bloom and fairy light.

I must be doing it well as they think I'm as excited as they are.

They have no idea at all what's really going on …

Chapter 2

It was Charlotte's idea, of course. Charlotte loved any excuse for a bash and she wasn't going to let this one go.

'Makes so much sense,' she announced, tossing back her mass of fair curls. 'We pool our resources, friends and legendary organisational skills and put on an extravaganza.' She threw out her arms as if to include the multitudes. 'I'm thinking the pavilion. Broadstairs won't know what's hit it.'

Wine had been taken so immediately a committee was formed. Charlotte would be Chair, because traditionally she threw the best parties. Fay would be treasurer as she ran her own business; Roz quickly offered to take the notes, grasping an excuse to say as little as possible, until she'd figured out how the hell she'd manage this, while Sherie had laughed and smoothed back her expensively-streaked blonde hair.

'And I shall sit and look decorative.'

'There's a change,' Fay had growled.

'You can be Artistic Director,' said Charlotte decisively. 'Colour schemes?'

As they fell to discussing the various merits of silver and black against burgundy and grey, Roz had felt the familiar tightening in her stomach. Now, three weeks later, as she looked at the notepad on her lap where she'd rapidly listed the latest ideas tumbling from Charlotte's mouth for a party she couldn't begin to finance, her anxiety deepened. She could barely afford the coffee they were drinking and Fay had just waved her hand for more.

'We need to fix this date,' Charlotte was saying, lounging back comfortably on the squishy leather sofa in 'Le Café', the town's latest coffee lounge. 'The pav is knee-deep in weddings, of course, in June but they have got a Saturday in July–'

'We could always do a Friday–' said Sherie.

'But people who are travelling a long way might be at work till six.' Roz smiled tightly. 'Some of us have fixed hours!'

'The Saturday is the 28th,' said Charlotte. 'Shall I book it then?'

'Depends who wants to wait and who wants to do it early,' said Fay briskly.

Charlotte's birthday was just four weeks away in May, Roz's in late June. Fay's birthday wasn't until August and Sherie was the baby of the group, hanging on to forty-nine until late September. Or – knowing Sherie – several years longer.

'The mid-way point,' continued Fay, always the one they turned to for mental arithmetic, 'is around the 20th July, so that would work. She looked at Sherie. 'Are you OK with it being so long before yours?'

'Absolutely! I can be smug. I'll still be forty-nine.'

Sherie was smiling but Roz thought she looked anxious too. She was playing with a strand of her hair the way she used to at school when they had an exam looming that neither of them had revised for. Roz knew that for all the lightness of tone, that Sherie was the one struggling the most with her impending big birthday.

'Yes, well you're married and have children,' Sherie had

said sharply, when Charlotte had said that personally, she didn't give a fig about age, wrinkles or being menopausal.

'And I'll be young for one more week!' put in Fay. 'I think that timing will be perfect for me – I'll have just about got over the hangover when you all come round for cake.'

'Cake!' Charlotte's eyes lit up. 'Now what do we think? Are cupcake towers a bit passé – how about a profiterole mountain?' She settled herself deeper into the cushions. 'One of my clients had a sort of waterfall wedding cake with all these fish leaping down it – hundreds of them in different coloured sugar. They gave each guest one to take home. It was amazing – she's got pictures up on Instagram if you want to see.' Charlotte grinned. 'It cost two grand.'

'Lunacy,' said Fay dismissively, as Roz shuddered.

Roz knew that if she said anything about being worried, Charlotte would pay. Charlotte had settled the bill in the wine bar last time, picking up on Roz's unease as the evening wore on and the bottles kept coming, automatically being as kind and generous as she always was. 'I've just had a fat commission,' she'd said casually. 'Let me.'

Charlotte always seemed to have just landed a lump of money – her one-woman estate-agency-come-house-styling enterprise was booming. Word was getting around that Charlotte could secure top prices for homes in Thanet – often from well-off city-dwellers looking to relocate, referred to locally as the DFLs (Down from London) – and her bold, de-cluttering approach to getting the property ready for sale was going down a storm.

'Are you manic as well?' Charlotte asked Fay now, as the empty cups were cleared.

Fay rolled her eyes. 'Crazy. April's always busy but we're working flat out.'

5

Charlotte nodded. 'Did a woman from Waldron Road contact you? Place stuffed with antiques – I told her you were the best in the business.'

'Yes, thanks – I'm quoting tomorrow. Going to Sevenoaks. Thrilled with you. Thought you were bloody marvellous.'

Charlotte laughed. 'Even though she ignored most of my advice. You'll have your hands full moving her.'

'Can't be worse than Sir Wotsit with his grand piano ...'

Roz felt her usual pangs of inadequacy. There was Fay with her removal business and a dozen men working for her, Sherie with her jet-setting life as an art consultant, Charlotte with not only her own success but Roger bringing in a ton as a corporate lawyer. And then there was her. Single mother, lowly gallery assistant, struggling to find her council tax let alone the French school trip Amy had set her heart on ...

'You OK?' Sherie was looking at her.

Roz nodded as Sherie turned to the young man who'd arrived with a tray. 'Have you brought soya milk?'

Roz saw Fay roll her eyes.

Charlotte was still talking. 'I'm thinking of taking someone on to help with the practical stuff – especially as I've got a couple of empties. I haven't got time to keep lighting flaming candles and changing the flowers–'

'I'll do it!' Roz heard the squeak in her voice. 'I'd enjoy that,' she added, trying to sound casual. 'If it would help you out ...'

Charlotte beamed. 'Really? God that would be fantastic – I've been worrying about how to find someone I could absolutely trust. Even with half the stuff in Fay's storage, the contents in the North Foreland house are still worth a bloody mint. It's just a case of opening the windows, changing the perfume oils, maybe a little light dusting–'

6

'I can do that.' Roz breathed deeply, not wanting to sound desperate. This could be the answer to everything. She met Charlotte's eyes. 'I was thinking of looking for another small job ...'

Charlotte nodded. 'I would be very grateful.'

Roz exhaled slowly. Charlotte was lovely like that – making it sound as if it were she, Roz, who was bestowing the favour. Charlotte knew things were tight for her but she didn't know how bad it had got.

Fay was rummaging in her handbag. 'Fag?'

Charlotte rose majestically to her feet, and stretched out her neck, pushing back her curls again. 'I think so!' As they both headed for the door, Fay's tall angular frame dwarfing Charlotte's much shorter, rounder one, Roz looked at Sherie.

'How's things?' she said lightly.

'I'm off to the States next week. Some hot young artist in Brooklyn is the next big thing and I've got three clients after him, and then I've got Mum coming at the weekend–' She shook her head. 'You know what she's like – I'm not sure I can cope. And I've had a stream of builders round giving estimates, because I really am going to get the fireplace knocked out–'

Roz put a hand on her arm.

'Sticks?'

Sherie shook her head.

'Nothing.'

It was their joke. Sherie was gorgeous. All blonde hair and cheekbones and glossy lips – she spent more on facials than Roz put by for the gas and electricity bills combined – with a fantastic figure. 'You should be beating them off with sticks,' Roz had once said. Yet Sherie's relationships never lasted more than a few months. She'd been internet dating on and off for years but never seemed to meet anyone with that special spark.

'Too damn picky,' Roz had heard Fay say. Roz knew it was more than that, but certainly Sherie had an exacting set of criteria. Mr Right had to be a good-looking, highly intelligent, kind but appropriately macho, tall, liberal cat-lover who shared Sherie's taste in music and films, with a penchant for salad. The last hapless applicant for the role had been despatched in short order when it was revealed that he did not fully appreciate the beauty and brilliance of Cillian Murphy in *Peaky Blinders* and also took three sugars.

'A sort of possible on Meet-your-match,' Sherie said now. 'But listed one of his interests as junk food. I really can't be doing with–'

'It may have been irony,' interrupted Roz. 'Or he might be writing a dissertation on the subject. You can't dismiss someone before you've even met him, just because he might like the odd Big Mac.'

'Hmmm.' Sherie pursed her lips. 'Charlotte's putting it on again, isn't she?'

'She looks the same to me.'

'She really shouldn't be smoking.'

'No. But she won't stop if you nag her.'

'Fay's such a bad example.'

'Charlotte would smoke anyway – if she wanted to. In any case,' Roz was trying to be reasonable, 'don't they say that stress is the killer? Charlotte's the most laid-back person I know.'

'Well she hasn't got anything to worry about, has she!'

Roz glanced at her oldest friend. 'I expect she has her ups and downs like most of us,' she said mildly.

Sherie didn't have an awful lot to worry about herself, as

far as Roz could see. She had a beautiful apartment, a fabulous job, good friends and she looked a million dollars. But Roz knew there was little point debating it. As far as Sherie was concerned, Charlotte had the husband so Charlotte had nothing to complain about, ever. Nor did Fay, who had chosen to unceremoniously kick her husband Dave out, and since Roz said frequently that she barely gave men a thought these days – too tied up with Amy and trying to keep their heads above water – Sherie reserved all her sympathy on the relationships front for herself.

Sherie could be thoughtful and funny but Roz had noticed a bitterness creeping up in her as she got older on her own. She looked again at the list in front of her. 'Char's certainly wanting to push the boat out for our birthdays!'

She waited, hoping Sherie would say it was all too extravagant, that they didn't need to supply champagne on arrival or hand round the sort of canapés Charlotte was after. That the cash bar could start sooner, and a live band wasn't essential. So she, Roz, didn't have to.

Sherie nodded, flicking through the various pieces of paper Charlotte had left on the table. 'Yes, when she comes back, I really must say something about the catering.' Sherie smiled at the young man proffering a small jug, took it and began to pour soya milk carefully into her coffee. 'It's rather a lot to spend per head–'

Roz nodded. 'Yes it is. That's what I–'

'–if we don't accommodate all tastes.' Sherie lifted the cup to her lips, looking disapprovingly over the rim. 'Has she even thought about gluten-free?'

'So, the Princess is lactose intolerant now, is she? I thought it was yeast or wheat or something that was the devil?' Out on the pavement, Fay leant back against the bricks, inhaled sharply and blew out a long stream of smoke.

Charlotte shook her head. 'I don't keep up with it. When she comes to mine I let her inspect all the packets and bottles in case there's any fatal additive lurking in the gravy that might strike her dead and then she eats what I've got or she doesn't.' She took another drag on her own cigarette. 'Bless her!'

Fay rolled her eyes. 'Funny how nobody had food allergies when we were kids. I can just imagine my mum buggering about with tofu on a bed of quinoa or whatever it's called.' She laughed. 'Meat and two veg we had and God forbid if you didn't finish your potatoes.'

Charlotte laughed too. 'Becky's a veggie now. They all are on her floor apparently. I've told her she'll be cooking for herself in the holidays.' She blew smoke out. 'Unless it means I can finally get Joe to eat something green! If we can agree on 28th that will be great actually,' she went on. 'Becky will be home from uni – Joe will have broken up. Oh and so will Andrew of course. It will make it more relaxed for him and Laura – maybe they and Stanley will stay a few days. I miss Lu so much since Andrew got that bloody headship in Gateshead. I can't wait to see them.'

Fay frowned. 'We're not having kids?'

Charlotte stubbed her cigarette out on the wall and dropped the butt into a litter bin outside the second-hand shop next door. 'We're obviously having mine,' she said firmly. 'And Stanley is as good as family. And almost an adult!'

She strode ahead of Fay back into the coffee bar. 'And there's Amy,' she said over her shoulder. 'Come on! Let's get this show on the road.'

'Amy probably won't want to come,' Roz said, trying to keep her voice bright. 'Far too embarrassing.'

'Of course she'll come,' said Charlotte. 'I shall tell her I'm expecting her. AND she's got to put up with you mum-dancing.'

Roz shook her head. 'She really will go home then!'

'Anyway, no other damn kids apart from your own,' said Fay, swivelling her dark glossy head round to fix them all with a stern look. 'Plus a special dispensation for the son of Charlotte's best friend. Because they are coming to stay,' she added grudgingly.

'I thought we were your best friends,' Sherie was smiling.

'You are – but Laura is my longest-standing best friend and fulfilled the role on her own before I met you lot.'

Fay was still on a mission. 'Can't be doing with them running around screaming. Did I tell you about the little bastard in M&S?'

'Ours are all teenagers,' said Charlotte, shaking her head. 'Of course no small children – it's an adult party.'

'I gave his mother the benefit of my opinion I can tell you,' said Fay, satisfied. 'Offered to scream the place down, and then throw *my*self in the chilled chicken. See what *she* thought.'

Roz laughed. 'We have some right little sods on the school trips to the gallery too.'

'So, are you going to confirm the booking, Charlotte?' Sherie was looking bored.

'Yep. I'll call in to the pav and see Dan tomorrow. Tell him the Big Bash is on!'

'And sort some vegetarian options?'

'He's used to all that. You saw the list – there'll be a selection–'

11

Sherie looked doubtful. 'I think we ought to mention it. And put a note on the invitations saying to let us know about dietary requirements.'

'Or tell them to eat before they come if they're that fussy,' said Fay. 'Which is what I'm about to do. I need to get home, I'm starving.' She got up and swept towards the counter.

Sherie put her sunglasses in their case and also stood up. She was holding a ten-pound note.

Roz felt in her bag for money, hoping a fiver would be enough, but Fay returning and putting a card back into her wallet, shook her head.

'You get it another time,' she said easily. Roz swallowed. As if it were that simple. Which it was for the other three. If next time, the bill came to forty quid instead of twenty, they'd pick up the tab without thinking.

'Swings and roundabouts,' Charlotte would declare, if she ended up paying more than her share. Not realising that if Roz got the wrong sort of ride when it was her turn, she'd have to plunge even deeper into debt.

'Can't stand faff about the bill,' Fay was fond of saying as she'd swiftly divide by four, not knowing that the only reason Roz had been on water was that she was desperately trying to keep that bill to a minimum.

Charlotte scrutinised her as she said goodbye. 'Amy all right?' she asked.

Roz shrugged. 'You know – fifteen!'

She thought of her daughter's face earlier, screwed up with rage and disappointment. 'WHY can't we ask Granny?' she'd said over and over while Roz tried to explain.

'I just can't – the boiler was different – we had to be warm – I couldn't let you have no hot water. It was a necessity and you going to Paris isn't. And I hated doing it even then.'

Amy had pouted. 'Granny said she never minds helping – if only you were a bit more grateful. She said when she gave you the deposit for this house you barely said thank you.'

'Nice of her to be so supportive,' Roz had said tartly as Amy had banged out of the room.

One of the things Roz resented most about her mother was her total lack of loyalty and her indiscretion. When Amy went on her twice-annual visit to Carshalton to stay beneath her parent's well-appointed mock Tudor beams, she came back with a new set of clothes and a fresh tale of Roz's ingratitude.

'She wanted me to abort you,' Roz felt like saying. 'Because they thought a single woman in her thirties getting accidentally pregnant was too low-rent for words.'

Instead she tried to explain the difficult nature of her interactions with the woman to whom her status at the Rotary and Golf Clubs was everything and who had never forgiven Roz for being the one two hours away when her sainted brother had emigrated, when it would have suited her so much better had the geography been reversed.

Roz used words like 'beholden' – not wanting to be – and 'self-sufficient', something she'd hysterically promised herself in the hospital when her mother had brought a shawl and a stiffly-signed cheque for a thousand pounds and her father hadn't been allowed to come at all. But Amy barely listened, increasingly resentful of Roz's low-income and her own fatherless state that she blamed for money being so tight.

'Terrible teens,' Roz added to Charlotte now.

'Nightmare, I remember it well.' Charlotte looked at Roz harder. 'Everything else OK?'

Roz nodded, her stomach churning.

'So I'll text you about getting together so I can show you round both places and give you the keys, and we'll talk dosh. I was thinking an hourly rate.' Charlotte hugged her. 'I'll pay well as it's you, love.'

Roz squeezed her back, touched and terrified. The extra earnings would be good but she needed the job for more than that. For a moment she felt lightheaded as bile rose in her throat. Charlotte was the best sort of friend. Roz dug her nails into her palms to stop her feelings of panic overtaking her. Charlotte trusted her to complete exactly what was required. What would Charlotte say if she knew what Roz was really going to do ...

Chapter 3

'I really don't know what I'm going to do.'

Charlotte sat at her super-sized kitchen table, hands clasped around her empty mug, and stared at the piece of paper she'd been looking at for at least an hour before Fay had arrived.

Fay picked it up. 'In itself it's not exactly conclusive, is it?' she said, raising her precision-plucked eyebrows.

'There was the message as well.'

'And are you sure that was the same number?' Fay enquired.

'Yes. No. I don't know. I think it had seven, nine, five in it.'

'So do half the mobile numbers in the country.'

Charlotte sighed. 'I called you because you have an analytical mind and will take a practical approach. What shall I do?' Charlotte said again, a plaintive note in her voice. 'It doesn't feel right.'

Fay ran a hand thoughtfully through her short dark hair and pulled her chair a little closer to the table. 'OK. Let's go through it again. Roger was looking shifty and then he got a phone message ...'

Charlotte twisted the mug around again. 'No, he wasn't looking anything. His phone was plugged into the charger

15

over there. I was right by it when the message came in and I could see the first line of it as a notification on the screen. There was a smiley face and '*I'll put you through your paces on Wednesday when ...*' I couldn't read any more without unlocking it. And I couldn't do that because he was in the doorway as it beeped and the next thing he'd shot across the room and picked it up and read it. And put the phone back in his pocket.'

'Which isn't actually an admission of guilt,' put in Fay.

'So later,' Charlotte went on, ignoring her, 'when he'd left it on the side again, I tried to unlock it and it isn't the same code any more! Why would he change the number, unless it was because he didn't want me looking in his phone?'

'Well, why *are* you looking in his phone?' Fay fixed her with a searching look. 'Why not just say: who was that from?'

'I did – and he said it was someone from work.'

'Well, maybe it was. You know, a bit of banter. You should hear the way my blokes go on. They–'

'Well it clearly wasn't,' Charlotte interrupted hotly. 'Because later still, I asked to use his phone – saying I wanted to WhatsApp Becky and I'd left my phone upstairs and couldn't be arsed to go and get it – and–'

'He didn't want you to?'

'He handed it over as smiley as anything!'

Fay frowned in confusion. Charlotte's face was grim. 'And guess what? The message had gone. He'd fucking deleted it.'

Charlotte's voice rose. 'And it wasn't someone from work anyway, cos their number would be stored wouldn't it? It would say Fred or Dick. This was just a number ... It's some woman he's met in a chat room.'

'Oh come on!' Fay's eyebrows had risen further. 'That's

going nought to ninety a bit quick. Could be a colleague he rarely deals with–'

'Why the banter then?'

'Or someone he usually speaks to in person so they're not in his phone. OR–' Fay looked inspired, '– it was simply a wrong number. Which is why he deleted it. And he came across quickly because he was *expecting* someone from work …'

'You're not listening!' Charlotte said tetchily. 'He said 'someone from work', which is also odd because usually he'd say the name.'

'Why don't you just ask him again?'

'Because if he is up to something, I'm going to catch him at it. I'm not going to be made to feel paranoid this time.'

Privately, Fay thought it might be a trifle late for that. She frowned again. 'This time?'

Charlotte hesitated, still turning the mug round and round on the table. 'There was this girl in his office,' she said. 'Hannah. Bit of a bunny boiler. She had a crush on him and he was lapping it up till I found out.'

'Most men would. Did anything happen?'

'He said not. They had some drinks … She used to text him all the time though. Suppose she's back?'

'How long ago was this?'

'Six years or so. Laura warned her off initially before I got hold of it. By then Roger was panicking anyway because she wouldn't leave him alone and eventually she moved away.'

'Unlikely she'd reappear after all this time.'

Charlotte shrugged. 'I've looked for her on Facebook but I couldn't–'

Fay put hand on arm. 'Don't!'

Charlotte shook her head. 'I know! I hate myself for being like this and I hate Roger for making me.'

Fay spoke firmly. 'Now come on. We don't know he has yet. If that Hannah caused him trouble before, he'd hardly engage with her now, even if she did turn up again. And this Marion could be anyone.'

They both looked at the piece of paper Fay was still holding – displaying the name and mobile number in Roger's handwriting.

'A client for example' said Fay.

'He doesn't have clients any more does he? He's the in-house lawyer.'

'Who's negotiating a string of take-overs – he told me about it when I came for the curry. CTG are snapping up all sorts of smaller wealth management outfits, aren't they? Marion could be some hot-shot chief executive he had to phone back – or her secretary!'

'Yes, she could be. But my gut tells me she's the same woman who sent the sexual message. And I feel like I did last time. When I *knew* there was something up but I couldn't put my finger on it.' Her voice became bitter. 'And he denied it of course.'

'Well of course he did.' Fay's tone was matter of fact. 'You said – he was panicking.'

'And I have the same feeling again,' Charlotte went on. 'That he's hiding something.'

'Your birthday present?'

'I don't think so.'

'Look,' Fay leant her elbows on the scrubbed wood and looked hard at Charlotte. 'You don't have to wind yourself up like this. You simply say: Roger, I read that message and it sounded like innuendo and I couldn't help noticing when I was having a poke about, that you've changed the code on your phone. Why?'

'But then he'll make up something plausible that makes me sound like a mad, jealous old shrew and then I'll feel worse. And–' Charlotte stopped abruptly and stood up. 'Do you want a glass of wine?'

Fay looked at her watch. 'Yeah ok. Len's at the office. I don't need to go back.' She pulled out her phone and glanced at it. 'Just one.'

Charlotte crossed her kitchen and opened the huge fridge, returning to the big pine table with two goblets of white and a bowl of peanuts.

She sat down and took a swallow. 'What I'm going to do,' she said, putting the glass down and surveying Fay with what appeared to be fresh determination, 'is see what happens on Wednesday.'

She took another mouthful of her wine. 'If he's got a rendezvous planned then he'll have to make some excuse to be back late. So then I'll know. And if she – whoever she is – has been putting him through his paces, he'll find it was nothing to what I'll be doing when he gets home!'

'OK,' said Fay. 'So that's a plan. Sounds good. Now, how are we getting on with the party?'

She watched Charlotte, as her friend reluctantly allowed the subject to be changed and brought Fay up to date with her investigations into cake designs and balloon prices. 'Two hundred in silver, a hundred in this sort of pale lilac, and a hundred in burgundy – they look really stylish grouped together. And the pale ones will have burgundy lettering – The Big Five-O!'

'I like it,' Fay nodded. 'Helium?'

'Of course. Long strings so they come up from the floor, with shorter ones for the tables.'

'Brilliant.'

'I thought we could let them all go over Viking Bay at the end. Video it!'

'Yeah, great.'

There was a small silence. Charlotte had finished her first glass of wine and was pouring a second. Fay put her hand over the top of her own glass. 'Got the car.'

'If I even feel like having a party then–' Charlotte added.

'You will!' Fay ate a peanut.

'I wish I was more like you,' Charlotte suddenly burst out. 'You're so, so – *sure* of everything.'

'You are like me!' Fay grinned at Charlotte. 'First time I met you – when you were still with Wainwright's and there was that bloody woman with the poodles whose mortgage hadn't gone through – do you remember?'

Charlotte shook back her curls. 'How could I forget? You had two vans of her furniture outside and she was wailing and all those damn dogs were yapping.'

'We were already short of a driver – that's why I was there – and we had another job to load up the same day. I was about to land her one when you turned up.' Fay laughed. 'I can see you now. 'Enough!' you said. 'Calm down.' And even the dogs shut the hell up.'

Charlotte smiled.

'I knew then that you were my sort of woman,' finished Fay. 'We don't fuck about. We're toughies.'

When Fay had left, Charlotte poured another drink, pulling a face as thirteen-year-old Joe, arriving home from school and dumping his rucksack and sports bag in the middle of the kitchen floor, frowned at her. 'You're not drunk, are you?'

'Of course I'm not.'

She supposed it made a change from his usual repertoire

of grunts and for once he wasn't surgically attached to his phone or Xbox either. 'Fay was round,' she said, aware as she said it, of the effects of the wine on her largely empty stomach. She took the last handful of peanuts. 'Have you had a good day?'

Joe shrugged.

'Homework?'

'Haven't got any.'

'Don't believe you.'

He grinned at her and she heard his feet thumping their way upstairs, his bags and blazer left behind where they'd been dropped. She knew she wouldn't see him again until she called him for dinner and that he'd disappear straight after. She sighed. The house felt different without Becky. They'd done nothing but row before she left for uni – it was time for Becky to spread her wings – but Charlotte missed her daughter more than she could ever have imagined. If it had been Becky standing here, who'd seen that text, she would have tackled Roger at once. 'What's this Dad? Who's putting you through your paces? Sounds a bit strange ...'

Last time, she'd tried to keep it from the kids, but Becky had picked up the tail end of the hoo-ha. Knew there'd been a woman chasing her father and had been none too impressed.

Charlotte rose and opened the fridge door, pulling out a bowl of chicken pieces she'd dragged the skin from that morning.

Fay was right. It wasn't necessarily a repeat of anything like that. Roger had promised her. They'd made a pact never again to keep anything hidden, however bad. For a moment Charlotte felt a stab of guilt. She'd had a long conversation with Laura on the phone this morning. Lu had said she should be talking to Roger ...

She pulled a baking tray from the drawer next to the Aga and began to spread out the thighs.

She was fond of Fay – as Fay had said, they'd hit it off straight away. Now they often ended up with shared clients and Fay was always reliable and straightforward. Fay kept her life uncluttered. No commitments, no husband, no kids. She worked hard, played hard – saw things in black and white. Charlotte found her entertaining and she'd filled a gaping hole when Laura had moved away. Laura was emotional and sensitive and if she were here now would have listened endlessly to Charlotte's uncertainties and doubts. Fay was a fixer, but Laura would have hugged her and allowed Charlotte to debate the situation until Charlotte felt calm again.

She took a small sharp knife out of the drawer and began to slash at the chicken in front of her – squeezing more lemon juice over the rosy flesh she'd left marinating, trickling olive oil, adding herbs and black pepper.

As she sliced onions and crushed garlic, she wondered if Fay was right and she should just tackle Roger when he got in. But a part of her wanted to test him – to see whether he would be late on Wednesday, to prove to herself that the uneasy feeling in her solar plexus was the intuition that had been right before, and not the menopausal neuroses she could see Fay suspected.

She was chopping chillies when she heard his key in the lock. Hastily shoving the piece of paper out of sight, she listened to the familiar evening sounds, the jingle of his keys as he dropped them into the bowl on the hall table, the thud of his briefcase on the bottom stair – his low call of hell-oo as he walked into the kitchen already shrugging off his jacket.

Her gut twisted as he came in, big and smiling, the way he'd come in a thousand times before. He leant round her, bending to kiss her cheek. 'Smells good.'

'That's just the oven pre-heating.'

Roger looked at the tray of chicken, as she scattered the finely chopped chillies and sloshed in red wine. 'I can see it will smell good soon then!'

She bent to put the tray in the Aga and then turned and searched his face. He looked as he always did. 'You seem happy.'

Roger nodded. 'Yep, all going well. I've got a dinner with the chief exec of AG next week but it's all going through remarkably smoothly and–'

'What night?' It was out – too sharply – before she could stop herself.

'Err Thursday I think – is that a problem?'

'No,' she shook her head, turning away and pulling a bag of spinach leaves towards her. 'Just wondered. What about the rest of the week? Have you got a lot on?' She swung back to watch his face.

He looked surprised. 'About the same as usual. Do you need me to do something?' Was she imagining it or had that been a flicker of anxiety?

'I might need to be out a couple of evenings myself, that's all,' she improvised. 'I want to get together with the others about the party and I'm seeing a new client – she can only do after 8pm ... Just thinking about Joe ...'

'I won't be late any other night ...'

She felt the relief wash over her as she continued to gaze at him. He was looking pretty good at fifty-two. Grey hair suited him. He was a bit heavier than he used to be but he had the height to carry it off. He was still an attractive man.

Women would still be interested, but he was coming home to her. He smiled again. She could see he was wondering why she was so uptight.

'I had a funny text exchange with Bex today,' he said. 'She sounds buoyant.'

'Oh.' Charlotte pushed down the pang in her solar plexus. 'I haven't heard from her.'

Roger shook his head. 'It was only because she sent me a photo. Some bloke sprawled out in front of the TV watching football surrounded by beer cans.' He laughed. 'She said it reminded her of me. One of the boys down the corridor is an Arsenal supporter – she said the way he went on about it was like listening to me and Joe.' He draped an arm around Charlotte's shoulders. 'I'm sure she'll be onto you soon. Wanting advice on how to cook something – what was it last time – artichokes?'

Charlotte nodded.

'She sent you her love, anyway,' Roger added.

'That's nice,' Charlotte said brightly, wondering if this was true or her husband was just trying to make her feel better.

She smiled at him. 'Want a beer?'

'I'll just get this suit off.'

His suit jacket was still hanging on the back of one of the pine chairs, when the beep came. Charlotte waited. He didn't look towards it.

'Sounds like you've got a text,' she said lightly.

'It'll be Don. He was going to let me know about squash on Sunday.'

'Oh.'

She walked to the doorway. 'Joe!' she yelled, hating the way her stomach had clenched again. 'Chilli chicken!'

When she turned back, Roger had retrieved the phone and was looking at the screen. As she came towards him, he snapped it off and dropped it back into the pocket.

'Yep,' he said. 'Don's booked a court for nine.' Roger patted his stomach. 'It's going to be hard work – I've lost fitness doing all these long hours–'

Charlotte tried to read his expression. Was this an act for her benefit? Reminding her of the demands of work so she wouldn't question it if he came home late? Was it even really his friend Don who'd sent a message?

'Well, don't have a heart attack!'

'Nah, we'll take it easy – a couple of old gents together.'

Charlotte suddenly and inexplicably felt close to tears.

She knew how the others saw it. 'Hostess-with-the-mostest', Sherie always called her. She knew from the outside her life looked idyllic – the big family home in Kingsgate, the loving husband, the great kids, regular holidays and frequent entertaining. And it *was* good – she'd always known how lucky she was. She was the one the other three relied on to always look on the bright side, to feed and nurture everyone, to open a bottle, stick a roast in the oven and make everything all right again. She was a regular, if ageing, Pollyanna. Wasn't she?

Except now she felt strange. Lost somehow. Even when she was talking and laughing, these days she was always touched with a low-level dread as if something terrible was about to happen. For the first time ever, she lay awake at 4.a.m. worrying about things she'd usually not give a second thought to. She dithered over what to wear, felt anxious about something happening to one of the children. Or Roger. Bloody Roger – it was all his fault she was stressed like this.

Roger was supposed to be her best friend who she'd trust

with her life. She had once. She'd forgiven him for Hannah but she realised she'd never been completely at ease since.

As Joe ambled into the room, Charlotte busied herself getting the tray out of the Aga so neither of them would see the tears in her eyes.

Fay might think that Charlotte was as tough as she was, but Charlotte knew she wasn't at all ...

Chapter 4

Fay cracked three eggs into sizzling oil and expertly flipped the sausages browning under the grill, throwing a look at the young man lolling in her kitchen doorway. She remembered the evening she'd told the others about Cory.

'It's the perfect arrangement for both of us,' Fay had explained, smiling at Sherie's look of amazement. 'I get a lithe young body in bed with me and he gets a decent breakfast. When Cory stays with Tiffany or whatever her name is, it's chipped mugs and a biscuit if he's lucky.'

Sherie had looked appalled. 'You *know* he's got someone else?'

Fay had snorted. 'Of course he has! He's twenty-three – wants to be at it all the time – and I don't want him round more than once a week. I love to see him come–' she gave a dirty chuckle '–as it were, and I'm happy to see him go again–' Fay had enjoyed the way the others were gawping at her. 'Confident that he will return because he gets double bacon and toast with proper butter.'

Charlotte had given her a huge grin. Roz nodded with admiration. But Sherie, as usual, persisted. 'But don't you want–'

'Something long-term or permanent?' Fay was brisk. 'No thanks – I tried that and it didn't suit me. Can't be doing with someone hanging around all the time. I go through my front door and I shut it behind me and I thank the Lord it's just me. The only bit that bothers me is why on earth I didn't give Dave his marching orders earlier!'

'How long ago was it?' Sherie always wanted the detail.

'I don't know,' Fay's tone suggested she couldn't be bothered to work it out. 'Seven years or so. Best thing I ever did.'

Sherie had opened her mouth and shut it again.

As Cory came up behind her, and put his arms around Fay's waist, there was a moment when she thought what she'd told Sherie might almost be true. She pictured Dave walking away from her down the path, a rucksack slung over one shoulder, a bulging bag in his other hand. She'd sat quite still on the bottom stair, watching through the still-open front door. She had stayed there a long time.

Fay jerked back to the present as Cory nuzzled into her neck. 'Are we having hash browns?'

'I've got some fried potatoes in the oven.'

'That's why I love you.'

'Pah!' She nudged him off as she crossed to the coffee machine, blowing air out dismissively. 'Through your stomach.'

He often said things like that. The young were supposed to be thoughtless and self-absorbed and she'd have expected him to be off like a long dog once the wake-up shag was over, but he was always tactile and affectionate in the mornings. Would hang about after breakfast if it was a weekend, and talk to her about his job at the bakery, his family, his mate Josh who was earning a fortune in Canary Wharf but sleeping so little and sticking so much coke up his nose that Cory worried he would fall apart.

He asked Fay questions too but she told him little. He

knew she was running the business her late father had started when she was a baby, that she was divorced, that she spoke reasonable Spanish and could knit. But she was careful about anything more.

'Nothing heavy,' she'd warned, when he'd first come home with her after pitching up at Green's wine bar with a couple of pals, the night she was running the quiz. 'We're just doing each other a favour.'

She hadn't expected to see him again but back he came, week after week. Now he'd suggested they spend this entire Friday to Sunday together but Fay had just laughed. 'Do you really want to look at me sprawled on the sofa in my pyjamas with a facemask on?'

He laughed too. 'You wouldn't be!'

'I would. Weekends off are my down time. You can come Friday night and bugger off in the morning. And if you're very good, you can pop in Sunday afternoon for a cup of tea and a scone.'

'You sound like my nan.'

'I expect I'm older than she is.'

She certainly had a couple of years on his mother. Cory had mentioned his mum's forty-seventh birthday a few weeks ago. No doubt she'd be as horrified as Sherie if she knew where her little soldier had spent the night. Fay gave a small chuckle to herself as she pressed the button to take the roof down on her red Mazda MX5, liking the feel of the cold air on her face as she reversed out of her driveway and headed along the Eastern Esplanade. The sea was grey and choppy today, but the sun was bright.

Fay turned into Rectory Road and down through Nelson Place to Albion Street, looking at the restaurants and cafes that now lined the bottom of Broadstairs, so many more than when she'd been a child. She swung the car past Costa Coffee, wrinkling her nose in disapproval – she had banked there when it was still Barclays! – and up York Street, headed for the Pysons Road Industrial Estate where Sternhouse Removals had its home.

She put her foot down as she left the last roundabout, finding the wind whipping through her hair exhilarating. It was a lovely cold, sharp day. She would have liked to have reason to take the car for a belt up the motorway but the office called. Reluctantly she slowed down and turned onto the estate following the winding road round until her empire stood before her.

She felt the small rush of pleasure and achievement she got every time she saw the row of distinctive brown and orange lorries, parked outside the small glass and steel reception area with the huge storage facility stretching behind it. The business had been here for nearly fifty years – but it had tripled in size since she'd taken over.

'Morning Ma'am!' A young man in a dark brown boiler suit, with the orange Sternhouse logo, jumped down from one of the cabs and saluted her smartly as she walked towards the main doors. Fay grinned. 'Good morning, Toby.'

She crossed the small carpeted space with its four chairs, coffee table and water cooler, and through the door at the back. As she walked through the drivers' room, shaking her head at the discarded cups and day-old newspapers, a stocky man in his fifties looked up from a computer screen in the corner.

'How we doing, Len?' Fay kept going into her own office, propping the door open for him to follow. He rose and strolled after her, a blue folder under his arm.

'The Waldron Road woman has booked. But she wants to go on the 21st now. Which is tricky because we've got three other big ones the day before and her packing's going to take a day on its own.'

Fay threw her jacket on the hat stand in the corner of her office and flicked the switch on the coffee machine. 'Get some more bodies in from the casuals list.'

'I already have.'

Fay nodded as Len continued. 'We'll have to put Toby and Will on her job – can't trust that to just anyone – have you seen how much china she's got?'

'I did the quote didn't I? Speaking of which, I've got three more to do this morning. I hope Elaine's on time for a change.'

'It was only one morning,' Len's tone was mild. 'Her grandson was off school and her daughter had to get to work.'

Fay snorted. 'Elaine needs to get to work! There are a stack of invoices to go out as well.'

'It's not even quarter to nine yet.'

'Hmmm. Want one of these?' Fay slotted a pod into the machine and pressed the button, apparently intent on the dark stream of espresso that began to trickle into her cup.

'Yeah go on then.' Len sat down in her other office chair. 'How's your mum?'

'Still away with the fairies.'

'But OK? Being looked after.'

'She still thinks she's staying in a hotel but she's almost stopped asking when she's going home. Says the food is mostly OK but they can't cook liver. Wants me to have a word ...' Fay gave a sudden shout of laughter. 'I would but offal hasn't once been on the menu!'

'Ah,' said Len, affection in his voice. 'I liked your mum. Jean was a good woman. Your dad was devoted to her.'

'I don't know why – she was never off his back. Always bloody creating about something.'

Len raised his eyebrows and gave a small smile. Fay removed her cup and put another in its place. 'Don't look at me like that. I only create when it's justified.'

Len smiled again. 'That was just her way. She was kind to me. Sent round casseroles when both the kids were born.'

'I know – you've told me before. Are you angling for me to make you one or something?'

'Can't imagine you cooking anything like that.'

'Well, you'd be surprised.' She laughed again. 'I'll buy you a pint and a pie next week.'

'By the time we're the other side of this lot, we'll need it. And talking of kids–' Len pulled a large pink envelope from the folder. 'For Matthew and Lisa. We've had a whip round for flowers and a toy for the baby. Just waiting for you to sign now.'

Fay fished in her handbag and then held out a twenty-pound note. She didn't look at the cover of the card, just opened it and signed her name briskly in the bottom left-hand corner, before pushing it all back towards Len.

'Having kids costs a fortune these days,' Len said conversationally. 'And Matt has shaped up good. He's well past his probation period and I was thinking–'

'How much?'

'Another couple of grand a year – bring him in line with the other younger ones now he's trained.'

'I'll get Elaine onto it with the next payroll. Now what have we got in the pipeline to pay for all this?'

By the time the older woman arrived, Fay had been through the next week's job sheets with Len and he'd disappeared to round up the lads he needed for a relocation to

Hemel Hempstead. Through the window, Fay watched him cross the yard.

She'd been twenty-seven when she'd been called back from her teaching job in Spain because her father had collapsed with a heart attack. Len had been thirty-three then but he'd worked with her Dad since he was sixteen and knew what to do. She thought back gratefully to how he'd taught her the ropes in those awful early months, made sure the younger men showed her respect, came in early and stayed late even when his wife was kicking off, quietly supporting her as she threw herself into running and later expanding the business.

Now she could run it herself with one hand tied behind her back. But she wouldn't want to – she was glad Len was there to oversee the daily detail, work out the rotas, get the lorries serviced and make it all happen. He was a brilliant right-hand man, good at knowing instinctively who to employ, who to let go, not afraid to disagree with her if he thought she'd got it wrong. She'd tried to look out for him too, since his divorce, often taking him to the pub on a Friday – feigning polite interest in the pictures of his grand-children even though–

Fay gazed at her computer screen open on an excel sheet. Elaine was tapping away in the adjoining room, her back to Fay, everyone else was out on jobs.

She hadn't looked for days. It had been better since she'd banned herself from using the computer at home. Left her laptop at the office. And taken the app off her phone.

Fay's eyes locked on the icon in the bottom left hand corner of her screen. She'd sworn she wasn't going to do this any more. She hesitated, then almost robotically she double-clicked. Went through the usual motions till there it was. The mop of dark hair thrown back, the laughing face, squinting in the sun – if it were her, Fay, she'd have been wearing sunglasses. And in her arms ... Fay felt the familiar tightness in her chest, she was holding herself rigidly as if by keeping very still, she'd feel nothing. She breathed out slowly, looking at the golden-haired toddler, clutching the pink plastic spade. There were no new pictures. Nothing had changed.

She'd told Len she was trying to create a proper demarcation between work and leisure. He'd been approving – said she worked too hard, that the business was flourishing and everything was under control. She should have proper days off ...

He didn't know she left the laptop here, to save her from herself.

Chapter 5

Sherie pushed open her front door, dumping her case on the polished hall floor and walking rapidly to the foot of the stairs.

'I'm home! Where are you?'

Her heart quickened as she heard a small thump and his feet coming across the floor above her. 'Come and see me!'

She waited while he trotted down the stairs, then she knelt down and swept Marquis into her arms, burying her face in the back of his neck. 'You gorgeous thing – my beautiful boy – I've missed you so much!'

'Well here I am.' She straightened. Her neighbour, Nate, was standing in the doorway of her sitting room, in jeans and bare feet. She flushed. 'Oh, I was–'

He grinned. 'It's OK, I didn't think you were referring to me!'

Sherie smiled too. 'Has he been OK?'

'He's been fine. We've been watching TV like you said. Last night he enjoyed *Pointless*, got a bit restless during the news and went upstairs for a kip as soon as *EastEnders* started ...'

Sherie laughed, still hugging the silver tabby. 'Thank you so much. I am so grateful.'

She picked up her handbag from the floor where she'd dropped it, and began to pull out her wallet. 'How many hours –'

Nate frowned. 'I don't want paying. I like being here with the old chap.' He looked around him. 'Who wouldn't enjoy hanging out in a place like this? The light down here is amazing with those windows on all sides – quite different from upstairs.'

'I must give you something. It made all the difference knowing you were looking after him. I missed him but I didn't worry.'

Nate shrugged. 'Take me for a drink sometime.' He hesitated. 'Now even? I'm ready for a beer. Once you've unpacked. We could go over the road. We could eat there?' He stopped as she said nothing. 'Sorry, bad idea – you're probably exhausted.'

Sherie shook her head as Marquis wriggled in her arms. 'It's not that. I am really tired but that's not the problem – I've got to meet my friends in Green's. Sorry. We're–'

'Oh sure – well over the weekend or something.'

She groaned, lowering the cat onto the shiny floorboards. 'I've got my mother staying.'

Nate turned away, bending over to retrieve his battered leather mules from the corner of the hall. But not before she caught sight of the disappointment on his face.

'Nate, we will go for a drink as soon as my mother's gone – seriously, I'd really like to.' He was pushing his feet into the shoes, feeling in his jeans pocket for his keys. The last of the day's sun coming through the glass panels of the front door, lit up his blonde curls like a halo.

Sherie bent and stroked Marquis who was still rubbing himself round her legs, purring. 'Hey come on, let's have a quick drink now before I have to get ready. I've got some lager or wine? Or how about a G&T?'

'I don't want to hold you up.'

'You won't be. I'm shattered – the gin will perk me up. And I want to hear all about how Marquis has been and the new painting ...'

She walked ahead of him down the hall into her kitchen. 'Any more domestics from next door?'

After a moment, he followed her, perching on a stool at her breakfast bar as she opened the fridge. 'She was crying outside on Saturday night,' he told her. 'I asked her if she was OK but she'd clearly had a few and then he came down so I left them to it.'

The beautiful old flint house was divided into four apartments of various sizes. Sherie owned one of the larger ones – a two-bedroom maisonette taking up half of the first two floors. The other half was occupied by the Wilsons. He worked in the city and left at five each morning for the hi-speed train, she was apparently some sort of designer who worked from home. She seemed, however, to spend a lot of her day wandering about the shared gardens with a coffee mug in her hand, which Sherie strongly suspected sometimes contained vodka.

Nate, artist and lecturer, rented a one bedroom flat on the third floor above Sherie. Something she'd only discovered when he'd dropped a card through her door, inviting her to his students' end of year show because he'd heard from one of the Wilsons she was an art buyer.

She hadn't been able to get to Canterbury that evening but she'd made a point of seeking out Nate, hoping if she were honest, he might turn out to be fifty, cultured and distinguished-looking instead of a slightly scruffy, bohemian and young-looking thirty-two who could easily be mistaken for a student himself.

But he had immediately endeared himself to her over his appreciation of her gorgeous Marquis, exclaiming over his unusual markings and later presenting her with a sketch of the cat attempting to catch a bumble bee down by the lilac bushes. This was now expensively framed in her sitting room, opposite her favourite small sofa near the French doors onto the garden. Nate had said more than once he would also like to paint her.

'How's it going?' she asked now, dropping ice into two long glasses.

'Slowly. I've had loads of assessments to do but I'll get it finished by Easter now we've broken up.'

'I can't wait to see it – you know how much I love your work.'

'You can come up when it's done.'

'Did you sell the other one?'

'Not yet. I'm keeping it back for the show in the Old Town – did I tell you about that?'

'I don't think so.' Sherie measured out gin, and sliced lemons, squeezing a little of the juice into the cold spirit before adding the segments to the glass, listening as he told her about the exhibition of local artists with the theme of seaside that was being put on just along the coast in a small gallery that was the latest addition to the arty quarter of Margate.

She smiled at Nate. 'I'll be tempted to buy it if nobody else does – I love those bold colours.'

'Will you come to the preview?' He smiled back. 'Warm wine, bendy crisps – you know.'

'Yes, of course. If I'm here. What sort of tonic do you want? I've got light, ordinary or elderflower–'

'How posh!'

She laughed. 'My friends would tell you I'm just fussy.'

She used a long decorative glass stirrer on both drinks. 'There you go. Tell me that isn't the best gin and tonic you've had this week!'

He sipped. 'I think it's the best I've had ever. Down!' He added as Marquis sprang onto the surface and poked a paw at the other half of the lemon.

'How did you do that?' Sherie asked, as the cat jumped meekly back to the floor. 'He never takes any notice of me.'

'He knows you don't mean it.'

'You're right.'

As Marquis jumped back up further down the counter, she reached out and cuddled him to her. She knew she would never get tired of the warmth of his thick soft fur, the little chirruping noise he made when he ran towards her. 'I love him so much,' she said. 'I woke up in my hotel room and it felt all wrong because he wasn't on my feet.'

'He's the most indulged cat I've ever met.' Nate took another swallow of gin and grinned at her. 'I couldn't believe it the first time I saw that row of little pots of home-cooked this and finely-shredded that – all with his own little labels on.' He grinned again. 'Just in case he gets confused.'

'He really doesn't like cat food.'

'I'm not surprised.'

'No, honestly. I've tried all the different brands – including the expensive stuff. He'll eat the biscuits but he just cries if I give him anything else. It has to be fresh chicken or ground steak or tuna in spring water.'

Nate shook his head. 'He eats better than I do. He is funny though,' he went on. 'He loves that remote-control mouse, doesn't he? We must have played with that for half an hour.

Before I tucked him up with his cocoa and read him a bed time story, of course. Sprinkled a little lavender oil on his cushion so he'd have soothing dreams, reminded him to clean his teeth and pop his cashmere bed socks on ...'

Sherie laughed loudly. The gin had relaxed her and she felt warm and mellow sitting here with Nate in the last of the fading light. She crossed the room and put the under-cupboard lighting on, adjusting the overhead spotlights so they weren't too bright.

'I wish I wasn't going out,' she said. 'I'm bushed. I'd like another gin and a long bath and to snuggle up with my cat and hear what he's been up to. How many birds he's chased and what he thinks of your taste in TV.'

'Do you have to go?'

He was echoing her own thoughts.

'I'd better,' she said reluctantly. 'We're having this party together – a sort of joint birthday thing.' She avoided saying which one. 'Charlotte is doing most of the organising and she's bringing us all up to date with the menu choices and stuff. They already think I'm being a prima donna because I said it was all a bit pastry heavy, and they arranged it tonight especially so I'd be back – the others really wanted last night so if I cancel now–'

She swirled the ice in the bottom of her glass. 'Fay gets fed up with me at the best of times, and even Roz who likes me the most – we went to school together – she won't be impressed ...'

She stopped at the look on Nate's face, his expression of incomprehension mixed with pity, making her wish she'd said nothing. 'Sorry I'm making them sound–'

'Not all that kind,' he finished for her. 'Why do you hang out with them if they make you feel bad?'

'They don't really, I'm just tired and–' She stopped. 'I'm seeing things bleakly.' She drained the last of her gin. 'We have some fun times. They're my best friends in actual fact. I like them and I need them.' Sherie spoke firmly and then gave him a rueful smile. 'And they're all I've got.'

In the beginning she'd only had Roz. When she'd finally bowed to parental pressure and moved back here, her old school friend was the only one left she knew. Roz had met Charlotte a couple of years before when Becky and Amy had joined the same dance school and she had asked if she could bring Sherie to one of Charlotte's parties.

Sherie remembered Charlotte's big, noisy, crowded kitchen, the way Charlotte had thrown an arm around her – pressed a glass of champagne into her hand, introduced her loudly all around the room. 'The more the merrier, here, Love,' she'd said, adding 'literally' and going off into peals of laughter, and Sherie had been so touched and grateful she'd nearly cried.

'So you're glad now, aren't you?' Her mother, settled on Sherie's sofa the following day in an annoying flowered frock and a droopy cardigan and clearly limbering up for the usual address, never passed up an opportunity to say 'I told you so'. 'If you hadn't come back here, you wouldn't have these new friends of yours and you wouldn't have *him*–' she pointed a finger at Marquis who was sprawled across Sherie's lap. 'You couldn't have kept a cat in that poky flat.'

Sherie sighed. The poky flat had been a million-pound studio overlooking the Thames but there was no point debating it. Here, yes, she had big rooms, and high ceilings, and access to a beautiful garden and her beloved Marquis. He made it all worthwhile.

'Mind you, I suppose you might have met someone up there.' Her mother didn't waste a chance to have a dig either. 'But it's not too late,' she went on brightly. 'Just because you're too old to have children doesn't mean you can't find someone who's on his second time around.'

'Yes, thank you!' Sherie remembered to try to slow her breath, to draw in oxygen in a way that inflated her belly not her anxious chest, to let it out unhurriedly through her nostrils, to repeat the mantra she'd been repeating since her mother arrived. *She'll be gone tomorrow. Tomorrow she will be gone ...*

'And it's so important you're here to support Alison, especially with this move going on – she says you're a very good auntie ...' Her mother's tone had an air of faint surprise. 'Strange how life goes, isn't it? You were always the pretty one but Alison had the boys after her. And Luke couldn't wait to marry her and start a family, could he? She was pregnant before they'd even got back from honeymoon.'

She was pregnant before they went, you silly cow. For a horrible moment Sherie thought she'd said it out loud. Her mother was still talking.

'I know these young girls don't bother getting married any more, but I still say it's better for the children ...'

Sherie recognised her father's wisdom being repeated. 'How IS Dad?' she asked with a deliberate edge to her voice. 'Still ruling the roost?'

'He's been very busy in the garden.'

'If you moved here too, he could see more of his grand-children.'

'He doesn't want the upheaval.'

No, it was OK for Sherie to be pushed, nagged and bludg-eoned to move back to the town of her childhood – to be nearer to her sister when the youngest of her three nephews was diagnosed with slightly-impaired hearing, dyslexia and ADHD, but her father had managed to avoid following suit.

They were still in the cottage in Wye to which her father had wanted to retire for the walking opportunities, and from which he seldom travelled except to drive her mother to Thanet every third week and pick her up twenty-four hours later. One month she'd stay the night with Sherie, the following time the pleasure would fall to Alison. Her father would come in for a brief cup of tea when he collected her mother the following afternoon. If it had been Alison's turn to participate in this joy he would have invited himself for Sunday lunch first.

'What about what you want?' Sherie enquired. 'Wouldn't you like to be back here where you could pop round to see Alison and the kids whenever you wanted? Do some babysitting? She could do with that. Why don't you tell him?'

'Your father doesn't like—'

'Everything is about what he doesn't like.'

Her mother looked irritated. 'Don't start that again.'

Sherie couldn't help it. 'You eat what he wants to eat, watch what he wants to watch, you don't drive because he wouldn't let you, he decides how you spend the money—'

'It's called being married – you wouldn't know about that.'

Sherie looked back at her mother and held her gaze. 'It's called coercive control – there was a very interesting programme on it the other day. You should listen to *Woman's Hour*, Mum. You'd like it.'

'You always have to try to outdo me, don't you?' Her mother had gone pink. 'Show me how clever and educated you are with your history of art degree and your long words.'

Sherie was immediately, as always, washed over by rage

and shame. This was also her father speaking – he had long regarded his eldest daughter as 'above herself' and a subversive influence. Her plainer, dumpier younger sister with her children and dutiful attentiveness to husband and offspring was a safer bet and he made no secret of who he preferred.

'I'm sorry,' Sherie said more softly. 'But you really would like *Woman's Hour*. They had Sheila Hancock on the other day.'

'Your father doesn't like the radio.'

Sherie kept her voice even. 'Well have it on when he's in another room. You said he spends all morning reading the paper and doing the crossword. Why don't you listen in the kitchen? You've got that Roberts radio I bought you.'

Her mother's mouth made that little twist it always did if anyone confronted her. 'Why are you always trying to change me?'

'I'm trying to help you have a happier life.'

'Well try helping yourself – you're the one who's on her own.'

Her mother didn't mean it unkindly, Sherie told herself as she stirred the ragù sauce she'd made specifically because her father did not approve of pasta. Evelyn genuinely thought she was the one better off because she was married and 'secure' – even if she was constricted in almost everything she did.

Sherie thought of the scorn with which Fay would view her mother. Sherie sometimes wished she could be like Fay – so sorted in her singleness; revelling in her one-night stands. Fay implied that all one needed to be content was sex from time to time and she didn't seem to have any problem in getting it.

It wasn't sex for Sherie – although that would no doubt be nice. She wanted to fall asleep at night in the curve of another's body, to feel an arm tighten around her waist at dawn.

She wanted to feel the sort of love and devotion for a man she had only managed to sustain with Marquis. Though that wasn't strictly true – she shuddered at the memory of the times when she had felt that devotion and it had been misplaced.

'Too intense,' Rick had admitted eventually, when he'd started to make excuses not to see her.

'Didn't know we were married,' had been Phil's response when she'd discovered another woman's lingerie at the foot of his bed and dissolved into tears.

Scott, of whom she had once held such high hopes, had always been kind, even when he told her sadly, he couldn't offer 'that level of commitment'.

It had still broken her.

She didn't want to think about all the men from her various dating sites who hadn't even pretended to want anything more than sex. What was it about her? Was she too dull for meaningful conversation or a theatre trip? Too needy for someone to love her back? She'd tried being cool and aloof. They left even faster then …

After dinner, she put on a family drama because she knew her mother would like it, aware of the vague thump of Nate's music upstairs, suddenly wishing she was in the pub with him instead. Nate would be easy to talk to – she wouldn't have to choose her words, hopping across the subjects as if watching out for mines.

Her mother nodded as the credits went up.

'That's the trouble today. Everybody expects too much.'

Sherie kept her voice level and kind. 'You didn't, did you?'

Her mother gave that little sniff that always sent Sherie's nerves jangling. 'No, well, you didn't then. You accepted your lot in those days.'

Sherie had found before that if she made her mother a large enough gin, the truth would seep out.

'Do you ever wish it had been different?' she asked. 'That you'd pursued your career – been a legal secretary like you wanted to, instead of having us and staying at home? Or gone back to it later, when we were at school?'

He mother didn't look at her. 'No point wishing. We didn't want latchkey children. We wanted to give you and Alison the best possible start.' Her voice had taken on that slight drone as if reciting. 'But I did have a brain,' she said suddenly, in a different tone.

Sherie leant forward, almost dislodging Marquis who gave a small chirp of indignation. 'Of course you did – you do. You're a very intelligent woman. And it's not too late, Mum. You're only seventy-five – it's nothing these days – you could do an open university degree–'

'Poorh!' Her mother's lips vibrated with disdain.

'Or take up painting, or join a writing class – you like keeping your diary. You could expand it – write a memoir.'

Even as she suggested it, Sherie wondered what would go in into such a tome. An endless account of serving cups of tea and listening silently to a catalogue of bigotry and Brexit bile?

For a tiny moment, her mother looked sad. Then she sniffed again. 'I'm fine as I am, thank you very much.'

She looked across at her daughter. 'I know you're unhappy because Alison has the children and you haven't, but it was

46

your own choice. You wanted the big job.' There was a note of triumph in her voice as she took back the upper hand and delivered the customary coup de grace. 'And so you missed your chance.'

Chapter 6

'It was too good to miss.'

Roz, sick to her stomach as she let herself into the huge seafront villa on the cliffs at North Foreland – the most expensive stretch of coastline in the area – remembered the first time her colleague had explained where she got her apparently endless money from.

Melody, tall, dark and smiling had looked Roz directly in the eyes when she'd finally plucked up the courage to ask. They did a similar job at Turner Contemporary, the iconic gallery in Margate, and Roz was pretty sure, knowing her own salary, that she couldn't be funding her lifestyle from there.

Sure, Melody had a five-year-old who spent half the week with her dad and not a cash-draining teenager who was there full-time, and she'd been at the gallery longer so worked four days, whereas Roz rarely did more than three. But even so, working it out pro rata, Roz still couldn't see how Melody did it.

She'd noticed the clothes and the shoes and the handbags straightway and assumed her workmate had an inheritance stashed away or a generous boyfriend, but as the months went on, it appeared neither was likely.

Melody's parents lived in a council flat, she told Roz cheerily, and her last boyfriend was a waster she'd dumped when she caught him going through her purse.

'You'll be all right one day then,' she'd said, when Roz – loosened up by the leftover wine she'd had, clearing up after a preview – had confided that she had a difficult relationship with her well-off parents and had always tried desperately hard to avoid asking them for anything – even when Amy was a baby.

'There's nobody to leave me anything,' said Melody. 'What relatives I've got left have got bugger all!'

So when she came in, proudly dangling the keys to her new car, and was heard announcing the booking she'd just made for ten days in Lanzarote, Roz couldn't contain her curiosity – or desperation – any longer. Melody had to be in debt – she must have a fistful of credit cards maxed out. But as Roz knew to her cost, this could only last so long. She told herself it was concern that drove her to check out the younger woman's finances.

'Melody,' she began cautiously, 'I know it's none of my business ...'

Melody had listened in silence, given Roz a long appraising look, during which Roz had felt herself squirm, and had then broken into a wide grin. 'I'll tell you after work,' she'd said. 'Can't discuss it here.'

They'd gone their separate ways for the rest of the day – Melody to help set up the Foyle Room for a corporate event and Roz to sit on a chair in the South Gallery upstairs, to make sure nobody was taking snaps of *My Dead Dog* – a gigantic plaster cast of a flattened Alsatian – or pinching the artistically scattered 'ashes' of said deceased hound that were mingled with the array of withered flowers, which one particular visitor – probably off his meds again – had been attempting to do on a daily basis.

By the time the two women were sitting in the Lighthouse

49

Bar at the end of Margate's Harbour Arm, with large glasses of rosé, Roz was in a lather of curiosity and fear. She'd decided it had to be some sort of fraud – shoplifting wouldn't fund a new car – not unless she was stealing by the sackful and had a very good client base on eBay – and the only prostitute Roz had met in Margate was a sad, downtrodden woman who was barely paying the rent.

'It's totally the easiest, best way I've ever found of making money,' said Melody, clearly enjoying keeping Roz in suspense a little longer. 'I get to dress up, drink champagne, do a bit of play-acting – you know I like my am dram like you do – and I work from home, hours to suit me. I'm providing a service and I'm coining it in.'

'You're doing escort work?' Roz could hear the disapproving note in her voice, despite her best efforts to sound neutral.

'Nope!' Melody grinned. 'It involves men for sure – but I'm not sleeping with them.'

Roz waited.

'I thrash 'em!' Melody giggled joyously. 'Oh, Roz your face. I'm a domme!'

Roz gawped.

'You know, high black leather boots, fishnets, whip ... Or sometimes tweed suit and sensible brogues if they're having a strict teacher fantasy. I've got a plimsoll I use for a couple of clients and a proper old-fashioned cane if they want six of the best. Love, I only started nine months ago and they are queuing up, I tell you. One-hundred and fifty pounds an hour, two-hundred and fifty pounds for two. I've got more work on than I can handle–'

'And you don't have to–'

'Absolutely not!' Melody took a mouthful of wine. 'No

touching of any kind. I am very strict when I get going – they wouldn't dare. And I make it clear in the email I send first. Everything is on my terms and quite honestly I'm having the time of my fucking life – without the fucking.' Melody laughed. 'I can help you get started if you fancy it ... it's dead easy.'

Roz's heart was pounding in shock and excitement. As one half of her brain was reeling at the image of Melody strutting about with a whip in her hand, the other was calculating the income.

Eight hours would bring her in a thousand pounds. Even if she just did that once a month it would make all the difference in the world ... But imagine if she did sixteen hours. There would be money for school trips galore, and she could start to pay off her credit cards ...

'I don't think I could ...' she said, already wondering how she might be able to. 'I mean where–'

Melody had it all sorted. 'Well first, we'd get you an ad up on bendover.com and a Twitter account and then–'

'I mean where would I do it? Could I go to them?'

Melody shook her head. 'Not usually. I do it when Emily's at her dad's. One of my mates borrows her friend's house when the friend is working nights. She's a nurse,' she added helpfully. 'You don't need much – just a room and a chair really. Do it on your day off when Amy's at school.'

'Oh, I don't know,' Roz's stomach was fluttering nervously. 'I think I'd be too terrified.'

'Only at first,' said Melody. 'The first time I did it, I was shaking all over. I hit the vodka and by the time he arrived, I'd got so drunk I could barely walk. But he was such a sweetie. Eighty if he was a day and just over heart surgery. Said a damn good thrashing was the only thing that cheered

51

him up.' She looked wistful. 'I couldn't bring myself to do it hard – thank god it was only a slippering – but he was very complimentary. Brought his own cane next time and told me what to say while he stood in the corner. That's the good thing about domestic and school discipline,' Melody rattled on. 'All you need is a cane, slipper, hair brush and belt – costs nothing. My friend Julie spent fifteen grand kitting out her dungeon with all the leather harnesses, cages and queening stools! Mind you, she's earned it back threefold ...'

Roz sat in stunned silence, with no idea what the latter list of equipment was or what you'd do with it.

'But how did you know about all this?' she eventually asked faintly.

'I'm a bottom in my private life,' said Melody, matter-of-factly, 'so it makes me a good top – I understand what they want. But I don't take it for granted,' she went on, 'I take it seriously. I ask all the right questions beforehand so I can give them the time of their lives.'

Roz tried to visualise herself in thigh-high black boots, hitting someone's nether regions, and failed.

Melody sounded almost evangelical. 'The gratitude really makes it worthwhile. And you get given lots of stuff too – flowers, booze, jewellery, lingerie. Know that Anya Hindmarch bag you liked? That was from a punter who just wanted me to tie him up and then poke him with a stick while he licked my feet.'

'Really?'

'And then asked me to pee on him.'

'Oh my God!' Roz's hand had flown to her mouth. 'I just couldn't–'

'But that's the thing,' Melody said calmly. 'You don't have

to do anything you're not happy with – that's why you have the conversation in advance. If you don't like the sound of it, you just politely decline. You can always hand 'em on to me, just in case it's something I don't mind.' Melody chuckled. 'I've got a bit more broadminded since I started ... and the cash started rolling in.'

Roz's brain was still whirring like a fruit machine. Melody was now talking about her 'profile' and discussing 'speci-alities'. 'Doesn't take long,' she was saying. 'Come round to me one evening and we'll set you all up. Think up a name and I'll take a photo.'

Roz frowned. 'But suppose someone who knew me saw my picture? There's Amy to think about ...'

'You don't have to show your face. I've just got a photo of my legs in high boots and stockings, with a whip trailing down beside me. My friend Nina has her hair down over her face – you can just see her lips. Some of the girls are shot from behind – wearing a basque or something. Here – look.'

Melody dug in her handbag for her iPhone and began tapping at the screen. 'Some of them don't care at all. See this Sharon? That's her real name – she works in the Co-op.'

'Gosh.' Roz peered at the redhead in the low cut top staring into the camera with a stern expression. 'Suppose her kids' teachers saw it?'

'Well they're hardly likely to bring it up in assembly, are they?' Melody grinned. 'You'll get loads of interest as soon as you register – the chaps are always all over someone new. Email with them first – make sure they're not nutters or after anything too disgusting – and they'll tell you what they want. You need to use the right words. One of my regulars likes me to say 'smack bottom' not 'spanking' and I've got another one who wants me to hit him with one of the shoes he's wearing. You'll soon get the hang of it.'

Melody drained the rest of her wine in her glass and gestured towards Roz's glass. 'Take the money before you get started and remember they've probably got more to lose than you have if anyone else found out, so don't worry about that ...' She stood up and began to move towards the bar.

'We can do a two-hander one night if you want,' she said casually over her shoulder. 'I've got one regular who'd love two of us going at him. Give you a taster of what it's all about ...'

As Roz walked tentatively across the spacious panelled hall of the house Charlotte had entrusted her with, and pushed open the door to the vast sitting room with its large inglenook style fireplace and sumptuous sofas, her heart pounded at the memory of that first evening.

Melody had told her to dress as an 'authoritarian' – a school mistress perhaps, she'd added helpfully, or some sort of forbidding character. 'If you haven't got tweeds,' she'd instructed, (*tweeds?*), 'then think Ann Robinson on *The Weakest Link*.'

Roz had looked hopelessly at her wardrobe of sweatshirts and jeans before putting on one of the simple straight black skirts she wore for work and teaming it with a high-necked blouse and some pearls her mother had given her. She still looked rather timid and mousey.

But Melody had nodded, substituting Roz's low heels for a pair of her own perilous ones as soon as Roz arrived, and handing Roz a dark lipstick to apply. 'You'll do!' she said, grinning at Roz while Roz looked wildly around her wondering which door on the landing led to the bathroom in case she actually had to throw up.

'I'll do the talking,' said Melody as they went back downstairs. 'You just follow me.'

Roz had been unable to make more than a squeak in reply before Melody, dressed in a severe black suit with her hair in a bun, opened the front door and ushered in a weedy-looking bloke called Clive, who looked as terror-struck as Roz felt.

Clive had sat in the middle of the sofa while Melody, towering above him, had kept up a ten-minute tirade about the Clive's poor performance at work and then ordered him to drop his trousers.

Roz instinctively recoiled and looked away but Melody, handing her a leather slipper and giving her a small encouraging shove, stepped smartly forward to where Clive was bent over the arm of the sofa and brought what looked like a riding crop with a wide leather end down on his lower regions with an alarmingly loud crack.

Roz clapped a hand to her mouth as a small, shocked squeal escaped before she could stop it and Clive yelped in pain. Thwack! Melody brought the crop down hard again and Roz gasped once more. 'Miss Sterling is very disappointed in you, too!' said Melody, looking disapprovingly at Roz, who shook her head faintly. She looked queasily at Clive's quivering buttocks encased in a pair of green underpants decorated, somewhat incongruously, with a pattern of holly and reindeers. 'I'm not sure ...' she began, but Melody was issuing further instructions.

'Upstairs!' she roared. 'Now we're going to do it properly!'

Roz felt a small bubble of hysteria rise in her throat as Clive scuttled up the stairs after Melody, holding up his trousers.

'Bare bottom!' Melody yelled as Clive draped himself over the foot of the bed and Roz shot backwards onto the landing in alarm.

'I really can't ...' she spluttered, as Melody began to apply a matching leather slipper to one side of Clive's behind, beckoning to Roz to do the same. Roz took a deep breath, trying not faint with embarrassment, before stepping forward, and giving the unappealing white flesh a timid tap with the footwear in her hand.

'Harder,' hissed Melody, bringing down her arm with spectacular force. 'Please stop!' howled Clive.

Roz immediately dropped her slipper, nearly falling off Melody's heels, but Melody, not missing a beat, retrieved it and stuffed it back into Roz's hand. 'Not said the safe word,' she mouthed, giving Clive another magnificent wallop. 'Any more fuss,' she said to him sternly, 'and it will hurt even more ...'

She nodded to Roz. 'Go!'

Roz raised her arm and brought it down as firmly as she could. Clive whimpered. 'Six more!' said Melody, as Roz raised her arm again and they rained down blows in unison while Clive squirmed. Then it was over and Clive was dressed and downstairs and pushing notes into Melody's hand while thanking her profusely.

Roz sat weakly on a chair in Melody's kitchen as her friend counted out eighty pounds and handed it over. Roz looked at the four twenty-pound notes in her hand. The whole encounter had lasted barely half an hour. But she still felt light-headed.

She'd decided then that the only way she could do it again was to make an absolute rule about no exposed flesh, and to treat it like a role in a play.

Hadn't she received rave reviews for her depiction of a

wounded wife in *Where Does He Go at Night?* at the Sarah Thorne Theatre, when she'd gone for a part with the Hilderstone Players?

That nice lady afterwards – Sue someone – had suggested she auditioned for Mrs Gargery for the annual Dickens Play as a result. And *she* was a dominating sort.

Channel your inner Mrs Joe, she breathed to herself now, trying to still the hammering in her chest as she moved around the elegant rooms.

She'd had a string of part-time jobs before the position at the gallery had come up, always acutely aware that she had to fill the shoes of two parents for Amy and wanting to be there for her. She had taken the decision – perhaps wrongly, she thought ruefully – to live hand to mouth so that she could pick her daughter up from school. She'd worked in shops and pubs, as a dinner lady and a hotel chambermaid, so that the hours would fit, claimed what meagre benefits she could, just about scraping along and hanging onto the thought of finding something with a proper salary when Amy was older. Not realising how very difficult that would be, when she'd been out of the marketplace for so long.

When Amy was small she didn't really notice how poor they were – or show any concern about her lack of a father – but she sure did now.

'Perhaps if you'd bothered to stay in touch ...' she'd said nastily, as Roz tried to explain the limitations of just one income against a rising tide of bills and why high-speed internet could not be a priority.

Roz sighed. Didn't Amy think her mother longed to stop the constant juggling, the endless calculations, the daily decisions over how much to allow for food so that the hot water could still go on. Didn't she think Roz *wanted* to be able to give her nice things? 'Ask Granny then!' Amy would snarl. And so it would go on.

That was why she was doing this, she reminded herself, as she looked around for a final time, and waited – heart still banging – for the doorbell to ring.

She'd dusted, changed the flowers, rubbed a little essential oil along the tops of the radiators, so the place would smell lovely when the heating came on for its hour twice a day, and opened the windows wide in the downstairs utility room which had a tendency to damp. She'd ticked off everything on Charlotte's list before stripping off her jeans and changing into the high heels and short, yet demure dress that she thought would fulfil 'Colin's' desire for someone 'sexy yet prim' to beat the living daylights out of him.

She'd taken Melody's advice and entered into a detailed correspondence with the three men who'd been in touch since her legs, neatly crossed in a pair of high heels, appeared on the website.

She'd withdrawn from 'Mark' quite quickly when he'd expressed a polite desire for her to smear him in peanut butter (if she didn't mind) and then spread it on toast and eat it, and was still waiting for 'Jimmy' to reply with his exact requirements. So far it just seemed to involve him standing in the corner while she threatened him.

But Colin had seemed unfussy apart from wanting to have a clear view of her legs, and as long as it 'really hurt.' Roz looked at the cane Melody had given her and the leather slipper. Oh Christ, could she really do this?

She'd been pacing the hall for ten minutes, braced for it, but she still jumped wildly when the doorbell rang. Her palms were sweating so badly she was likely to drop the bloody stick before she could use it.

For a moment she thought about hiding in the coat cupboard till he went away, or telling him it had all been a mistake. Or even denying all knowledge and pretending he'd been the victim of a terrible hoax.

Then she thought of Amy's face when she told her she could go on the trip to Paris after all.

Roz took a deep breath and opened the door ...

Chapter 7

I left it so long because I didn't believe it. Nothing fitted with anything I'd ever read or heard. Breast lumps – I thought – were small and hard and you discovered them in the shower. Like a pea – that's what everyone always says. This wasn't even in my breast really – it was above it where there's a muscle anyway. It wasn't even a proper lump, just a sort of … thickening … It felt like something that could have happened because I'd pulled something. Or lifted too much.

Or knocked it.

I've been waiting for it to go away.

But it hasn't.

It's got bigger. And I can no longer pretend. I've Googled of course. And I thought at first it was probably a cyst. Easily drained and removed. Some go away all on their own. But not mine.

But I've felt stressed and stress can lead to all sorts of things. It could be some sort of inflammation caused by too much cortisol.

Or a fibroadenoma. 'A very common benign breast condition' the website says. Describing a lump that is rubbery and moves when you touch it. I think mine moves. I'm not sure. I've prodded it so much it's sore. Unless it was going to hurt anyway – in which case it can't be cancer, can it? Cancerous lumps are usually painless – it says that on several pages.

Apart from the forum where the terminal women were talking.
But everyone knows you don't go to chat rooms with good
news ...
If this happened to any of the others, they'd be decisive, and
go straight to the doctor and God knows they'd expect me to
as well.
I don't know what's stopping me. It is a lump now for certain.
So it's not as if I'm making a fuss about nothing. I will phone
tomorrow. I really will.
I'm just so, so scared ...

Chapter 8

Charlotte threw down the newspaper in disgust. 'Have you read this stupid woman interviewed here? She's saying she actually felt grateful to God when her husband went on blood pressure pills and they made him impotent!'

Charlotte glared at Fay. 'She says she's spent thirty years in a constant state of anxiety waiting for him to stray and now she finally feels confident she has him all to herself.'

'While presumably needing to stray herself,' said Fay drily.

'No, she says she's not bothered about sex and if she is at any time, frustration is a small price to pay for peace of mind.'

Fay pulled a disparaging face. 'Hasn't she heard of vibrators? Silly cow.'

'But how horrible to be always uneasy about what your husband is up to.' Charlotte gave a sudden wail 'I do not want to be like that!'

Fay sipped at the coffee Charlotte had made her and looked at her watch. 'I need to be at the office as soon as I've had this, Hun. Tell me what's happened.'

'That first Wednesday – Roger came home at the usual time and said he'd had meetings all afternoon. 'All very dull,' he said. But there was just something. He sort of didn't meet my eye ...'

Fay waited.

'But what could I do? He was here so if he'd seen that Marion then presumably it was in working hours and he couldn't have been with her long because he phoned me at two and he was in the car driving and then I phoned him at half four and he was driving again – said he was popping back to Ashford to go into the office for an hour and then he'd be right back. And he was here by seven so he must have come straight home. In fact, sometimes he's later than that if he leaves at half five and the traffic's heavy–'

Fay sighed inwardly. This wasn't going to be quick.

'So basically, he'd been at work.'

'I think so, yes, but yesterday–' Charlotte paused and Fay waited again.

'Yes?' Fay knew she sounded sharp, but she'd told Len she'd be there by ten latest and surely Charlotte had stuff to get on with as well.

'I phoned him around 3 p.m. and his phone was switched off. Went straight to answer phone. So I called him at work, and Libby said he was out of the office.'

'Right.' Fay drank a bit more coffee and resisted the urge to tell Charlotte to get to the crux.

'And she wasn't sure where.' Charlotte's tone suggested this was loaded with significance.

Fay sighed audibly now. 'Well, perhaps he hadn't told her. Doesn't mean he was up to no good.'

'Lib organises his diary. She's the most efficient woman on the planet. There is no way Roger would be in a meeting she didn't know about. She was covering for him!'

Fay shook her head. 'If she was, why not just lie and say he had a meeting with the ABC company and have done with it?'

63

'In case I checked I suppose.' Charlotte looked irritated. 'When I persisted, she was all vague about how he could be *here* and he'd mentioned he might pop in *there*. I didn't believe a bloody word of it.'

'Anyway,' said Charlotte impatiently as Fay looked sceptical. 'I was talking to a client the other day who said she's got some sort of tracking on her two kids' phones – so she can see where they are if they're late home from school or the daughter goes out in the evening. Says it stops her worrying so much. And I was thinking – that maybe you'd know about it. So I can do it to Roger.'

'What?' Fay heard herself almost squawk. 'You want to put a tracker on your husband's phone?'

'Yes.' Charlotte looked defiant. 'I do.' She got up and reached for the coffee pot. 'She said it's a feature on an iPhone – you do family sharing or something. I pretended I wanted to keep an eye on Joe. But I've Googled it and I don't know how to do it without getting into Roger's phone – and as I told you, he's changed the pass code. I wondered if you'd have any ideas.'

Fay frowned. 'Why would I know how to hack into someone's phone and why would I want to?'

'I suppose,' said Charlotte. 'I could ask him to do it for me and say I've been worrying about him having a car crash and also about Joe cycling back from football practice and could we all track each other's so we all know where we are all the time. I could say I was going to ask Becky too.'

Fay shook her head. 'He'll think you've gone crazy – and any self-respecting eighteen-year-old is going to tell you right where to get off. Anyway,' she went on. 'How would tracking him help him not to have a car crash? You could see that he was on the M20 but you wouldn't know if he was

64

whizzing along merrily listening to Drivetime or pulverised in a forty-car pile-up!'

'But if he refused,' – Charlotte was in no mood for logic – 'it would show he didn't want me to be able to see where he was going.'

'If he refused,' said Fay deliberately, 'it would be because he didn't want to go along with a wife who didn't trust him or want to allow him any personal freedom! How would you feel if Roger came home and said he wanted to track *you*?'

'I'M not doing anything wrong!' said Charlotte heatedly. 'He'd say no because then if he goes to this Marion's house, he'd know I'd be able to see which road she lived in. I've got a feeling it's in Maidstone.'

'Why?'

'There was a receipt for a coffee from the Wealdstone Hotel there. Look!' Charlotte got up and rummaged in her handbag. She slapped a small piece of paper on the table between them.

Fay looked at it, unimpressed. 'So? He could have been waiting for someone – or killing time before a meeting. It's not even two coffees, for God's sake.'

'Or waiting for her husband to go out before he went round ...'

Fay stood up. The conversation was making her feel sick and shaky inside. She spoke firmly. 'This is crazy. You haven't got a shred of evidence to support that there even is 'this Marion'. Why don't you simply ask him where he was yesterday afternoon at 3 p.m.?'

Charlotte scowled. 'I did, of course,' she said crossly. 'He said he'd gone over to Arnold Greaves – it's a company they're buying. But if that were true, Lib would have known.'

'Not if he popped in on the way somewhere else. Just to drop off some paperwork–'

Charlotte had topped up her own cup and held the pot towards Fay. She looked hard at her friend. 'Why are you defending him?'

Fay waved the coffee away. 'I am trying to be the voice of reason. Somebody needs to be!'

Charlotte sat back down and picked up her iPad. 'Well, if you won't help me do the phone, I will have to go to plan B. I've been looking at private detectives to get him followed. They can put some sort of tracking device on the car or follow them in person. But I can only do it on Wednesdays to start with, cos the one I spoke to wanted nine hundred quid a pop.'

Fay who had been heading for the door, spun back round, alarm flooding her. 'OH for God's sake! That's ridiculous. What ARE you thinking of? I'll follow him myself if you're going to spend that.'

Charlotte leant forward. 'Would you? Really?'

Fay walked back towards the table and leant both hands on it, looking straight at Charlotte. 'If I did, it would only be because you were getting so upset – not because I think it is justified in any shape or form. And because I can't stand by and let you waste money like that on some shyster who saw you coming.'

'He's been in the game for thirty years,' said Charlotte calmly. 'He was very nice actually. He's called Pete and he specialises in philandering spouses. I told him everything and he said it did sound as if Roger had something going on.'

Fay snorted. 'I'll bet he did.'

'He said he probably has a second phone anyway, and is contacting her on that.'

A dull rage thudded in Fay's chest. Second phones were something she did know about. 'Good old Pete!' she said coldly. 'It's what private dicks *do* – feed your fears so you cough up vast amounts for them to go on a wild goose chase for you.'

Charlotte continued as if Fay hadn't spoken. 'He said in 99% cases if a wife felt her husband was playing away, he usually was. He said he trusted my instincts.'

'And your credit card.'

'He said he could park near Roger's office next Wednesday and trail him.'

'So could I. And I'm free.' Fay spoke sternly. 'But there are going to be conditions. And we are not doing it yet. We'll see what happens first.'

Charlotte was looking at her like a hopeful child. Fay swallowed hard.

'So – this is the way we are going to play it. Next Wednesday morning you ask him what he's got on that day, and then you phone up and double check during the day with him or Libby or both. If he's gone AWOL a second time, at the same appointed hour, I will help you investigate. But not till then – OK?'

'OK.'

'No talk of phone-hacking or Dickhead Pete's illegal devices till then either.'

'OK,' said Charlotte again, with reluctance.

'Because you're being a bit manic about this Hun, and it's not good for you.' She stared at Charlotte for a moment longer. 'It seems very odd to be having an affair at the exact same time each week,' Fay went on. 'Has it occurred to you that Roger could be doing something private? Going to AA? Having therapy?'

Charlotte smiled for the first time. 'So, you don't think my husband would shag another woman but you are quite prepared to believe he's a drunk or a loony?'

'You'd better not let Sherie hear you say that! Doesn't she go to something where they all sit in a circle and tell each other their woes?'

'It's a chakra-cleansing meditation class.'

'Knew it was something bonkers.'

'It may be the only time the woman's available – or he's paying for her and it's when *he* can get away!' Charlotte looked aghast at her own new theory.

'Or perhaps he's having treatment for some strange medical condition he's embarrassed about,' Fay smiled, hoping to persuade Charlotte how farcical it all sounded. She didn't like the way her friend appeared to losing her grip on reality.

Charlotte shook her head. 'Oh no, believe me he'd tell me – he wanted me to look at his toenail the other night in case I thought it was poised to in-grow. I told him to go to a bloody chiropodist.'

Fay put her handbag back over her shoulder and prepared to leave again. 'Well there you are then – that's probably where he's been. Marion is probably shaving off his bunions as we speak ...'

'I wonder how old she is.'

Fay tried to be patient. 'We don't even know she exists.'

'That bit of paper– they'd arranged to meet for a drink.'

'It was someone he needed to phone. He'd scribbled it down when someone gave him the message. If she'd given it to him herself, he'd have put it straight into his phone.'

'No, he'd be afraid I'd see it.'

Fay stood up straighter. She was at the end of her

tolerance for this and needed to get to the office. 'I've got to go.'

Charlotte had lit a cigarette and seemed to be talking to herself. 'Hannah was younger of course – and that's the thing. You can't even breathe out and sleep easy when they're in their fifties. Nobody wants to look at us then but there are still all these young things impressed by an older man.'

She pushed the cigarette packet distractedly across the table towards Fay.

Fay picked it up. 'Speak for yourself!'

'Still seeing Cory?'

'Keener than ever. He is, I mean,' Fay added hastily.

'And you don't ever think–?'

Fay took a cigarette and abruptly changed the subject. 'Isn't it time we all went out for another drink? Discussed the party?'

'Everything is under control.'

'Well we may as well meet anyway – a gathering will cheer you up.' The sooner Charlotte's mind was on something else, Fay thought, the better. 'And we can talk about getting the invitations printed. And how many people we can each invite. We never got onto that last time – it wasn't exactly a bundle of laughs was it? Sherie wound up like a spring and Roz looking all traumatised. Did you find out what was wrong with her?'

'No, not really. I think Amy's being difficult.'

Fay inhaled. 'I'm glad I haven't got kids if they make you that jumpy. When you asked her how the cleaning had gone she looked as if she was being held at gunpoint. And wasn't she pale?'

'She'd had a bad night's sleep, she said.'

Charlotte ground out her cigarette and put her head

briefly in her hands before looking up. 'Fay – thank you.' For a moment, Charlotte seemed about to cry.

Fay twitched with her usual unease at displays of emotion.

'Charlotte,' Fay leant across the table and put a brief hand on her friend's arm. 'I'm going to be honest and then I really am leaving.' She took a deep breath. 'You're going over the top on this one. I've always thought you the most sensible woman I know. But – honestly Hun. Your reaction is totally out of proportion to what's happened. To what you actually know has happened – not what your fevered imagination is telling you.'

Charlotte opened her mouth as if to protest and then shut it again looking hopeless.

Fay looked at her friend hard. 'Is this only about Roger? Or is there something else going on?'

Chapter 9

'Where's it all gone?' Sherie looked around her younger sister's kitchen in surprise. 'I've never seen the place look so tidy.'

'Charlotte insisted,' Alison laughed. 'She's good, isn't she? She's absolutely transformed the place – go look in the lounge.'

Sherie went back into the hall and through into the other room. 'Wow!'

'Problem is keeping it that way,' Alison called after her. 'Containing all the kids' junk to their rooms is a nightmare. But I couldn't put their things in storage.'

There was a thunder of feet down the stairs. 'Shereeeee!'

Seven-year-old Oliver threw himself at his aunt, head-butting her in her middle so hard she gasped. The small boy threw his arms around her waist.

'Are you staying for tea? Are you? I want to sit next to you. It's my turn, isn't it, Mum? You said!'

Sherie crouched down and gave him a hug. 'I'm not staying this time,' she told him, looking straight into his eyes and speaking as clearly as she could. 'I've just come for a quick visit to see your mum. I'll sit with you next time ...'

'Why isn't he at school?' she asked when Oliver had been distracted from his disappointment and had thrown himself

71

through the back door and was hurling a football about. 'I was only whizzing in for ten minutes – I thought you'd be off to collect him soon.'

'We had an appointment with the educational psychologist – wasn't worth taking him back for only an hour or so.'

'And?'

Alison shrugged. 'They just want to monitor him for the moment. He thinks his behaviour may settle once we get the full learning support in place.' She sighed. 'It's been such a long bloody haul.'

Sherie reached into one of Alison's cupboards and pulled out a box of peppermint tea. 'Did you try what I said? Magnesium and zinc?'

'Yes, I read your email. I'll think about it.' Alison was suddenly brisk. 'It's not always easy to do fad diets with a family to feed, you know ...'

Sherie dropped a teabag into one of Alison's mugs and emptied the kettle onto it. 'It's not a fad,' she said, keeping her voice pleasant. 'Cutting down sugars and increasing foods rich in minerals is quite simple. You can give Ols avocados and bananas and nuts, and as a family you focus on lean proteins. It can only be healthy for you all to cut down on processed foods and eat more fish, fruit and vegetables, surely?'

'Yes, ok! I'm going to look at it.'

There was a pause. 'I'm glad Charlotte's been helpful anyway,' said Sherie lightly. 'Had many viewings?'

'A couple. But Charlotte's got six lined up for the weekend. All DFLs, she says. Mainly media people – apparently Margate is now the place to be.'

'Well I hope it goes soon, so you don't lose the other one. Sounds fantastic.'

'Well it will be when we've done it up. I can't wait for Oliver and Ant to have their own bedrooms, I tell you. They fight the whole time – it's doing my head in.'

'So Fay's storing your stuff is she?'

'Yep! And Charlotte said we should use her to move us as well.'

'Oh yes – she'll be very good. Have you met her yet?'

Alison shook her head.

Sherie removed her teabag and flipped it neatly into the swing bin. 'I think you'll like her. One of these salt-of-the-earth types – what you see is what you get and all that. Let's you know about her Northern, working class roots – calls a spade a spade and proud of it.' Sherie smiled. 'Even though she's been down here for ever and has a massive house on the esplanade. She is funny. I think she likes shocking people. But Charlotte says her service is brilliant.'

Alison nodded. She walked into the cramped utility room at the end of the narrow kitchen and opened the chest freezer. 'You can stay for tea if you like,' she said, delving into it. 'If you're prepared to eat sausages. They are good ones,' she added, with mock pointed-ness. 'From the butcher! Made with free range pork. Oliver would be thrilled and the others will love to see you when they get back.'

'I can't. I've got a date.'

'Oh?' Her sister raised her eyebrows.

'Though I don't know why I'm bothering – it won't be any good. It never is.'

'Well it won't be if you go with that attitude,' said Alison, suddenly sounding like their mother. 'Where did you meet this one?'

'Online of course, as always. Where else would I meet anyone?'

Alison put a large frozen package on the work surface and reached into the vegetable rack for potatoes. 'I don't know – where do most people find a partner?'

'I really have no idea!' Sherie knew she sounded sharp. 'He seems ok – good-looking enough in his photo, and we had quite a nice chat on the phone, but I don't know, it seems such an effort.' Sherie shook back her hair. 'I never appreciated how easy it was to be young. When you just slapped on a bit of make-up and got a pair of heels out of the cupboard and everybody thought you looked lovely.' She sighed. 'It takes hours now to even look OK.'

Sherie stepped into the hall and pushed her face towards the mirror. 'Ugh – look at my neck.'

'You look fantastic and you know you do,' said Alison flatly.

'There's so much to live up to nowadays,' Sherie went on, ignoring her. 'I was reading an interview with Kylie on the plane. My goodness she looks brilliant at fifty-one. Barely a line on her face, her arms all toned ...'

'Probably airbrushed,' said Alison. 'And stop fishing for compliments. You know your face looks loads younger than you are. Should do after all you spend on it,' she added tartly.

'Seriously–' Sherie began, feeling her voice wobble. She'd come here wanting to confide in her sister. Alison was five years younger but so often seemed the more mature of the two of them, with a wisdom Sherie didn't feel she herself possessed. She wondered what Alison would say if she told her everything. 'I'm tired of all this,' she went on tentatively, thinking she might ease her way up to it '–chasing around looking for a man, having to wax and pluck and exfoliate and moisturise and rub my dry heels just in case someone wants to take me to bed–'

Alison frowned in warning as Oliver reappeared, mud on his face.

Sherie smiled at the small boy. 'I sometimes wish I lived in a fairy tale and could just kiss Marquis and he'd turn into my prince.'

'Hmmm,' said Alison. 'You might have a problem with his breath.'

'Honestly, she's like my grandmother sometimes.' Sherie leant against the back of the wooden seat in Green's and rolled her eyes at Roz. 'Remember before she met Luke when she could be fun? She makes no effort at all now – no make-up, shapeless old tracksuits. She only dresses up to go to work and that's a sensible blouse from M&S. I bought her a beautiful top from Zara for her birthday – never seen it on her.'

Roz shook her head. If Sherie ever went on Mastermind her specialist subject would definitely not be 'Being In Another's Shoes' or 'Attempting Empathy'. 'Well looking after three kids is hard work,' she said. 'Is she still at the surgery?'

'Just in the mornings. She was supposed to be going fulltime but she wants to be there for Ols after school. Especially now.'

'We can't all be as glamorous as you ...' Roz smiled.

'I don't feel like that.' Sherie picked up her gin and tonic and sipped, looking suddenly emotional. 'Thanks for meeting me anyway.'

'What's the matter?' Roz twirled the plastic stirrer in her own glass and looked at Sherie quizzically. 'Is the big five-o getting to you that much?'

'It's not just that–'

'What then?'

'Oh, I don't know.' Sherie sighed. 'I'm too tired to explain.

I think I'd rather be spending the whole evening with you than meeting this bloke,' she added. 'I don't have the energy for it tonight.'

'Well at least you've had a stiffener.' Roz said practically. 'And you can say straightaway that you've got a very early start and can't be late. You can always change that later if you're having a wonderful time, but at least you've got an escape if not.' She looked at her watch. 'If you're with him at eight, you can slide away at nine thirty if he's a dork.'

'He actually sounded very bright. He's a marine engineer or something. But says he reads the *Times*,' Sherie sounded approving. 'And we talked about the direction of Three Billboards and he really rates Frances McDormand too, so that was good. And—' Sherie smiled. 'I asked about cats and he said he liked all animals.'

'What, even rats and headlice?' Roz smiled too. 'Well he sounds promising then, and you liked his photo. Who knows – he may be The One.'

'You've been saying that for years.' Sherie took another mouthful of her drink. 'They had a repeat of The Likely Lads on the other evening – I watched it because I couldn't be bothered to switch it off. I thought about us. It's such a sad theme song. 'What became of the people we used to be?' Have you ever listened to all the words? It really made me feel miserable.'

Roz shook her head. 'Hey come on – we're still here – just a bit older and more wrinkled. Well you aren't,' she added hastily. 'You look amazing – you really do.'

It was true – in the soft light of Green's Wine Bar, Sherie's complexion was flawless, and line free. Her eyes were luminous, her beautifully-shaped and darkly-lipsticked mouth dramatic against her pale skin. But once again there was a nervousness about her. For Sherie, Roz guessed, the milestone birthday was a reminder of what she saw as her failure to have nailed down a relationship. Sherie shrugged off all her other achievements – everything was about getting a man. And now, Roz suspected, she felt time was running out.

'You're beautiful,' said Roz honestly. 'You look years younger than the rest of us. Hey – could that be him?'

Sherie swung round to peer past the end of the booth they were in. 'Oh God yes, I think it is.' They both gazed down the long room to where the tall, fair, jacketed man was speaking to Sarah behind the bar. 'He's a bit bloody early.'

Roz downed the last of her wine and gathered keys and bag. 'Looks quite attractive from here. I'll pay for the drinks and be off. You can give him a wave in a minute.'

Sherie grabbed her arm. 'Don't go just yet. I've suddenly got cold feet about this ...'

She woke in the early hours, feeling warm breath close to her cheek. For a moment she was startled, her body jolting into a sitting position in alarm. Then she looked round, her muscles relaxing as she sunk back into the pillows with relief, as she remembered.

Greg was indeed attractive. And attentive. And generous – he'd insisted on paying for their food and wine. He'd listened with interest while she described her job and wanted to know about her family. He was wearing a very nice shirt. Sherie had felt herself unwind as they shared a seafood platter and drank a crisp, cold Chablis, dismissing her earlier misgivings as nerves.

She heard Roz's voice in her head about snap judgements and making allowances for the bloke possibly being nervous too. So when he'd made a slightly dismissive comment about the gender pay gap, she'd reminded herself he worked in a very male-dominated environment – there were no female marine engineers at all on his shipping line, he told her – so he probably simply hadn't really thought it through.

He was, after all, a champion of women generally – he described his two sisters in glowing terms – going into considerable detail about Jennifer's abilities as an accountant and Sylvie's talent as a music therapist. For a moment the reverence with which he spoke about both of them made Sherie uncomfortable, but then he explained sombrely that his mother had died when he was fourteen so his older siblings had been like parents to him ...

Sherie found herself admitting that her relationship with her own parents was not always easy and he had nodded sympathetically, confiding that he hadn't seen his father since he'd left home at eighteen. 'A terrible temper,' he said. 'I would never shout at a child the way he yelled at us.'

But he didn't regret not having children himself – he had five nephews and nieces who all loved Uncle Greg. He had laughed and got his phone out to show her a picture of a group of grinning kids in a garden with a trampoline in the background, and she had been able to tell him about her beloved Oliver and how worried they had all been when he was having such a hard time at school.

Sherie wasn't used to revealing so much personal stuff on a first date. At first she answered his questions awkwardly but Greg seemed genuinely to want to know all about her and was open about his own life – explaining how he'd never married or even lived with anyone for long – being deep-sea so much. But that now he'd retired from that and was working on the cross-channel ferries, he was hoping to meet someone he could have a 'normal' life with. 'And to be honest,' he added disarmingly. 'I was too selfish when I was younger. I like to think now, I have a better understanding of what a woman wants ...' He was looking at her in a way that suddenly made her wonder what it would be like if he kissed her and she dropped her eyes and took a swallow of wine, afraid her thoughts showed on her face.

She'd made the speech about the early start but 9.30 p.m. came and went and it was he who looked at his watch just after ten, expressing concern that she should get enough sleep.

She assumed they'd get separate cabs but he immediately took the lead ordering one that could drop her off in Reading Street on his way to Westgate. Sherie, used to having to do everything herself, liked the way he did. He held the door of the taxi open, stood back while she got in. On the back seat he sat next to her, not touching but close enough for their clothes to brush. As they drew up outside her apartment, she felt a small thrill run through her as he softly kissed her cheek and took her fingers in his for a brief moment. Almost from a distance, she heard herself say it, against all her usual safety considerations and first date risk assessments. 'Do you want a quick coffee before you go home ...?'

She'd gone through her front door, mellow on wine and good conversation, thinking she might go to bed with him.

She couldn't pinpoint later where her slight sense of unease had set in.

He didn't make any move when they sat on the sofa. He asked about the art on the walls, admiring the sketch of Marquis – who had disappeared through the cat flap shortly after they arrived – and wanting a quite detailed lowdown on Nate in a way that felt a little odd.

'I can't understand why you haven't been snapped up,' he said, stretching his long legs out in front of him and looking at her with a slow smile. 'Or have you had strings of lovers and broken their hearts?' It was said in a teasing way, but Sherie felt flustered.

'I wish,' she said lightly, feeling uncomfortable now the way his eyes lingered on her. She said it only to cover her confusion. 'One last coffee?'

He sprang to his feet. 'Let me help ...'

'You are very special,' he murmured, as he followed her back into the kitchen to watch her pour milk into his mug for a second time.

She knew he was going to do it and it was as much the fear of hurting his feelings as any physical response, that made her kiss him back when he put his arms around her.

But there was something about the way he held her – the way he gazed into her face – that made her shrink inside.

'I think I'd better get some sleep after this,' she said, pulling gently away, ignoring the hope in his eyes. He had wanted to arrange their next meeting there and then but she'd suggested they text. He was talking about a restaurant in Whitstable he wanted to take her to and, not being sure what else to do, or even understanding her own hesitancy, when he'd done nothing wrong, she'd said it sounded lovely.

Still she heard herself exhale lengthily when his cab had finally hooted outside and she'd been able to climb upstairs with Marquis.

Now she shifted the cat off her pillow and repositioned him further down the bed as she stretched out, glad to be here on her own and not having to make morning-after conversation. On the bedside table her phone beeped. She picked it up, scanning the number on the screen. He'd texted when he got home last night thanking her for a 'wonderful evening' and saying he would be in touch soon. She hadn't yet stored his name.

Sherie raised her eyebrows as she took in the opening lines of the text sent at 6.30 a.m. The experience of spending time in her company had been upgraded to 'magical'. Which seemed a tad over the top.

Then she read the next one and frowned.

Chapter 10

Ding dong!

Roz strode to the door, heels clicking across the expanse of parquet flooring.

She threw it open and gazed sternly at the tall man on the doorstep. He was younger-looking than she'd imagined. He looked at her hesitantly and offered a shy smile. 'Err – would you be–? I'm so sorry–' He spread his hands apologetically. 'I've forgotten your name.'

'Miss Sterling, to you!' she snapped.

'Oh! Right!' The man coloured slightly. 'I've erm just come round because–'

He was going too fast.

She glared again though part of her wanted to giggle. 'Silence! I know why you're here.' She held her head erect and tried to look down her nose towards him, in an attempt to appear forbidding, but ended up eyeballing his chest. 'You'd better come in,' she said coldly. 'You have some explaining to do.'

Damn. She'd got it wrong – he'd thrown her off track by speaking. He was supposed to say nothing at all until she said: 'Yes, Boy?' He was probably nervous too, she decided. Well, nothing lost. She'd get them back on script now.

She led him into the opulent sitting room where she'd just arranged fresh roses, and stood in front of the fireplace.

'Sit!' she commanded, nodding towards the huge brocade sofa. She could see his mouth working slightly – and he was shifting uneasily against the cushions. He was clearly new to this too and unsure what to do. Or was this him getting into role as well?

She raised herself to the full height allowed by her sensible shoes and brushed imaginary fluff from the sleeve of her fitted tweed Hobbs suit – an absolute find in the charity shop at the end of Margate High Street after she'd done some Googling on strict headmistress attire – before fixing him with another icy stare.

'So,' she said, with slow menace. 'You have been sent to see me.'

'Er yes. I was–'

'QUIET!' For a moment she felt a small bubble of hysteria at the back of her throat. He was acting scared well, as he shrank back slightly on the sofa. 'And sit up straight!' she roared, beginning to enjoy herself. 'I will not tolerate slouching in my school!'

Now he looked genuinely alarmed. He stood up and moved towards her and she stepped forward and pushed him hard in the chest so he sat abruptly back down again.

'How dare you!' she spluttered, not understanding why he'd come out of character, when he'd been so specific in his requests. Perhaps this was all part of the game. 'You sit still until I've finished.'

To her surprise he stood up again, looking at her warily. 'What the hell is going on here?' he said. With a sick lurch in her stomach, she saw his bewilderment was real.

Roz felt her face burn. Her heart was pounding.

'You're not Sebastian?'

The man in front of her slowly shook his head. 'Sadly

83

not. My name's Jamie. Charlotte asked me to pop round and take a look at the ground at the back to see if it might make a building plot.' He smiled and held out a hand. 'And you're Rosalind. I've just remembered ...'

Even after he'd got her a glass of water, Roz still thought she might be sick.

Jamie, he explained calmly, was a chartered surveyor from Canterbury. He had been given a key to the side gate but Charlotte had told him to be sure to ring on the doorbell first. 'She didn't want you to worry if you saw a strange man wandering about in the garden.' He had smiled again then. 'She thought you might be scared,' he added. 'Which is somewhat ironic since I found you absolutely terrifying ...'

He'd shown her the key as if she might not believe him, but she was still breathing too hard to speak.

Suppose he'd knocked when she was in the middle of seeing the real client. Suppose he'd gone round the back and then looked through the window ...

'I'm so sorry,' she managed eventually. 'I was just – I'm rehearsing for a play,' she improvised desperately. 'The chap I was expecting is going to be in it with me ... I haven't er met him yet but we were going to go through our lines.'

She tried to laugh as though it were all perfectly normal and jolly and heard herself give a strangled yelp.

Jamie was backing away from her again, his hands held wide in front of him in a shrugging gesture.

'It's none of my business,' he said.

Roz's heart was still beating too fast. The real Sebastian would presumably arrive any minute. What the fuck was she going to do?

Then she remembered he'd given her a number. She'd have

to head him off. 'Are you going to go and look then?' she squeaked. 'At the garden, I mean.'

He nodded slowly, 'I think I'd better,' he said meaningfully.

'Here, come through this way,' Roz scuttled through to the conservatory beyond the sitting room and twisted the handle to open the French doors onto the flagstones that led to the immaculate lawns. 'I'll just – just be in here,' she said, catching sight of herself in the huge mirror in the hall as she rushed back to the vast kitchen to find her phone.

What the hell must he think of her in her tweeds and stout lace up shoes? Her face was bright red, her hair escaping from the bun now. Oh Christ, had he noticed the cane propped up in the corner? Thank God it hadn't been the day for Andy when she had to put on the fish nets and boots.

Her hands were shaking violently as she scrabbled in her handbag for her phone, frantically scrolling through for the last email from 'Sebastian' with his number on the bottom. **Running late,** she texted, jabbing at the keys, praying he wouldn't ring on the bell before she'd finished. **Please arrive 4.30.**

She pressed send, breathing heavily, sending as an afterthought: **You can spend the time reflecting on how bad you've been,** so he might think it all part of the service. He should be in a lather of anticipation when he did finally arrive, she thought wryly.

Through the kitchen window she could see Jamie strolling up and down, pointing what looked like an electronic measuring device towards the swimming pool and apparently talking to himself. He was voice recording his notes, she imagined. Oh Christ, suppose he was also recording what she'd said, all the better to tell Charlotte. She had to stop him ...

By the time he came back in, she'd got her hair back in place, and more lipstick on and trusted herself to speak normally. She repeated her excuse about the play.

'That's why I'm dressed like this,' she offered. 'I find it helps me to remember the lines if I get into role early.'

'Yes, I thought it must be something like that,' he said solemnly, his chin twitching slightly as if trying not to laugh.

'It is,' she said more firmly. 'That's how I always approach a new drama.'

Jamie looked amused. 'Er would you like to go for a coffee somewhere?' He gave another small smile. 'Perhaps with a brandy in it? You do still look a bit shaken.'

'I've not got time. My co-star – well co-performer, I wasn't trying to say I'm the lead or anything,' she stumbled, embarrassed. 'In fact, it's quite a minor part.'

'I'll have to come and see it,' Jamie said pleasantly. 'When is it on?'

'We haven't got a date yet.'

'Even though you're already rehearsing?'

He raised his eyebrows, leaning back in the doorway, looking relaxed and stylish in his well-cut suit trousers and clearly-expensive shirt with silver cufflinks. How could she have thought he wanted to be bent over and beaten with an old plimsoll? But Melody had insisted she'd get all sorts ...

'The playwright is still working on it – it's in development,' she said. 'Steven's a friend of mine. We are trying it out for him,' she added, inspired. 'And when he's finished writing it and had feedback from the proposed cast, then he will schedule it. It will probably be on at the Sarah Thorne Memorial Theatre,' she finished, for extra authenticity.

'I'll look out for it,' he said, still in the same measured tone. 'What's the play called?'

'It's only got a working title at the moment,' she said desperately. 'Er – *STRICTLY SPEAKING*. It's about a boarding school,' she added. 'With a very stern headmistress.'

Jamie smiled. 'I could see that.' He looked around him. 'So where is your fellow thesp?'

'He'll be here any minute. He's running late.'

'Ah.'

Roz suddenly felt as though she might cry. 'Please don't tell Charlotte,' she blurted. 'I hadn't asked her about rehearsing here and I really should have done. I will do – I will of course, but if you could not mention it, so it comes from me–'

Jamie nodded – his brown eyes fixed on hers. She couldn't decide if they were still amused or disapproving.

'As I said,' he replied lightly. 'It's really none of my business ...'

'Oh, I love it!' Melody gave another long peal of laughter. 'That happened to me once. Poor bloke had only come round to talk me into faster broadband and by the time he'd managed to explain, I'd already chained him to the radiator.'

Roz smiled uneasily. Melody seemed utterly delighted by this tale but it just made Roz feel sick all over again.

'When the real bloke arrived, I didn't feel up to it,' she said. 'I went through the motions but I expect he was quite disappointed.'

'Probably didn't even notice,' said Melody, taking another swallow from her mojito. 'Most of 'em are quite easily pleased. Want to do another two-hander with me on Tuesday night? He likes at least a couple of hours but he'll give us five hundred. Stockings and suspenders.'

Roz nodded. She'd be safe at Melody's house. That night after Jamie, she'd determined never to do it again, but then when her credit card statement had arrived at the same time as her ancient Volvo was due its MOT, and Colin had wanted to rebook, she'd found herself agreeing to the same time and place and just praying that Charlotte wouldn't send anyone else round, or more horrifying to contemplate, decide to call in herself.

So far though, her friend had always warned her if there were any viewings booked. And Roz had formed a plan.

'I leave the chain on, and look through the peephole to check it IS the proper client,' she told Melody, 'and then once he's in I bolt the front door from the inside so nobody else can let themselves in. Charlotte would have to ring the bell and I could get rid of whoever it was, out the back. I've got a pair of tracksuit bottoms and a baggy t-shirt I can throw over fishnets, while I'm pretending to be coming to the door. I can tell her I saw someone dodgy outside and was being security conscious ...'

'Bleeding hell – you have thought it through,' Melody was admiring. 'That should cover it, all right.'

But Roz was suffused with shame at her elaborate scheme to deceive someone who was her dear friend. She could switch operations to her own home, but recoiled at the thought of doing anything like that in the place where her daughter lived. And the neighbours would wonder about all these strange men ...

'You still look very worried though.' Melody finished her drink and picked up Roz's empty glass too. 'Is it just all the bills?' she asked sympathetically. 'Or is something else wrong?'

88

Chapter 11

*T*here's a poster on the wall at the surgery listing five signs you may not realise could mean breast cancer. I know every sign and symptom and type and outcome – I have spent hours on research. None of it sounds like me. I look around me at the others waiting. Apart from the bloke in the corner who appears to be coughing his last, nobody else looks particularly ill. I wonder if any of them are sitting here, heart thumping painfully, because they have something growing on them.

My GP is kind. He can see I am terrified and is brisk and reassuring. He only touches my stress-lump briefly and then goes back to his screen and begins to tap at his keyboard. He thinks it is a cyst but of course we must get it checked out. I am to attend the breast clinic and an appointment will be made for me within fourteen days. The NHS works fast when it might be serious. He asked me how long the stress-lump had been there and I saw the look in his eyes when I told him. He thinks I should have come earlier. But if it is only a cyst, it won't matter …

But you think it's a cyst, I say, just to hear it one more time. This time he hesitates for a fraction as if tugged at by sudden doubt. 'I think so,' he says. 'But the clinic will tell you for sure.'

He asks me if I have support. And my heart tightens. Why do I need it?

I haven't told the others – I will when my stress-lump has been removed and I am back to normal. It will seem funny then.

Chapter 12

'Ha ha, bloody hilarious, Love.'

Charlotte put the birthday card from Fay on her kitchen windowsill with the others and began to open the package. 'Thought we said no presents, as we're doing the party.'

'It's only small.'

'That's what you've all said.' Charlotte waved a hand towards the Jo Malone candle Sherie had brought her and the bouquet of flowers from Roz. 'OH – thanks Love – that's gorgeous.'

She put the beaded clutch bag down on the table and opened the fridge. 'Champagne?'

'I should say so. And it's the real stuff as well!' Fay picked up one of the flutes from the counter and held it out as Charlotte poured.

'My husband presented me with a case of it this morning.' Charlotte's voice was even. 'As well as this.' She held out her arm to display a tasteful gold bangle. 'Says I'm getting my proper present at the party.'

'Gosh,' said Roz, faintly behind her.

Charlotte didn't look round. Her eyes were still on Fay, eyebrows slightly raised, expression meaningful. 'He's being very attentive.'

'Of course he is,' Fay kept her voice brisk. 'It's your

birthday!' She turned towards Roz and Sherie and raised her glass. 'Many Happy returns.'

They all chorused.

'This looks amazing,' Roz said, surveying the plates that were covering Charlotte's long kitchen table. 'When you said "nibbles" I was imagining a couple of bowls of crisps.'

'At Charlotte's house?' Sherie laughed. 'You're kidding. It does look great though.' She picked up a strip of yellow pepper and dipped it in the homemade guacamole. 'Must have taken you hours.'

Charlotte shook her head. 'I got the pâtés and the quiche from that new deli in Charlotte Street – have you been yet? Brilliant cheeses. I only whizzed that up and chopped the veg and made the salad and the garlic bread. Dig in!'

'Or we'll be eating it all weekend!' Roger appeared among them. 'And Becky's insisting on some Thai or Chinese or–' He looked at Charlotte. 'What is it?'

Charlotte addressed the others. 'The new Fusion place on Northdown Road. Bex is coming back tomorrow morning – just till Sunday night. I said she didn't have to but–' She grinned. 'It will be really great to see her. And all be together for a family dinner. Even Joe is looking forward to it.'

'I'm not.' Joe didn't look up from the end of the table where he was tapping on an iPad. 'Can I go now? I'm playing Sam at half eight.'

'Only for an hour,' Charlotte said. 'You've still got school tomorrow, remember.'

Joe rolled his eyes. 'Oh I'd completely forgotten. Though there's no point going on Fridays – we don't do anything.'

'Funny that! My copy of your timetable says double maths ...'

Charlotte pulled him towards her as he started to walk

away, giving him a noisy kiss. 'Love you!' she said loudly. Joe gave a small, embarrassed shrug. 'All right mum.'

'Poor boy!' Fay laughed. 'All these females clogging up his kitchen.'

'Helen and Marie will be here in a minute too.' Charlotte was getting another bottle from the fridge. 'Told them to pop in for a quick one after Rumba or Zumba or whatever it is they do.' Charlotte shook her head as if whatever it was, it was not to be recommended. 'Cheers – here's to the Big Five-O!'

Roger put an arm around her shoulders and kissed her before looking round. 'Who needs another drink?'

Fay watched Roger as he moved around the kitchen, topping up glasses. He did not look like a man with a guilty conscience. He smiled at Charlotte as if he loved her to bits, and seemed perfectly at ease. She hadn't seen him look at his phone once.

'How's work?' she asked, when she'd taken the opportunity to manoeuvre him into a corner.

'Busy!'

'Still empire building?'

Roger smiled and made a gesture of collapsing with exhaustion. 'One last acquisition to tie up – for the moment! It's the smallest firm we've bought, by a long chalk, but they're making it more complicated than all the others put together.'

Roger shook his head. 'The contract's the size of the Magna Carta and they've got me running back and forth there constantly. It's a tiny two-pot financial advisor set-up. I'd have walked away by now – but one of the senior partners is keen. Think there's something going on under the old-pals act. Probably went to Oxford with the MD ...'

93

'Where are they based then?' Fay asked, sipping her champagne.

'Back end of Maidstone.'

Fay smiled at him. 'Ah, I remember we did a relocation for a big nursing home there – was a right bloody nightmare. Took about three days. The Matron was a right dragon who messed my blokes about a treat. I had to go up in the end – we used to go in this tatty old hotel – the Wealdstone was it? – to eat. Don't know if it's still there ...'

'Yes – it's being refurbished. I was there the other week.'

'How funny,' said Fay.

She had considered coming straight out with it – which was her preferred way of doing things – and simply telling Roger that Charlotte had noticed he'd been going AWOL and so if he *was* up to anything, he'd better put an end to it double damn quick. Or he'd have her to answer to, let alone his wife.

But Charlotte would be furious if she did that and this more subtle approach was working. Roger had volunteered he'd been to the hotel Charlotte had found the receipt for – which seemed to indicate that particular visit was above board. Fay was surprised at the depth of her relief.

She opened her mouth to try to casually find out what he'd been doing there – a meeting? A business lunch? – but as she began to form the words, the doorbell rang and Roger excused himself with what Fay tried not to interpret as indecent haste, and bounded off to answer it.

Marie and Helen were friends of Charlotte's from the days when she worked at the estate agency Wainwright's. Fay had met them a couple of times before and found them annoying. As usual, they spent the evening standing together like a couple of Siamese twins, taking turns to regale Charlotte with the marital woes of various of her ex-colleagues.

Fay, helping herself to some more of the cream cheese roulade and breaking off a piece of what tasted like genuine made-in-France French bread, couldn't have cared less that someone called Janine had lost a stone since she'd found out Gareth was leaving her for the woman who groomed their dog, but it had sent Charlotte into high dudgeon.

'Bastard!' she said loudly. 'They're all the bloody same.'

'Well that may be a tad sweeping,' Roz was trying to steer the conversation elsewhere. 'Hey Sherie – you haven't told me about your date the other night? Was he as good as he looked?'

Roz left Fay persuading Charlotte to have something to eat and hurried after Sherie. She waited till she emerged from the downstairs loo.

'What's the matter?' Roz scanned Sherie's face. She'd clearly applied more make-up but her eyes still looked pink. 'Nothing happened, did it?'

'Oh no – I'm sorry. I'm just tired and–' she gave a weak smile. 'Emotional. Birthdays do that to me sometimes. I've probably had too much champagne.'

Roz frowned. 'So what did happen on the date?'

'He was fine – he was charming and interested. And he even came back for coffee–'

'And?'

'I don't know. He asked me to go out again, but I'm not going to–'

'Why not?'

Sherie looked at Roz. 'He seemed a bit *too* keen ...'

'Oh Sherie, for heaven's sake.' Roz knew she sounded exasperated. 'They can't win with you! What do you *want*?'

She saw Sherie flinch and her eyes fill with tears again.

Roz immediately felt guilty but that somehow made her even crosser. She'd been listening to Sherie's woes about men for decades. How many hours had she spent hearing what was wrong with pretty much every single one of them? Apart from the few that Sherie had decided were entirely perfect for her, who had failed to call.

'As a general rule, if they didn't have dietary, artistic or sartorial shortcomings, they weren't enthusiastic *enough*.' Roz glared at her friend. Did Sherie ever stop for a single moment to think about how she, Roz, might feel about anything? How maybe Roz would have liked a nice man to be a bit too keen once in a while. Sherie had no concept of what life was like for Roz. Especially at the moment ...

'You don't understand,' Sherie began, feeling in her handbag. 'I'll show you–'

She stopped as Fay swept towards them. 'What you two having a mother's meeting about?'

'Nothing at all interesting!' Roz saw the look of surprise on Fay's face at her sharp tone. She moved sideways so Fay could open the loo door. 'Sorry,' she muttered.

Fay shrugged. 'Doesn't make any odds to me what you're talking about,' she said. 'But it's got to be better than listening to those two boring on for Britain in there. You'd better go and rescue Char.'

Sherie had already walked away down the hall, whatever she was going to show Roz, forgotten. Roz sighed, feeling suddenly exhausted.

She'd had a long day at the gallery with two separate school groups to take round. And it would be another long one tomorrow as it was the start of changeover week and they were all expected to work late.

The new exhibition was about depictions of wealth. Tracey

Emin's photograph of her stuffing bank notes between her legs was getting an outing and Roz had seen photos of a giant red money box with a chute going down the inside of it into which one could, after climbing a blue stepladder, deposit yellow plastic coins.

Roz wandered back into the kitchen, thinking of the way she'd been scrabbling about for change this morning to get enough to give Amy for lunch. And the house insurance that was due for renewal, the size of the electricity bill that would mean larger direct debits for the foreseeable, the broken microwave she had promised Amy she would replace as soon as she was able.

The dominatrix work was the only thing keeping her head above water. She might live in terror of discovery but it made everything just a tiny bit more manageable. Life with Amy was calmer now she mostly had a little cash to give her. And she could go to Paris with her friends. But it wasn't a solution long term. The empty house wouldn't be there for ever. Charlotte, smiling as she offered Roz another drink, had just this minute said someone was interested – especially since Jamie had confirmed they'd be likely to get planning permission for a second home on the plot.

'You made quite an impression on him.' Roz couldn't read Charlotte's face – did she know? 'He asked me for your email or phone number.'

Roz could feel her heart thumping. 'What for?'

'Dunno! I didn't give it to him. Said I'd have to check with you first.'

'Well please don't.'

Charlotte raised her eyebrows. 'Jamie's lovely. Divorced, solvent ...' Then she laughed. 'On the other hand, he might be trying to recruit you onto the PTA – in which case yes, good idea, keep a low profile!'

She laughed again. 'Though you've got to hand it to him. It's unusual for anyone to do any fund-raising much at secondary school, isn't it? I mean at primary we all ran around and made the cupcakes but usually by the time they get to the next school ... but Jamie's right into it. He's Chair and he puts on all sorts of things. I'm surprised you haven't come across him before.'

Roz frowned. 'I thought he lived in Canterbury?'

'Oh he does, but his daughter goes to Highcourt with Amy.' Roz's heart performed an unpleasant jerk as Charlotte went on. 'Pretty sure she's in the same year.'

Roz tried to look as if this meant nothing. Jamie wouldn't say anything to his daughter, would he? No, of course he wouldn't. But suppose he did – suppose he told her what had happened, just by way of a funny story, and Charlotte had told him her surname and he repeated it. And this daughter said: *oh there's a girl at school called Drawthorne.* It was an unusual name – she only had to ask Amy if her mum was called Rosalind ... But no. Why would she? Roz breathed hard, trying to stay rational.

'Are you all right love?' Charlotte was looking at her curiously. 'I wouldn't want to be on the PTA again either – I give fifty quid a year to their lottery thing at Chattenden instead, to salve my conscience. And I did make a sponge for their charity day except my super-organized son managed to leave it at home!'

'I'm fine,' Roz took a larger than intended gulp of her drink and coughed.

Charlotte clapped her on the back. 'I didn't mean to scare you. I imagine he's been struck by how gorgeous you are – I did tell him you were single – and thinks he'll take you out for dinner ... In fact, I know that's what it is. He said as much ...'

'I don't– I wouldn't–' Roz stumbled as Charlotte continued to grin at her. 'I'm not gorgeous,' she said in confusion.

'You are! You've got that lovely skin and calm eyes. You have a–' Charlotte was speaking in the deep-and-meaningful drawl she dropped into after copious amounts of alcohol. '–Inner serenity,' she pronounced slowly. 'Like a nun or something.'

At this Roz did actually choke and had to allow Charlotte to clap her on the back even harder, while Fay snorted. 'Can't see any of us allowed within ten miles of a convent, frankly!' Fay laughed loudly.

Roz watched as Charlotte waved the bottle at them all again. Her heart was still thumping harder than usual. What would she say if she knew about Roz's inner whiplash? If she knew about all the debts ... and everything ...

'I think I need a cup of tea.' An hour later, Fay was looking at a clearly-sloshed Charlotte. 'Shall I put the kettle on?'

'Sure! Help yourself.' Charlotte swept an arm around her to indicate the rest of the kitchen. 'All of you, help yourselves to anything, everything! Roger can open another bottle when he comes back down. I bet Joe was still on that bloody Xbox. Roger's probably had to confiscate the controller.'

Fay was rooting in the cupboard for mugs. 'Do you want a cuppa?'

'No I bloody don't. It's my fiftieth birthday. I want a fag and another glass of fizz!' Charlotte gave Fay a grin. 'So, I'm going to have a wee and then go outside with both!'

'OK!'

As Charlotte marched out of the kitchen, Fay raised her eyebrows at Roz and Sherie. 'Tea for either of you?'

'We've noticed her drinking a lot lately too.' Beside her, Marie's voice was low and confidential. 'Haven't we, Helen? She had a glass of wine on the go just before five when I popped in the other day.' Marie glanced around the kitchen, knowingly.

Fay's eyes immediately narrowed. 'So you think that makes it OK to stand here gossiping about your hostess, do you?'

Marie flushed. 'I wasn't–'

'You were.' Roz saw Marie shrink from Fay's icy gaze. 'I am Charlotte's friend. And you are a guest here. You don't stand in her house and badmouth her to me!'

Fay kept her eyes fixed on Marie while she pulled a cigarette from her packet with slow deliberation and then moved towards the open back door, speaking over her shoulder. 'Didn't I hear you say you were in early tomorrow?'

Roz and Sherie exchanged glances as Fay stepped out onto the patio and clicked at her lighter, inhaling with ferocity.

After a couple of minutes Sherie followed her. 'I don't like her either, but you can't throw out a guest from someone else's house.' Fay looked unrepentant. She nodded towards the far side of the kitchen to where Marie was hastily kissing Charlotte goodbye.

'I think you'll find I just have.'

She smiled and opened her packet of cigarettes as Charlotte came towards her, leaving Roger to show Marie out.

'They leaving already?' Fay called, pulling a cigarette out so that Charlotte could take it. While murmuring from the corner of her mouth towards Sherie: 'Tell Charlotte you want a coffee.'

* * *

'You've told me all this already.' Fay rubbed her arms. The temperature had dropped considerably during the evening and there was a chilly breeze out here now. She was cold and rapidly getting bored. She gave a grin to soften her words. 'You're getting a bit repetitive now, Hun!'

Charlotte ground out her cigarette beneath her foot and stooped to pick up the butt.

'You said after another Wednesday,' she said doggedly. 'Well, he definitely disappeared again. Whatever he does it goes on between three and five p.m. He never, *never* answers his phone then.'

'We were talking earlier,' Fay said. 'There's a company in Maidstone keep calling him in to sort out the contract for the buy-out ...'

'AND,' Charlotte continued as if Fay hadn't spoken. 'He also went missing after work. Said they had a drink for someone who was leaving ... but when I double checked the next day, his secretary knew nothing about it. So I told him that and he said it was a leaving do at one of the clients', and only he went as he was friends with this chap. But he didn't look at me and he blew his nose – that's always a sign ...'

Fay looked steadily at her friend who was rather red and had just poured yet another glass of champagne.

'I really think–' she began.

'You said you would!'

'I did and I will.'

'So you'll follow him next Wednesday?'

'Got a crazy day then – six jobs on.'

'But you–'

'I'll keep the one after that clear.'

'Promise?'

'Promise.' Fay held up her mug and Charlotte chinked her glass against it. Behind her back, Fay slowly uncrossed her fingers.

Coffee had finally been made and the four of them were sitting round the table, Roger having been instructed by Charlotte to put the bins out and Helen having scuttled after an embarrassed-looking Marie.

'Bloody lightweights!' said Charlotte, still defiantly drinking champagne but taking the occasional sip from the cup Sherie had put next to her. Sherie stifled a yawn. She badly wanted to go home and get under her duvet with the warm weight of Marquis on her feet.

'It's been lovely but I'm going to call a cab in a minute.' She looked around the table.

Roz nodded. 'I'll come.'

Fay dug in her handbag. 'Here, call this one.' She pushed a business card towards Sherie. 'All female band – they set up because they were sick of our usual mob being late. Len and I waited half an hour at the White Swan the other night – after the bloke said ten minutes. That's taking the piss. As I told him!'

Sherie smiled, picturing the scene. Fay nodded, striding across to stand in the still-open doorway to the patio. 'There's six of them so far, and they're working all round the clock to build it up. I said I'd put the word out.'

She lit a cigarette and blew the smoke out into the dark. 'I like seeing that – people using a bit of initiative instead of sitting around on their arses moaning because they haven't got any money.'

Sherie saw Roz's lips tighten. Fay was clearly gearing up for one of her favourite diatribes.

'Not everyone who's poor is sitting on their arse,' Roz said tightly.

'No, but a lot of them are.' Fay swept on. 'Elaine, who works for me, has a son-in-law who hasn't worked for a year. Her daughter has two jobs and when one of her brats was ill, Elaine was late in so she could look after him, because HE'D gone bloody fishing! Idle bastard.'

'Perhaps,' said Roz deliberately, 'he can't find a job. It can be very difficult—'

'He doesn't want to work!' Fay interrupted. 'If he did, he'd set up a business of some sort. He'd become a gardener. Thanet is stuffed to the gills with elderly women with a heap of money and nobody to cut the hedge.'

'Maybe he knows nothing about plants.'

Fay gave one of her snorts. 'He could learn. Or be an odd job man. He could sweep paths, clean windows. You know very well what I mean – you're just being argumentative for the sake of it.'

Sherie suppressed her choke of disbelief but Charlotte laughed out loud.

'Look who's talking!'

'That is a bit rich,' said Sherie mildly, when she'd recovered herself.

Fay tossed her head back. '*I'm* not arguing – I'm just telling you about a lazy sod who's got two kids to support and leaves it all to his wife.'

'And I'm just saying that we're not all the right personalities to be entrepreneurs,' said Roz heatedly. 'You always bang on about business and enterprise but the fact is that we can't all start selling flowers on the side of the road and turn into Marks and Spencer's. Some of us just have to go to work from nine till five and do all the overtime we're offered and still be fucking broke!' She had turned slightly pink.

'I wasn't talking about you,' said Fay. 'And if he isn't the type to run a business why doesn't he stack shelves in Asda? Or be a delivery driver?'

'I have no idea,' said Roz. 'So I wouldn't presume to judge.' She looked hard at Fay. 'I just know there are plenty of other people in this country doing the best they bloody can but they still simply don't earn enough money.'

'Then they should look for better jobs.'

'What about nurses?' Roz's voice had risen further. 'Where would we be if *they* all looked for better jobs? The staff in the NHS–' for a horrible moment Roz looked as if she might cry, '–do a fucking magnificent job and some of them are using food banks!'

'Yes, that's quite disgraceful, I agree.' Fay was unperturbed. 'But I wasn't talking about them either. I was talking about the people who actually can't be arsed to work – and *don't*–' she went on, as Roz began to protest – 'tell me they don't exist because they do!'

'Maybe some do,' conceded Roz, 'but on the whole–'

'I'm going to call this cab,' Sherie began tapping on her phone.

Roz tried again. 'I just feel that it's harsh to judge someone for not making their own wealth when you don't know the full circumstances.' She looked at Charlotte. 'We shouldn't do this on your birthday. I'm sorry.'

Charlotte shrugged. 'So is Fay! She knows all that, really.'

Fay looked unabashed. 'Only saying what I think.'

Charlotte leant across the table and squeezed Roz's hand. 'Don't wind yourself up.' Roz nodded. Again, Sherie thought she looked emotional.

Sherie gave Fay a challenging look of her own. 'Well maybe think a bit more occasionally, before you open that great gob of yours!'

Fay laughed good-naturedly. 'This great gob has got me where I am today!'

Sherie spoke into the phone, giving Charlotte's address. 'It's going to be fifteen minutes,' she said when she'd rung off.

'And it will be,' put in Fay. 'Right come on, a last toast to Charlotte on her birthday ...' She raised her coffee cup. 'Happy Big Five-O. Here's to the next decade ... Can't believe we're going to be *in our fifties*.'

'Elasticated trousers here I come!' said Charlotte.

Sherie gave a small shudder. 'Not yet!' she said, at the same time.

'Well we will be soon,' replied Fay firmly. 'And it's going to be great.'

'We hope,' said Charlotte as Roger reappeared through the door and came towards the table.

'It will be!' Fay looked round the table, her cup aloft once more. 'Here's to us and the fabulous times ahead.' She waved a hand around them all, her face now looking tired and a little saggy from all the booze. Her voice had taken on an evangelical note. 'All will be good!' she declared rousingly. Almost, Sherie thought, as if she were trying to convince herself ...

Chapter 13

Sherie's boss Geoffrey had not got any less eccentric in the three weeks since she'd seen him. He was wearing a mustard yellow corduroy jacket over a purple silk shirt and electric blue trousers. A purple and green silk scarf was elaborately knotted around his neck and his mad-professor grey hair was over-due for a cut. Again.

'You look like something out of a Dickens novel,' she said, as he put two cups of peppermint tea on the big leather-topped desk and proffered a plate of shortbread.

Geoffrey ignored her. 'So spill. How's the boy Byron?'

'His work is amazing.'

Sherie folded back the case of her iPad and propped it up between them so Geoffrey could see the screen. She began to swipe through pictures of artwork. 'Charles Saatchi is rumoured to have bought this one—' she paused on a photograph of a twisted metal sculpture depicting an entwined couple without heads. 'And these are the two paintings I offered on for Edwin.' She clicked through to a pair of black and white abstracts.

'And?'

'Coming back to me. But he'll sell. He's got this 'agent' who's playing hard to get. Full of bullshit. But I said that was absolutely our final figure and that I'd be securing something else for the client if I didn't hear by today.'

'Edwin's very keen. You could go up a bit.'

Sherie shook her head. 'Let's not set a precedent. Edwin is bound to want more.'

Geoffrey nodded. 'He does like a protégée. Someone he can 'discover'.'

'Yes and this one is right up his street. Very unusual style. And he's very strange himself.'

'All the best people are.' Geoffrey scrutinised her. 'Are you all right? You look a bit pale. On one of your silly diets again?'

Sherie spoke tersely. 'No I am not. And just because I do not stuff my face with sugar and lard all day long, does not make what I eat silly.'

'I'm going take you to Rules for lunch,' Geoffrey said, unabashed. 'And have the steamed steak pud. With an Oyster.'

Sherie pulled a face.

'You can have fish,' he added.

Sherie was still moving through the photos. 'I've found another one too. Rosemary Tallow. She's graduating from Cornell. Her end of year show collection is sensational. I think we should recommend her to Lownden Price for the foyer. But we commission something special. She's done this incredible painting which is her dead father's face – from a distance. Up close it is hundreds of smaller fragments – all her childhood memories of him. Look!'

Geoffrey peered at the screen.

'I was thinking she could work from a photograph of the founder's face,' Sherie continued. 'Or the current Chairman's–'

'Oh, he'd adore that darling. Ego the size of Milton Keynes.'

'And paint in things to do with the bank's history. Money and buildings and bridges, bags of gold, whatever ... They'd need to make some suggestions.'

'I said I'd see him once you were back. It's a brilliant scheme.'

Sherie nodded. 'I think she's going places.'

Geoffrey wrote her name on his old-fashioned blotter, which was covered with doodles. 'What else has she got? We should suggest a couple of pieces from the show for investment – if you're right about her, they'll soar.'

'I'd recommend these.' Sherie was already scrolling through to more. 'I think when she's settled into a style these will be the ones to watch. A really unusual use of space. It's very confident for someone so young ...'

Geoffrey leaned forward, his chin resting on his steepled fingers as Sherie worked through the rest of the photographs, listening intently as Sherie picked out the ones she thought showed the most originality, pointing out the work that had already sold before the night. 'The photo isn't doing it justice,' she said, tapping on a multi-coloured canvas. 'The luminosity she's achieved is astonishing. I spoke to her tutor. He said she's the best natural talent they've had through there in a long time. There's a buzz building among the collectors already.'

She stopped. There was a pause. Then Geoffrey brought his pen down on his blotter like an auctioneer who'd just closed a sale.

'Good! Let's do it!'

Sherie would have been happy to go straight to the station and head for home but Geoffrey was in expansive mood and wanted the full lunch experience. It was his way of showing he was pleased with her. And although she did not feel like eating, as usual she had to play the game.

As they walked through the sunshine from his Covent Garden office on the third floor above a print shop on Bedfordbury, towards Maiden Lane, Sherie reflected what a happy stroke of luck she'd had the night they'd been introduced at a private view in a gallery off Charlotte Street, some twenty-six years before.

'Geoffrey Davenport. Knows everybody,' her companion – a sweet young journalist called Simon she'd bonded with over the wait for champagne – had told her, as he'd led her across the room to the flamboyant figure in cravat and waistcoat. 'A terrible tart but what he doesn't know about paintings ...'

Geoffrey had shaken her hand and immediately demanded to know what she thought of the artist exhibiting. Not much, had been the answer, but – afraid she might be criticising a friend of his – she had gone to great lengths to justify her answer. Geoffrey had said nothing while she was speaking but when she'd finally tailed off, embarrassed, had given a whoop of triumph.

'Yes! Absolute crap, darling. Couldn't agree more!'

She'd somehow been tagged onto a group going for supper down the road in Chez Gerard and, sandwiched between Geoffrey and his much younger partner Richard, picking at frites, had loved the conversation about up and coming artists, the rise of the young British set and why Damien Hirst's sheep had been such a hit. Geoffrey had fired questions at her throughout. By the end of the night, Simon had asked her for a date and she'd been offered a job.

'I don't know anything about art-consultancy,' she'd said nervously. And Geoffrey had shrugged. 'Neither did I twenty years ago. You've got a good eye. It's all you need.'

She and Simon had fizzled out after a few drinks but Geoffrey had taught her about auctions and valuations and shipping and restorations and who to watch and who to talk to and now he no longer wanted to travel so much after his heart attack, and she had a fat contacts book and a good record of hitting the spot for his wealthy clients, she was his right hand.

He still enjoyed the wheeling and dealing and client meetings, would buy by phone or in person if it was London or home counties. But she was the one who flew around the world when flying around the world was necessary.

Even when there was a request from a big advertising agency in Manchester – it was she who got on the train. In return, Geoffrey was increasingly generous with bonuses and cuts of commission.

'Are you supposed to eat that sort of thing?' she asked him now, as he sat back at his favourite table in Rules and surveyed her across the thick white tablecloth, and the waiter poured red wine.

'The anti-oxidants in that, cancel out the fat content,' Geoffrey told her, indicating his glass.

Sherie smiled. 'If you say so.'

'I think it was you who told me.'

'I don't think it was.'

She heard her phone beep again from her handbag and kept her eyes on Geoffrey. 'You're popular today,' he said.

She shrugged. 'My sister's had an offer on her house. In a flap about moving.'

'Is that it?' He was watching her as if waiting for her to say more.

'How's Richard?' she asked, changing the subject.

'In a terrible sulk over the car. I want another Jag – he is absolutely insisting on some sort of Audi – won't listen to reason at all.'

Sherie raised an eyebrow. 'Doesn't sound like him.'

'Only I see the real Richard,' said Geoffrey theatrically. 'He is a nightmare, darling, an absolute beast when he wants to be ...'

Sherie laughed. 'I don't know how you've managed to put up with him these thirty years ...'

'Have I told you what I'm buying him for his fiftieth?'

'No, but do.'

'A string of lavatories would you believe!'

'No, I wouldn't.'

Geoffrey sighed. 'I offered a silk smoking jacket, a diamond encrusted money clip, a gold tooth-pick holder – all spurned! He wants a hefty donation made to Water Aid or some such, to pay chaps to build facilities in Africa. Charmingly known as bog-builders. He says it will help prevent the spread of disease. Apparently goats are so last year ...'

Geoffrey took a sip of wine. 'So I'm giving him a hundred of the things – it's setting me back five grand.'

'How lovely.'

'Yes, it is delightful of, me isn't it. And dinner at Le Gavroche, of course! I've been my own worst enemy over the years – given the boy such expensive tastes. It's all charity this and donation that and help the world's poorest. But he still wants lobster and Laurent Perrier when his birthday comes around.'

Sherie thought about her own impending big birthday and felt the familiar prickle of anxiety in her solar plexus. Charlotte was trying to organise another get-together to discuss the party. She must remember to text back later. As if on cue she heard her phone beep again, just as her grilled plaice was placed in front of her.

Geoffrey was too busy exclaiming over his pudding to notice. There was a companionable silence as he tucked in. Sherie leant down and slid a hand into her handbag, feeling for the side button that would silence the handset.

She took a small mouthful of the wine in front of her, not really wanting to drink this early in the day but knowing of old it was simpler to have a little bit than refuse altogether. She topped up her water glass and offered the jug to Geoffrey. He shook his head.

'I knew there was something else to tell you,' he said, dabbing at his mouth with the linen napkin. 'Edwin's got a friend who wants a 'statement piece' for his boardroom. In Newcastle of all places. Can you go up and see him?'

Sherie nodded.

'Marvellous. I'll send you the details. Edwin says he's loaded and will probably want something for himself at home if we play our cards right. He's built some sort of Bel-air style mansion over Whitely Bay– Oh look–' Geoffrey was immediately distracted. 'There's Dylan Rogers the old reprobate.' Geoffrey waved across the room. 'Wonder if Sotheby's have got anything interesting coming up ...'

Geoffrey had got to his feet and after briefly introducing her, was deep in conversation with 'Dylan' a few feet away. Sherie took the opportunity to delve into her handbag. She looked at her phone. There was indeed one text from her sister, but also ... The anxious knot tightened further.

She'd blocked him once and thought he'd gone but now here he was contacting her on WhatsApp under another number. She knew it was him immediately – **ball-breakers like you** ... She took a sharp intake of breath. What was wrong with the bloke?

'Not hungry?' Returning, Geoffrey looked at her largely untouched fish. 'I was hoping you'd join me in cheese ...'

She'd forced down a little stilton to keep her boss happy, but as she came up the escalator at St Pancras, Sherie still felt slightly sick. She wished she had told Roz the truth when she asked. Roz would have been calm and sensible. Would have said it wasn't Sherie's fault ...

Or would she? Still the nagging voice in Sherie's head reminded her that she had let him into her house. She had encouraged him to think ...

She shook herself. She had only kissed him back for a moment. And since then she had been kind and firm – she hadn't done anything to deserve this. Had she? She looked down to her mobile and the latest message. She would block him again but he could get through to her on yet another number. He knew her phone number and it wasn't something with her hundreds of work contacts that she could easily change.

He also knew where she lived.

Sherie had ordered a cab to collect her from Broadstairs station. The driver was one she often got. 'You all right, love?' he said cheerily, as he swung the car out of the station car park towards St Peter's. 'Good day in the smoke?'

She gazed out of the window with relief as minutes later, they turned into Reading Street and drove past the familiar cottages, glad that she'd only had to spend a short time in the capital. As the car went past the church and pulled up on the gravel in front of the graceful grey stone façade of her home, she smiled at the driver in the mirror.

'Thanks Tony.' She handed him a note, signalling him to keep the change, pushing down the unease that had dogged her on the journey and looking forward to getting out of her heels and formal clothes.

It was only half past six and the June sun was still warm. She would take her book and sit in the garden ...

She let herself into the bright hallway and began to shake off her jacket, jumping as she heard a small clatter coming from the kitchen.

'Who's there?' Her heart was pounding. Fuck. Had he somehow got in and was waiting for her? She couldn't stop herself screaming as a figure appeared beyond the stairs.

'Christ I'm sorry.' Nate looked stricken at her obvious alarm. 'I thought you may have been held up. Marquis was yowling – I came in to see if he needed feeding. I just gave him some biscuits and–' He held up the patterned tin. 'I'm sorry Sherie – I thought it would be OK to use the key. I thought you wanted me to check him if you were late and ...'

She swallowed hard. 'Yes, yes, it's fine – I'm so sorry. It was really kind of you. I – it just made me jump ...'

'You looked terrified. Is everything all right?'

He came towards her and put a hand on her shoulder.

Sherie flinched and he immediately dropped his arm.

'I'm sorry,' he said again, quietly.

'It's really OK. I um – I–' She stopped. What could she possibly offer as a reason for her behaviour? 'I thought perhaps I'd been burgled,' she finished, forcing a smile. 'So I'm really glad it was only you!'

He smiled too, watching her carefully. 'I'll let you get on.'

'OK thank you.' She had scooped Marquis up into her arms and was holding him against her, comforted by his warmth and the reassuring rumble of his purrs.

'I'll just be upstairs,' said Nate, his face still full of concern. He moved towards the front door.

'Shall we go for that drink later?' Sherie blurted it, suddenly afraid of the evening stretching ahead of her on her own.

He turned back and grinned. 'It's pie night. Are you hungry?'

Chapter 14

The White Swan, just over the road, was busy. Nate, calling out a cheery greeting to Kate the landlady, grabbed them the last table in the corner of the saloon bar and pulled out his wallet. 'Which one are you having?'

'Please let me.' Sherie stood up and picked up her bag. 'You've been so helpful to me.'

He didn't protest but sat back down while she got him a pint of Gadds and ordered their food. She was suddenly glad to be in the warmth and buzz of the pub and as she sipped at her rosé, the tight knot of anxiety in her middle loosened a little. Sherie made a conscious effort to push her worries to the far corners of her mind and gave Nate a big smile as she put his beer in front of him.

'Finished that painting yet?'

'Nearly.'

She'd put her phone on silent and buried it in the bottom of her handbag. She'd now blocked him twice. Surely he wouldn't have a third number to contact her with. He was clearly deranged and would soon be dating someone else he could obsess over. She'd looked at the site and he was still there, still available ...

She kicked the bag under the table and kept her eyes fixed on Nate as he told her about his choice of work for the

Margate show that was coming up. 'You still coming to the private view?'

'Sure. I've got the date in my phone.' Had she imagined the sensation of it vibrating beside her foot? 'Unless I have to go somewhere at short notice. My boss wants me to go Tyneside at some point soon.'

She began to tell him about the artists she'd recently discovered, relaxing further as they had another drink and began to eat. The pie she'd chosen was good – chicken and leek in a rich creamy sauce, the pastry buttery and flaky. For the first time in days, Sherie felt hungry.

'I hope I'm not being boring,' she said between mouthfuls. 'I can talk about art endlessly. Roz is always interested in what I've been doing – she knows a huge amount – she should be running that gallery – but the others begin to glaze over if I go on too much ...' She stopped and laughed. 'And my sister tells me to shut up!'

'Well I'm finding it fascinating.' Nate sounded sincere. 'It must be wonderful doing what you do. Being paid to hang out at art shows. My idea of heaven!'

'Well there's a stroke of luck!' Fay was suddenly towering above them. 'Last two seats in the house and they're next to someone we know!'

Sherie shuffled her chair sideways to make room. It wouldn't occur to Fay that she and Nate might not want to be interrupted. Len was looking apologetic. 'Are you sure–?'

'Of course.' Nate smiled easily, holding out his hand to the other man and introducing himself. 'Hi Fay – we met briefly when you–'

'Oh yes – I remember who you are.' Fay grinned at him and twisted round to look at the blackboard. 'So what do you recommend – steak or chicken? I suppose *you're* having organic lentils and mung beans?' She looked at Sherie and grinned again.

Sherie smiled back. 'The free-range chicken one is delicious.'

'I'll have that then. You're a red meat man, aren't you Len? What's everybody drinking?'

Half an hour later, Sherie had to admit, Fay could be fun. Nate was laughing uproariously at her account of that day's removals – 'right bloody mare of an afternoon' – and how she had dealt with a customer whose cup of tea had been knocked off the windowsill when her washing machine was being carried in.

Fay rolled her eyes. 'I mean, in fairness, Matt did look half-asleep and I had a word in his shell-like after, but give me strength. I went up there as a courtesy to check she was happy with everything – it's a house on four floors and she's been in overdrive for weeks about whether we'd be able to get the beds up the stairs – and she must have mentioned this bloody broken handle at least five times.'

'I was charm personified for quite a while and then I'd had it. 'It's a mug that came free with petrol,' I said. 'Not priceless china. Have a word with yourself, love."

Fay gave a bark of laughter. 'Funny thing is, I went and bought her another mug and she was thrilled to bloody bits with it. And I *had* got it from the garage!'

'Yeah, she was your new best mate by the end of it.' Len shook his head indulgently.

'Pah! Don't need any more of them.' She grinned at Sherie again. 'You lot are enough of a handful.'

Fay leant back and stretched as Len carried their empty dishes to the bar and Nate went for more drinks. 'Time for a fag I think!'

Sherie followed her gaze to the door, where a tall fair man was walking purposefully through. 'Oh my god!' Her hand flew to her mouth before she realised she was wrong. 'Er – sorry thought it was someone else.'

Fay frowned. 'You're jumpy. I noticed you watching the door earlier. Who are you expecting?' She looked at Sherie shrewdly. 'Or dreading?'

Sherie hesitated. 'You know I had that date Roz asked me about on Charlotte's birthday?'

Fay shook her head. 'No, not really. But go on.'

'Well I did, and he seemed very nice and I–' Sherie felt her face flush – 'I invited him back for coffee.'

'No law against that.' Fay gave a dirty chuckle. 'I think that's what I called it when I took Cory home with me the first time. And?'

'Well it was fine and nothing actually happened – well we had a kiss but I felt a bit – well I didn't want him to stay. So he went, and then the next day he sent these texts saying how wonderful I was and he couldn't wait to see me again. I woke up to a string of them. It was completely over the top.'

Fay shrugged. 'You are pretty well-preserved, love. Probably thought all his Christmases had come at once.'

'And then–' continued Sherie, 'the last one said he was a bit disappointed I hadn't taken my profile down from the dating site. That I was still 'making myself available' when we'd agreed we would see each other again. Well I had said, yes, we could have dinner but we hadn't actually made a firm arrangement – and we'd literally been out for one drink–'

'Clearly a nutter,' put in Fay.

'So I ignored all the messages for a bit and they kept coming so then I sent a very nice one – I thought – saying it had been a lovely evening but I wasn't sure we were really very well suited and I was sorry I had disappointed him but since I couldn't assure him of the level of commitment he obviously wanted it was probably better if he looked elsewhere and I hoped he would find someone lovely who would share his outlook.'

'I'd have told him to sling his hook and pronto.'

'And then,' said Sherie, hearing the slight wobble in her voice, 'the abuse started. He keeps talking about 'women like me' and saying did I get a kick out of playing power games and all sorts of stuff.'

She told Fay about blocking him and him re-appearing the next day with another phone number. 'It's like I've done something really awful. Honestly it's like I've jilted him at the altar.' She looked at Fay in alarm. 'Suppose he really is a nutter? Suppose he comes round?'

'Who?' Nate was standing beside them, carrying a beer for Fay.

'This creep who is plaguing Sherie,' announced Fay. 'Some loser she met on a dating site,' she added, apparently oblivious to Sherie's discomfort.

Nate looked at Sherie. She could see the disapproval written across his face.

'He won't come round,' Fay went on, blithely ignoring Sherie's furious expression. 'Men like him may give it all that from the end of a text. But he wouldn't have the balls to turn up.'

'If you need help, you phone me,' said Nate tightly. 'I'll be down in seconds.'

'I'm sure it won't come to that,' Sherie shot Fay another look. 'It's just someone I had a drink with – he's a bit keener than I was.'

She tried to smile, feeling mortified that Fay had announced the situation like that. Now Len was here and he too, was looking concerned. 'You should tell the police if someone's hassling you,' he said kindly. 'Don't let him make you afraid. Nobody should be allowed to destroy your peace of mind.'

Sherie nodded back – had she imagined it or had Len's eyes flicked towards Fay when he said that.

Nate wasn't looking at her, but his mouth was set. He probably thought she was sad and desperate to be meeting strangers she'd found online. Especially at her age ...

Fay looked thoughtful. 'Have you still got these numbers?'

'Yes, if I access the blocked list.'

'Give them both to me.'

Sherie felt uneasy. 'What are you going to do?'

Fay snorted. 'Make sure he doesn't bother you again. Text them to me now.'

'But how–?'

'Seriously Sherie. I'll sort it.'

She held up a hand as if that were the end of the matter. Len gave a small shake of his head and then nodded at Sherie's empty glass. 'You sure you won't change your mind? Let me get you another,' he said.

'OK, thank you. A small one.'

'I found Cory a bit over-enthusiastic at first,' Fay swept on, when Len had gone back to the bar. 'But he's settled down now. And of course he'll be off like a long dog as soon he finds someone his own age who's desperate to be up the duff.'

'How old is he?' Nate looked curious.

'Just turned twenty-four. I bought him a day driving a racing car. He was so excited he was like a kid – which is exactly what he is. He'll think differently when he's thirty.

It'll be all marriage and babies then and towing the line.'

Nate shrugged. 'Not all men want children.'

'Hmm.' Fay looked doubtful. 'Most of them do. Their over-inflated egos dictate that they go forth and replicate themselves, as if the future can't possibly do without them in the gene pool. All the men I know have felt compelled to spread their seed.'

'I don't.'

'No? Oh well, good for you – I mean I agree – I can't be doing with the little bastards either but–'

'Fay!' Sherie wanted her to stop now. 'My nephews are gorgeous.'

Fay ignored this. 'Generally speaking, a younger man is eventually going to want a younger woman. I know that and–'

'Not necessarily.' Nate hadn't looked at Sherie since the revelation about her dating disaster and still his eyes were averted.

Sherie saw Fay wink at him before she shrugged. 'Exception that proves the rule.'

There was a small uncomfortable silence. Sherie looked at her nails. Fay rose to her feet and picked up her cigarettes. 'Text those numbers now,' she commanded before heading for the door. Nate stood up too. 'I'll help Len with those glasses.'

Sherie leant under the table and retrieved her bag, fishing in it for her phone. Len was only bringing one drink and Nate knew it. He didn't want to be left alone with her. Embarrassed, probably, by the exchanges. She knew there was no point in trying to persuade Fay to be a bit less outspoken. Fay would probably only laugh and repeat anything she said when the others came back. There were no new messages. Relieved, Sherie started to put the phone back when a WhatsApp pinged in making her jump again. Fay had sent a smiley and one word. **NOW!**

Outside Fay leant back against bricks still warm from the evening sunshine, tapping at her phone screen.

Len appeared by her side and propped himself on the windowsill.

'I think it's illegal to make threats,' he said mildly.

'Do I look as if I care?'

She carried on tapping. 'I'm not threatening him anyway. I am simply giving him a friendly warning, quoting the malicious communications act of 2003 and pointing out, in my role as a community police officer—'

'What?'

'That he is contravening it by sending electronic missives designed to cause anxiety or distress to one of the residents on my patch. I have assured him that no action has been taken to date save the tracing of the details attached to the mobile numbers deployed, but should he persist in these offences, I will be handing it to one of my colleagues who will investigate further.'

Len shook his head. 'You're so funny.'

'If that doesn't work, we'll go and do his knees.' Fay gave a sudden hoot of laughter. 'Do you remember that bloke who didn't want to pay us? The one with the dogs?'

Len grinned and nodded. 'I was scared, never mind him.'

Fay laughed again. 'I told him to pay up or I'd have his legs broken. And he believed me!' She clapped Len on the shoulder, sounding thoroughly pleased with herself. 'Nobody messes with me.'

Chapter 15

'Please don't touch!' Roz got up from her chair in the corner of Turner Contemporary's large white North Gallery for the umpteenth time and strode towards the Victorian style bathtub artfully filled with papier mâché 'treasure'. The coins-into-money-box installation downstairs was proving hugely popular, with queues forming for a chance to climb the ladder and send the yellow discs clattering below, but some visitors were seeing this interactive opportunity as carte blanche to put their sticky hands on everything.

'Sorry.' The young man she'd addressed edged away but his pink-haired girlfriend stood her ground and glared at Roz. Roz nodded towards the notice nearby.

'Thank you,' she said curtly.

She was overdue a break and could do with a pee. Melody should have been up here five minutes ago. Roz pulled her radio from her belt and put a call out. When Melody did not respond, Roz sighed.

Now the couple had wandered out, the room was empty. Checking down the corridor to see if anyone else was approaching who looked likely to start prodding the exhibits, Roz signalled to Holly, who had just taken over in the gallery opposite, that she was shooting out – something that was highly forbidden even if there were nobody there – and went quickly to the top of the stairs, running down the first flight to see if Melody was on her way. As she came around the corner to the second flight down, she saw Melody standing at the bottom. Talking to –

'Shit!' Roz had instinctively turned and run back the way she came before her brain had fully processed what she'd seen. What the hell was *he* doing here? Her heart was pounding. If Jamie was asking for her, surely Melody would have the sense to tell him it was her day off or something. But then how would Melody know who it was? Roz had told her the story but she didn't think she'd used his name. And he wouldn't mention – would he?

Shaken, Roz stopped just around the corner and peeped back. They were still talking. Roz breathed deeply and tried to be rational. Him being here was probably nothing to do with her at all. He was probably just looking around in his lunch break and asking Melody some questions about the installations or what time the café closed ...

As she watched, Melody pointed up the stairs towards her and made a gesture to Jamie to follow. Roz shrank back and fled. Rushing past the exhibition she was supposed to be supervising, she pressed her pass feverishly against the door to the staff offices and threw herself into the room, perching herself on the edge of a chair to stare at the bank of CCTV screens. Paula from marketing was typing at a desk opposite. She looked up curiously. 'Problem?'

'No, no, just on my break.'

Roz looked at the screen. She could see the camera-jerky figure of Melody coming up the corridor, and into the gallery with Jamie in tow. She was looking around. Clearly wondering why Roz wasn't at her post. She and Jamie walked to the far side and looked into the adjoining gallery space. Now they were coming back and had stopped near the entrance. He was giving Melody something ...

Roz swung round as her boss Vivienne opened the door looking irritated. 'What are you doing skulking in here? You haven't left the bathtub?'

'No – Melody's there.' Roz turned back and pointed at the screen where her friend was just lowering herself into the chair Roz had vacated. 'I am on my break.'

Vivienne's eyes narrowed. 'You know we don't leave anywhere unattended. Ever.' Vivien fixed her with a steely gaze and stalked out again.

Roz turned back to the screens, breathing heavily. There was no sign of Jamie. Roz scanned the other viewpoints. She couldn't make him out anywhere else but there was a crowd downstairs now, gathered around the huge plaster sculpture of a polar bear that was gracing the foyer, and it was difficult to see exactly who was among it. She'd go quickly to the staff loo and then go back and quiz Melody. What could they have been talking about all that time?

She came back into the office a few minutes later and searched the screens again. A tall figure that could have been Jamie had his back to the bear. Roz came cautiously out onto the top corridor and peered into each room. Melody was turned away from her by the bathtub, talking to some students. Holly's gallery only had a couple of women in it. She tentatively checked the West Gallery. He definitely wasn't upstairs.

'What's he called?' A young man with long hair and a bandana stopped next to her as she stood near the Clore Learning Studio, deep breathing and gazing through the huge expanse of glass and out to sea.

'Sorry?'

She followed the man's pointed finger to where the cast iron figure by Antony Gormley rose from the grey rippling water.

'Oh, um, *Another Time*. It's one of a series of a hundred pieces,' she went on robotically, as the young man appeared to be waiting for more. 'That are installed all over the world.'

'Yes, but what's that one called?' he persisted.

'I don't think it has an individual name,' Roz said distractedly. Melody had told the last person who'd asked, the figure was called Charlie. 'Could you excuse me,' she said apologetically. 'I'm actually on my break ...'

Vivienne, who had chosen that very moment to stride past, stopped and glared. 'What is it you'd like to know, sir?' she asked, with a professional beam. Roz slunk away, heart sinking. She'd be offered even fewer extra shifts now.

'Where have you been?' Melody looked pleased to see her. 'You'll never guess who was here a minute ago ...'

Roz listened horror-struck as Melody regaled her. 'I clocked who it was straightaway, when he said he'd met you recently at a house he was looking at and your friend Charlotte had told him you worked here!' Melody gave a peal of laughter. 'So I said, yes, you'd told me all about it, and I was in the same game so I'd been able to just picture the scene!'

'Oh for God's sake, Melody!' Roz put her head in her hands. 'What did you do that for? He thought I was rehearsing for a play.'

Melody looked scornful. 'Of course he didn't! Anyway, he was really nice and charming and he said he needs to see you again.'

'Well I don't want to see him.'

'Why not? From the way he was reacting I reckon he's into a bit of S&M himself ... you can always tell. Wouldn't surprise me if he doesn't want to become a client for real. And it's always a bonus if you get a good-looking one ...'

Roz clutched at her middle, feeling sick. Now what she'd been doing had been confirmed for him, suppose he told Charlotte?

Melody was still talking. 'So I brought him up here to find you but you'd disappeared. He was going to wait but then his phone rang and he said he had to go and he dashed off. But he'd already given me this.'

Melody handed Roz a business card. 'Wants you to give him a ring.'

'I won't be doing that.'

Melody looked hopeful. 'I don't mind taking him on if you don't want to?'

Roz had no intention of letting Melody have any more contact with Jamie. She pushed the card into her pocket and then had a horrible thought. 'You didn't give him my number, did you?'

'No, of course not.' But there was something about the way Melody's eyes flicked away from her as she said it, that made Roz doubt her.

'I do hope you didn't,' she said sharply, resolving to add Jamie's number to her contacts so she would know if he was ringing and could leave the phone unanswered. 'I really wish you hadn't discussed me at all!'

Melody looked petulant. 'It's not a crime you know. I know you're worried about Charlotte finding out but you can sort somewhere else to work if she finds it a problem. It's a job. There's nothing to be ashamed of.'

Roz felt suddenly exhausted. Her shoulders slumped as

she shook her head, her voice grim. 'That's not how my daughter would see it.'

Amy had been surprisingly amenable when Roz got home, chatting about her art lesson and the trials of sitting behind younger boys on the bus. She'd even made Roz a cup of tea while her mother was unpacking the shopping.

Roz pushed the M&S lasagne – grabbed hastily from the garage outlet at Westbrook before she made her way home – into the oven and looked across at her daughter sitting at the tiny kitchen table, ostensibly doing Geography homework but mostly, as far as Roz could see, liking things on Facebook.

She thought about the business card she'd removed from her pocket and now stuffed in her handbag – not quite sure what to do with it – aware that the double-barrelled surname rang a bell. She knew it was a risk to bring it up in conversation but she was sure Amy had mentioned that name once before.

Roz tipped salad leaves into a bowl and began to slice tomatoes, keeping her voice casual. 'Is there a girl at school called something Lees-Parker?'

'Yeah, Lucinda.' Amy did not look up from her phone. 'I told you about her before. She's got a horse and a swimming pool – one of those!'

Roz smiled. 'You're not close then?'

'She's all right. Bit up herself at times. I don't see her much – she's in different groups. Why do you want to know?'

'Oh, Charlotte knows her Dad,' said Roz, as if it were of no importance. 'She just mentioned he had a daughter at school with you and I thought I had maybe heard the name, that's all.'

She breathed out, relieved, and picked up an onion.

'Funnily enough,' said Amy, still tapping on her screen. 'We were talking yesterday.'

Roz felt a pang of anxiety shoot through her middle and looked at her daughter sharply – was there something in Amy's tone?

'Really?' Roz heard a faint squeak to her voice and hoped Amy hadn't noticed.

'Well, she was talking to Chloe more than me ...'

There was a silence while Amy did a bit more tapping. 'They were moaning about their dads.'

'Oh?'

'Chloe's dad has moved in with this awful woman who actually used to be friends with her mum – so she's really unimpressed with that one.'

Roz waited, not wanting to ask. 'I can imagine,' she said eventually, when Amy did not appear to be planning on saying any more.

'And Lucinda said her dad brought loads of girlfriends home, and she didn't care most of the time cos she doesn't live with him, but when she is there, she gets fed up with it. Says it's a drain having to watch them pretend to like her and want to be her friend when they clearly don't give a fuck–'

'Amy!'

'–about her really, but just want to make themselves look like great step-mother material so they can get their hands on his money.'

'So he's well-off?'

'Loaded,' said Amy dismissively. 'I just told you!' She yawned. 'Anyway, they said I was lucky that you didn't see anyone and I said I wouldn't mind if you wanted to go

130

dating.' Amy raised her head and looked candidly at Roz. 'As long as you don't bring them home!'

The home that I live in and pay for, thought Roz, biting back any retort because it felt like a long time since she and Amy had talked like this.

'In fact,' said Amy. 'I wondered if you had been dating and not telling me.'

Roz's stomach gave another unpleasant jerk. 'What do you mean?'

'The other night when you went out – that meeting you were so mysterious about.'

'I wasn't being mysterious – I was having a drink with Melody, as I said ...'

'You seem to like her a lot these days.'

'She's having a bit of a rough time,' Roz improvised guiltily. 'She needs someone to talk to.'

She began to thinly slice the onion to add to the salad, hoping she sounded convincing, wondering what it had been in her demeanour that had made Amy suspicious. She hadn't changed into her 'stern' outfit till she'd got to Melody's house.

Amy put down her phone and continued to gaze at her. 'Mum–'

Roz recognised the deceptively soft, slightly wheedling tone and braced herself. Amy looked down and bit her lip. 'I was wondering ...'

If she stopped doing the dominatrix work altogether now she would really miss the extra income. Roz had two hundred pounds in cash in the drawer in her bedroom. It made such a change from poking about looking for change for a pint of milk or a bus fare.

'How much?' she said, smiling.

Amy shook her head. 'I wasn't going to ask for money.'

She grinned. 'But if you're offering ...' Then she was abruptly straight-faced.

'Tell me the story again – about Dad.'

Roz felt her heart quicken. Was there once more an edge to Amy's voice, a slightly weighted emphasis on the word 'story'?

She took a deep breath and carried on slicing. The onion was stinging her eyes, despite her leaving the root end on.

'We went out for a few weeks,' she said lightly. 'And we drifted apart. I think he went to work abroad. I didn't discover I was pregnant until much later.'

'And you didn't try to find him?'

'Didn't think I needed to. You and me against the world, eh?'

Amy didn't smile.

'But you must have thought to look since?'

'Not really. And anyway – where would I start?'

Amy looked scathing. 'Facebook? Google. You can find anyone these days.'

Roz shrugged, wondering where this had come from. The talk with the other girls? Amy had always accepted they didn't know where her father was. She'd gone through a stage, when younger, of making up fantastically wild stories about him being lost in a jungle or killed in a plane crash, when other children asked, but at home she'd not seemed overly bothered. Why was she suddenly asking?

'I've looked,' continued Amy deliberately. 'There are lots of Mark Johnsons. I've narrowed them down by age and I've made a short list – some on Facebook and some on LinkedIn. I need you to look with me.'

Roz's heart was really thumping now. She glanced at the piece of paper with the column of names and locations that

Amy had pushed across the table, knowing without looking that none of them was Amy's father.

She'd known this would come one day. Maybe she should have told a different tale but Amy had always seemed happy enough with just the two of them. Had seemed content to have been fathered by a mythical and remote figure who was tucked away in some forgotten corner of the world. Unless someone else was enquiring, her paternity didn't get a mention from one year to the next.

Roz took another deep breath. Amy was fifteen and had a right to know. She couldn't lie to her for ever. Amy was also dogged when she wanted to be and would not let this drop now she'd decided she wanted to find out more.

At the end of the kitchen counter her phone began to ring. Roz froze, staring towards it.

'Look properly!' Amy's voice was hard.

Roz shook her head. The phone was still ringing. 'He won't be on that list,' she said slowly, seeing her daughter's eyes narrow. 'He won't be there because his name's not Mark Johnson.'

Amy gasped dramatically. 'You *lied*,' she snarled.

'I didn't tell you the whole story.'

'Granny said—'

'Oh yes, I might have known she'd be involved ...'

'You'd always been very secretive ...'

'I wonder why.'

'Who is he then? Didn't you even ask his name?' Amy's voice was steeped in disgust.

The phone had stopped. As Roz looked at the stony face of her daughter there was a small beep to indicate that someone had left a voice message.

Swallowing hard, she reached out and picked up her

mobile. Praying that Melody's interference hadn't come home to roost as well. She looked at the screen and was gripped with alarm.

There was a missed call from Charlotte.

Chapter 16

Charlotte propped herself up in bed and reached for her glass of water. Her mouth was dry and she had a slight headache. 'I really, really, am not going to drink today,' she recited to herself, as she got up and walked towards the en suite, leaving Roger still slumbering behind her.

Her legs felt tired and heavy. She needed an early night and an evening of sticking to cups of tea. She'd promised herself that yesterday, but after a broken previous night attending to Joe, who was throwing up for England, and a day scurrying about between clients, on top of the stress of everything else, it had been only too easy to sink gratefully into the sofa and accept Roger's offer to open a bottle of her favourite Mâcon.

Except it was more than one bottle, she thought guiltily. And she'd drunk the lion's share. Mainly to blot out the stricken look on Roger's face that morning when she'd told him he'd have to take the day off work to stay with their son because she had too many meetings to cancel.

It wasn't strictly true – only one of them was with someone who'd come specially down from London and was in a hotel waiting to see the properties she'd found for them – and she could probably have asked one of the others to sit with Joe for a while. But she wanted to see what Roger would say.

'I don't want to leave him alone,' she'd said. 'He's still feeling rough and I think he's got a temperature. One of us needs to be here.'

'Of course.' Roger had made the phone call straight away but she'd seen the look of quiet despair in his eyes.

'And fancy – it's a Wednesday!' she'd said with grim satisfaction to Fay when she'd let her know her tailing techniques would not be required after all. 'Whatever it is he should be doing, he's pissed off to be missing out on it. I can tell!'

Fay had been matter of fact, probably glad to be off the hook, but Charlotte was determined to pin her down to next week. She pulled on her dressing gown and went downstairs. She usually liked this quiet time on her own, before anyone else got up, but today she felt rattled and edgy.

She put the kettle on and got milk from the fridge – leaning down to check the level in the second bottle of wine she'd opened. There were a couple of inches left. Tonight she'd make a big, healthy salad and drink lots of water. 'I'll give you a rest, you poor old thing,' she said out loud, patting her middle in the general direction of her liver and wishing, not for the first time, that she still had a dog to address.

None of the others had picked up when she'd called the night before. Her official reason for phoning round had been to suggest another get-together – the party wasn't that far away now and there were still details to discuss – but really she'd wanted someone to talk to. Joe had gone back to bed after a mug of soup, still looking pale; Roger was ensconced in his study, catching up, he said, on work emails after being home with his son all day.

Charlotte had sat on a kitchen chair in the open doorway, blowing smoke out across the patio, feeling, for the first time she could ever remember, lonely. She'd sent Becky a WhatsApp and her daughter had sounded upbeat – about to go to see a band put on by the Student Union – but not in the mood for a long exchange with her mother.

In the old days, before Laura met Andrew and they eventually moved away, she'd have phoned her and Laura would have been there in the kitchen – sharing a bottle, talking about anything and nothing. But last night she couldn't even call. It was Laura's wedding anniversary – they'd be out to dinner.

Now, Charlotte put her coffee on the table and fetched her iPad, thinking she would email Lu and see if she'd had a good time. She looked at the photo that was her screensaver – the smiley one from her birthday of the four of them, taken by the waiter at the restaurant, Becky and Joe beaming either side of her, Roger's arm draped across her shoulders. They looked like the perfect happy family ...

Idly, she flicked through other photos. Becky and Joe at Christmas wearing Santa hats, Andrew and Lu and Stanley when they'd come to stay for Broadstairs Folk Week last summer. She and Lu holding champagne flutes, standing outside round the barbecue. Suddenly Charlotte missed her old friend deeply. She swallowed.

'Why don't you see if Laura would like a visit for a couple of days?' Roger came up behind her and looked at the screen over her shoulder. 'It would cheer you up a bit. Joe and I can cope here.'

Charlotte cleared the screen and pushed the iPad away from her. 'Why are you trying to get rid of me?'

'I'm not. I was trying to be nice!' Roger looked irritated. 'We'll all go then,' he went on briskly. 'Make a weekend of it. Stay in a hotel and take Laura and Andrew out to dinner. Then you two can go off and do girly stuff and have a catch-up and I'll hang out with Andrew and Joe. Bound to be a match on and didn't Andrew say he was mates with one of the governors who could sort tours of the stadium in Newcastle? Joe would love that. Why don't we? We haven't been away for a while ...'

Charlotte nodded dumbly – suddenly wanting to cry.

'I'm sorry,' she said. 'I'm sorry to be a cow. I just miss Laura and I was thinking about Benson and how the house still seems so empty without him especially now Becky ...' She broke off as her voice cracked.

'Hey.' Roger sat down next to her and leant forward to give her a hug. 'You're tired. You were up all night when Joe was sick and, well–' he smiled sympathetically at her '–you did have quite a bit to drink last night. You know it makes you emotional ...'

Charlotte shook her head. 'It's not that.'

'Is there something else wrong?' Roger's eyes scanned her face. 'You have been a bit distracted lately.'

Charlotte hesitated. *Tell me where you go on bloody Wednesdays!* But if she said that then, she'd never know the truth. He would deny everything like he did before. Better to wait till Fay followed him next week and find out for sure. She wished it wasn't eating away at her like it was.

Roger had his hand on her shoulder. 'If you want another dog–' He gave her a squeeze, got up and moved towards the coffee pot. 'But we did say after Benson we wouldn't, didn't we? Because of holidays. You said – as the kids grew up you wanted to travel more ...'

She nodded.

'But if you want a dog, we'll get a dog.'

He was spooning fresh coffee into the cafetière. 'I just want you to be happy, Char.'

Charlotte looked up at him. He had his back to her.

'I'd like that too,' she said.

'You could try telling yourself you are!' Fay stirred her coffee vigorously and leant back against the leather sofa in Le Café. 'A bit of mind over matter perhaps?'

Charlotte snorted. 'Not like you to promote mumbo jumbo.'

Fay pulled a face. 'I just think you should give the poor bastard a break,' she said flatly. 'Roger isn't behaving like someone who is having an affair.'

Charlotte sighed. 'I'm not meaning to be rude, love, but how would you know? Because he suggests a weekend away – because he's being nice? Oldest trick in the book isn't it, be extra lovely to the wife to put her off the scent?'

'Not always,' said Fay tersely. 'I simply don't think—'

'Well we'll find out next week when you follow him.'

'I can't next Wednesday.'

Charlotte let out a hiss of annoyance. 'Oh bloody hell – why not?'

'Because, funnily enough—' Fay looked at her friend with a mixture of affection and exasperation. 'I have a business to run.'

Charlotte knew she sounded like a petulant child. 'You said you would.'

'Yes,' said Fay with exaggerated patience. 'And I will. But on that particular day I have three big jobs on the go and need to be in Thanet in case I'm needed. I also have a hospital appointment.'

'Oh.' Charlotte was contrite. 'Are you OK?'

Fay was brisk. 'Yes of course. It's a routine thing.'

Charlotte waited but Fay didn't expand. Instead, she

looked directly at Charlotte and spoke firmly. 'I'll do it as soon as I can.'

Charlotte shook her head. 'But you don't want to. Perhaps it's better if I book Private Pete.'

He had phoned the day before, to see if she'd had any more thoughts and there was anything he 'could do' for her.

His voice had been soft and soothing. 'I believe you, Charlotte,' he'd said. 'In thirty years in this business, I have rarely found a wife's instincts to be wrong ...'

Charlotte had wavered. Part of her just wanted to throw money at the problem, to let Pete follow Roger and get it sorted once and for all. But she had promised Fay she would wait for her.

Fay sounded annoyed now. 'Don't you dare waste your cash. Or let a money-making dick wind you up. I said I would do it and I will.' Fay pulled out her phone and tapped at it. 'I'll put it in now for the following Wednesday. If you still think there's anything to investigate. Which I think there probably isn't.'

Charlotte looked at her hard. 'Why are you so keen to defend him?'

Fay held her gaze. 'I'm keen to see you get a sense of perspective. I told you I did a bit of digging on your birthday and Roger didn't seem to me like a bloke with anything to hide.'

'Hmm.' Charlotte broke her biscuit in half and dipped it morosely in her coffee.

'I went to see Sherie's sister.' Fay abruptly changed the subject. 'She's completely different from the Princess, isn't she? I couldn't get over it. Old jeans, not a scrap of make up on – very down to earth.' Fay nodded approvingly. 'I liked her.'

Charlotte gave a small chuckle. 'Says the woman with three hundred lipsticks.'

'Thirty-eight at the last count. People take you more seriously if you are groomed,' said Fay. 'Especially when you get a bit older. But I still like a woman who doesn't give a shit.'

'I don't think she's got time to – she's got her hands full with those kids – especially the youngest one.'

'I quite liked him too, actually,' said Fay, sounding surprised. 'He told me 'all the crap' was in storage. Made me laugh. I said – yes it's my storage. And he said: 'well, you know then.'"

Charlotte smiled again. 'Sherie adores him.'

'Anyway – I've priced up her move but she says the exchange got delayed again? So the July date she'd told me isn't going to work? I thought you'd got it going bloody quick.'

Charlotte nodded. 'That was the deal – exchange within six weeks. And complete a week later. It still might happen – it's only the other side's bank dragging their feet and the solicitor being an arse. I'm on it. Keep it pencilled for the moment?'

Fay nodded. 'Good. Will do. You seen Sherie?'

Charlotte frowned as if trying to remember. 'Only very briefly. She was just going into Bodilight – as I was coming out of the Co-op. She's having some course of facials where they zap your jowls with these mini cattle prods. She's booked one a week till the party, says it lifts and firms. I couldn't be arsed personally but it makes her happy.'

'Don't know why she doesn't just try this.' Fay twisted her face into a snarl and opened her mouth wide, before clamping her jaws shut again. 'Twenty of those before you clean your teeth every night does the same thing.'

Charlotte shrugged. 'I wouldn't be arsed to do that either.'

'Stops you getting a double chin.'

Charlotte smiled. 'Yeah, your boat's looking pretty good too. I'm the only one letting myself go ...'

'Pah!' Fay looked cynical. 'I bet you've spent a fortune on an amazing dress for the party and you'll be glammed to the eyeballs.'

'I haven't yet. I've been too distracted by–'

'Didn't you say we were having another get-together soon?' Fay asked, interrupting before Charlotte could get started on Roger again.

'I'm still trying to find a day when we can all meet – you all seem to be so busy at the moment.'

Everyone was occupied. Charlotte pushed down the disappointment she still felt from her phone call with Laura earlier. Her good friend had explained brightly that she and Andrew and Stanley had too much on at weekends to get together before the party, and had then been much brisker than Charlotte was used to, about Charlotte's fears over Roger being up to no good.

'Oh Charlotte!' she'd said, when Charlotte had explained that the sofa cushions had been more than usually rumpled the other evening and she'd half wondered if Roger had had a visitor while she was out collecting Joe from Karate practice. 'Of course he didn't!'

She had moved straight onto quizzing Charlotte about mood swings and how hot she got at night, before suggesting a visit to the doctor for a blood test. Charlotte had pretended she would think about it and hastily changed the subject.

'Laura says I should be taking sage drops.' Charlotte gave

a brief laugh now, to show how silly it all was. 'She thinks my hormones are affecting my balance of judgement—'

'Well ...'

As Fay looked at her thoughtfully, Charlotte wished she hadn't said anything. She'd trusted Fay to be dismissive. 'Anyway, I'll have another go at gathering everyone next week,' she said tightly.

Fay looked at her watch. 'Do you fancy a quick one now? Greens? Just one before we go home. Len can lock up.'

'I wasn't going to drink today.'

'Oh, OK well no problem ...'

'But yes. Let's!'

The bar was quiet – the six o'clock crowd having not yet arrived. Sarah, one of the owners, was the only one behind the bar. She came round to the front and hugged Charlotte. 'Hey stranger! Feels like you've not been in for ages.'

'Wasn't that long ago, surely.' Fay gave her a kiss. 'We conceived the party here, didn't we ...?'

'Ah yes.' Sarah laughed. 'Invite of the year. Everybody's talking about it.'

'Course they are!' Charlotte laughed too. 'Laura's coming down for it.'

'Lovely. It will be really good to see her ... So, what are you ladies having? Is it a bottle of our finest house white or are we on the fizz tonight?'

Fay looked at Charlotte. 'The Cava?'

'Oh my god – they should have this on prescription.' Minutes later Charlotte carried her glass and a bowl of peanuts to her favourite table in the corner by the window. 'What is it about fizz? I've only had two mouthfuls and already I feel so much better.' She scooped up some nuts and took another sip. 'Just what I needed.'

Fay nodded. 'So where are we with this party then? Do you need me to do anything?'

'Just chase up your RSVPs. They're going to want final numbers the week before.'

Fay shrugged. 'I've not got that many coming that you haven't already included. All the chaps at work and their partners – saves me a staff outing. Elaine from the office and her old man if he can stay sober long enough to come. I did ask my cousin but–' Fay shrugged again. 'Her ladyship won't want to travel all this way for a party for me. Mingling in a crowd is a bit beneath her. And there's no point involving Mum – in the old days she'd have loved a party but ...'

For a moment Fay looked uncharacteristically sad. Charlotte spoke brightly. 'And Cory?'

'Haven't mentioned it. Hardly think a gathering of drunken middle-aged women doing the conga is going to be his scene.'

Charlotte mock shuddered. 'God forbid. I must make sure Sherie is on top of the flowers.'

'Not literally.'

Charlotte laughed. 'Thanks for suggesting this. It's good to spend time with you. And I hope you are right about Roger,' she went on. 'He is being very nice – just as he always has been really. Maybe you and Laura are right and I am over-thinking it all ...'

'I'm quite sure you are,' Fay said.

Charlotte drained her glass. 'I know I drink more than government guidelines,' she said ruefully. 'And I am going on a detox for a few days very soon. But when everything else is going wrong, booze makes me feel confident it will all be OK.' She looked at Fay, hesitating for a moment before saying: 'When I've had a glass of wine, I feel invincible again – that I can deal with it all, that whatever happens, I will overcome.' She gave a short brittle laugh. 'So is that the real me coming out? Or is the real me these days, this fucked-up, totally fretful mad woman, obsessed with what her husband is doing, even if he isn't doing anything?'

'They are both the real you,' said Fay. 'Different parts of you. But drink,' she said, looking seriously at Charlotte, 'probably isn't the answer!'

'I know,' said Charlotte, 'but it does make me feel happy.' She picked up her phone to look at the time. Then she shrugged off her cardigan, fanning herself briefly with a beer mat and leant back. 'Hey, you know what?' she said with fresh conviction. 'Joe's not being brought back till eight. I'll leave the car and get a cab home. Let's have another ...'

Chapter 17

*T*hey were kind at the breast clinic too. The first doctor was Polish, with beautiful skin. She frowned when I opened my shirt and showed her.

She made me sit on the bed and put my arms above my head and then lie down, while she spent a long time stroking the stress-lump looking quizzical. Then she smiled.

'We will be positive and say I don't think this is cancer,' she said. She gave another tiny frown. 'But I don't know what it is.'

She wants me to come back on Thursday but when I explain about work commitments, she says she will see if anyone is free to give me the biopsy today. She makes phone calls while I sit and twist my hands together, trying to remember what else I have Googled that the medical profession might not immediately identify. That looks like cancer but just might not be.

The radiologist is Polish too. She is older than me and motherly-looking. I keep my eyes on her face as she puts her ultrasound probe over my stress lump and I know immediately.

'Is there fluid in it?' I ask, hearing the hope in my voice and knowing it is misplaced.

'No,' she says, and I see her sympathy. She asks the young nurse to fetch things and begins to talk quietly about what the biopsy will entail.

'What do you think it is?' I ask her. 'On my report,' she says, 'I shall write "Indeterminate."' There is a pause. 'Slightly suspicious,' she adds, as if her conscience has demanded honesty.

When it's all over she smiles at me but her eyes are sad. 'Try to remain strong,' she says. 'There is nothing to be done before the results are here. That will be as soon as we can.' She pauses as if choosing her words. When she speaks again, her voice is full of encouragement. 'We do not cross the bridge yet.'

She shakes my hand and sees me out.

The door clunks shut and I hear it closing on the rest of my life.

Chapter 18

'Here's to the second half of your life!'
'Thank you!' Roz smiled around her cramped kitchen at her three friends. 'Fifty,' she added ruefully. 'How did that happen?'

'God knows,' said Charlotte. 'But you're looking pretty good on it, love. So let's get the fizz open!'

Sherie shook her head sorrowfully. 'I still can't believe I'm going to be that old.' She pulled a face. 'From now on, every time we're paid a compliment there'll be that unspoken *for your age* ...'

'And when you're sixty, you'll wonder what all the fuss was about!' Charlotte sounded uncharacteristically sharp. 'Let's just be grateful we're alive!'

As the others looked at her in surprise, she gave a brief smile and said in a milder voice. 'So we'll drink to that, shall we?'

In the slightly awkward pause that followed, Roz reached into the cupboard for glasses. She'd deliberately invited them all round in the afternoon – saying it was for tea and cake – so she could keep it cheap and didn't have to put on a lavish spread or spend a fortune on booze. But Fay and Sherie had both brought a bottle of champagne with them and Charlotte had produced two.

Charlotte popped the cork and began to pour, mouthing 'sorry' at Roz and handing her the first of the mismatched wine goblets. As Roz sipped at the deliciously cold bubbles, she was grateful. Amy was still largely monosyllabic and had stayed glued to her iPad for the entire journey back from her parents this morning and they had barely spoken since. Her actual birthday, the day before, had been a low-key, slightly strained affair and it was good to see her friends cheerily raising their glasses to her, instead of constantly judging.

'How was your mother?' asked Sherie, taking a chair at the small table. She looked, as always, effortlessly stylish in her jeans and heels, loose top and arty, chunky jewellery. Beside her Roz felt rather tired and drab.

'Oh her usual joyous self,' Roz pulled a face.

'She got you a cake!' Amy spoke accusingly from the doorway.

'Ah – come and give me a hug!' Charlotte held out her arms. 'You're looking so gorgeous.'

Amy coloured and smiled at Charlotte. 'How's Bex doing?'

'Partying extremely hard, as far as I can gather,' said Charlotte brightly. 'But sparing me the details. How is school – and what do you want for your sixteenth darling? Euros to spend in Paris?'

'Yes, she'd arranged a cake,' Roz told Fay and Sherie, as Amy chatted on to Charlotte with more enthusiasm than she ever displayed for her mother. 'We had dinner at the golf club and they brought out a strawberry gâteau with five candles and everybody clapped.' Roz looked at them with a straight face. 'Yes, I did feel about six years old, and yes she did manage to get in about six digs about my appearance before the main course.'

Roz raised her eyebrows. 'Have you thought,' she intoned, 'about a more structured look now you're that bit older? There was an article in Good Housekeeping about bobs to suit all face-shapes.'

Roz raised her eyebrows. 'Apparently mine is entirely wrong.'

'Your bob or your face-shape?' Fay enquired.

'My general lack of style,' said Roz, pushing back the soft brown waves from her face. She nodded at Sherie's classy blonde chignon. 'She'd like me to look a bit more like you.'

'You look lovely,' said Sherie. 'You have a beautiful face and your hair is fine as it is. What did she give you as a present?'

'Five hundred quid's worth of M&S vouchers.'

'Not to be sniffed at,' observed Fay.

'Presumably so I could buy clothes like hers,' continued Roz, adding guiltily: 'but yes, it was generous.'

'You can always blow it on yummy food, and champagne and scented candles,' said Fay. 'And there's knickers ...'

'Indeed,' Roz nodded. 'I do get my underwear there. And that particular drawer could certainly do with an overhaul ...'

'Oh, I must give you my copy of the Marie Kondo book,' said Sherie with enthusiasm. 'Honestly it really is life-changing – look!' She picked up her phone and began scrolling through her photos. 'I've got two more to do ...' Sherie held up her iPhone so they could see the screen. The picture showed an open drawer filled with neatly-rolled tights. She flicked to the next one and Roz and Fay peered at an array of make-up in small boxes sorted by type. Sherie appeared to own an astonishing number of mascaras.

'See?' Sherie sounded animated. 'And it really does spark joy every time I look at that.'

150

Fay made a peculiar noise in her throat but Sherie kept talking. 'Mind you, it becomes addictive. Once the inside of my cupboards were a work of art, I started moving the furniture and I did so much hoovering that I hurt my back.'

'Hmmm – that's unlikely to happen to me,' said Fay dismissively. 'I thought you had a cleaner?'

'Yeah, I do – Toni – but she's a bit hit and miss. Her child keeps getting excluded from school so she can't always come.'

Fay pulled a face. 'So glad I don't have kids.' She swallowed the last of her champagne. 'Hey Char, let's have some refills.'

An hour later they'd moved into Roz's small sitting room. Sherie had taken off her shoes and was sitting cross-legged on the floor doing occasional yoga stretches, Charlotte and Fay were sprawled on the sofa. Roz, several champagnes down, and propped up against the bean bag was beginning to feel in need of a bit more sustenance than a slice of Waitrose's Mary Berry celebration cake.

'Shall I make sandwiches?' she enquired of the room, aware that her voice was teetering slightly and she was in that place just before slurring began. She'd left her parents' house early, shaking away her mother's offer of breakfast, wanting to get home and the house tidied, before her friends were due. Longing for some sea air away from the stifling atmosphere of Carshalton polite society. There was bread, she had eggs and there was probably ham left lurking at the bottom of the fridge. She wondered if she dare ask Amy – who had disappeared again after her conversation with Charlotte to help. She must be hungry too ...

'Don't go to that effort, love.' Charlotte waved an arm as if brushing the idea aside. 'We'll go on Just Eat and order something. I'm famished as well. Where's Amy with her iPad? I find a teenager very useful in these situations ...'

Before Roz had a chance to reply, Charlotte had levered herself off the sofa and was at the bottom of the stairs. 'Amy darling! Us oldies need your assistance ...'

They finally settled, after much discussion and eye-rolling from Amy, who was tapping on a variety of menus and reading out the options, on an Indian take-away, including vegetable rice and paneer for Sherie, a 'fuck-off sized shish kebab' for an increasingly strident Fay, and a variety of chicken dishes that Charlotte had taken an executive decision on, for them all.

'Stick the order in, darling!' she instructed Amy. 'You can use my card.'

'Please let's just phone the restaurant direct,' begged Roz. 'I've heard these booking sites charge so much commission that for the business, it hardly makes it worthwhile.'

Charlotte looked at her fondly.

'Your mum,' she said to Amy, 'is such a very good person.'

Amy looked at Roz. 'Don't be so sure of that,' she said darkly.

'Garlic!' said Jean, three hours later. 'Pooh.'

'Yes, I've had a curry, Mum.' After the perfunctory hello kiss, Fay settled herself in the chair in the corner of the lounge next to her mother.

The TV was blaring as usual with nobody watching it. The three old boys on the sofa were all asleep with their mouths open and the other residents were variously engaged with staring into middle distance or wandering in circles muttering.

'Don't know whether they're coming or going – this lot,' remarked Jean. 'Where've you been anyway? Haven't seen you for months.'

'I was here Tuesday,' said Fay. 'And it's only Sunday now.'

'The doctor asked me if I knew who the Prime Minister was,' said Jean. 'I said – do you think I'm stupid? It isn't Tony Blair!'

'Who is it?' enquired Fay with interest.

'I don't know,' Her mother's tone suggested she didn't care much either. 'That one with the shoes.'

'Can we go in the conservatory?' Fay stood up. 'It does my head in, in here.'

She'd come on impulse. Sherie and Charlotte had shared a cab from Roz's but Fay had said she'd walk – it was only twenty minutes from the Broadway to the Esplanade. But as she'd come out of the end of the road, she'd seen a bus go past, heading for Margate, and had run to jump on it.

Maxine the manager had greeted her warmly when she arrived, used to Fay popping in at odd hours. 'All as ever,' she'd said in answer to Fay's raised eyebrows. 'Still complaining I don't know how to make steak and kidney.' She continued as Fay nodded in recognition. 'And she wants more oranges.'

'Bloody hell – what's she doing with them? I brought a dozen last time.' Fay smiled as the other woman shrugged. She sometimes wondered if her mother was squirreling all her bounty away somewhere and at some point a giant, rotting fruit mountain would burst out of her wardrobe or ooze up through the floorboards.

'That's better,' Fay said now – as they sat down in the cool and comparative quiet of the glass extension at the back of the home. 'I can hear you in here. What sort of day have you had?'

Her mother pointed to a large potted palm in the corner. 'They didn't water that.'

'But what have you been doing?'

153

'Shopping I think, but I don't know,' her mother stood up. 'Have you seen my room?'

'Yes,' said Fay, as she always did. 'It's got a lovely view of the garden.'

Her mother looked surprised. 'Yes it has. Have you seen it? Come and see it now.' Fay rose and followed her mother down the carpeted corridor where they went every time she came here.

The room was tidy – the hairbrush and comb lined up on the dressing table that had come from the house, the blue and white cushions propped up in the chair Fay had brought here from her mother's bedroom at home, the bed covered with the quilt she'd had as long as Fay could remember. Fay looked at the framed photographs of herself and her father. She wondered how long it would be before her mother no longer remembered who he was.

Her mother settled herself into the armchair as Fay perched on the end of the bed. 'Tell me why I'm here again?' her mother asked, sounding as if she'd forgotten some minor detail.

'Because you kept leaving the gas on,' said Fay. 'And the front door open,' she added. *And you tried to give the window cleaner three hundred pounds but thought twenty was enough for the plumber. And we never did find your post office card or what you did with the key to the garage …*

'You don't have to worry here,' she said. 'Maxine looks after everything.'

Her mother nodded. 'She's not a bad one.'

With perfect timing the manageress appeared in the doorway. 'I've brought your cocoa, Jean. Do you want one?' she looked at Fay.

'Smells like Horlicks to me.'

Maxine gave a wry smile. 'It is. But Jean calls it cocoa so we do too.'

'Don't like that chocolate muck,' put in Fay's mother. She took the steaming mug and picked up the shortbread finger from the plate below it. 'Are you going to marry Len?' she demanded.

Fay laughed, startled. 'I shouldn't think so.'

'Well he's going to ask you, so you say yes.' She regarded Fay beadily. 'If you know what's good for you.'

Fay gave a small snort. 'I really don't think he is, Mum.' She turned to Maxine. 'Len works for me. She hasn't seen him for years.'

'Oh, she has – he was here the other evening. Nice man isn't he? They played scrabble.' Maxine picked up the water jug from the bedside table.

Fay felt her mouth open. 'She can't do that any more ...'

'No, but she enjoyed putting the tiles out. They were laughing.'

'I like scrabble,' said Jean firmly. 'And I win.'

'She was brilliant,' said Fay, softly. 'The last time we played before she got this, she got one-hundred and seventy-eight with detoxify. That's when I knew – she was still doing the words but she couldn't add up the scores any more.'

As Maxine moved around the room, turning a lamp on, checking the en suite bathroom, Fay remembered her mother's satisfied sigh of triumph. In those days when she still played three times a week, beating her neighbour mercilessly on a Monday, the two long-suffering women she went to Bums & Tums with, on a Thursday after class, and trouncing Fay nine times out of ten when she visited on Saturday afternoons.

Jean always wanted to hear what Fay had been doing,

with a seemingly insatiable appetite for the minutiae. It was never enough to say she'd gone for a pie with Len, her mother had to know what was in it. Probably if her mother were still the full ticket, she would tell her what was going on now. Jean would have been brisk and bracing. Reminded Fay that the Sternhouse women were tough and strong – that you could get through anything if you believed you could, and held your head up high.

Maxine said goodnight and disappeared through the door. The Horlicks mug had been drained and her mother's eyes were drooping now.

Fay took hold of her hand for a moment, as she prepared to slip away too. 'Sleep well, Mum.' She felt the slightest squeeze against her fingers as she added softly: 'I miss you.'

Chapter 19

'You look lovely. I've missed you!'
Nate came into the hallway and looked at Sherie in her pale linen dress and jewelled sandals. 'Love the beads.'

Sherie smiled self-consciously. She'd felt awkward with Nate since the night at the Swan and had been attempting to avoid him, but he'd reminded her by text about the private view and she hadn't felt she could pull out. 'Thank you.'

Nate was examining her more closely. 'But are you OK? You look a bit–'

Sherie hesitated. 'Oh, I'm just a little stressed because–' she stopped and shrugged.

'That bloke isn't still bothering you?'

'No, no,' She gave a short, embarrassed laugh. 'I don't know what Fay did but whatever it was, it worked.'

Nate grinned. 'I wouldn't take her on.'

'I used to be a bit scared of her too! But Charlotte always says she has a heart of gold.' Sherie went quickly on. 'I was only thinking about an email I've just had. You know I'm having this fire put in?'

Nate shook his head.

'Oh, sorry I thought I told you. It's an amazing flame effect. There was one in a client's house and I honestly thought it was real. I really fancy one in the sitting room for

157

the winter. So I'm having the fireplace enlarged and the gas supply needs to be rerouted – they said it could take a couple of days. But now I've got to go to Birmingham to see an artist and I don't want to put the fire people off because they're doing me a really good deal as they're quiet at the moment and they said it had to be next week ...'

She stopped, aware of how agitated she sounded.

Nate's tone was reassuring. 'No problem. School's out. I'm around now, aren't? I can let them in and let them out and even make them a cup of tea. Are you away overnight?'

'No, I'm back in the evening. But it might be late. And the next day I have to meet with Geoffrey. I can let them in myself if they start really early but–'

'Sherie, it's fine. I'll be on hand to supervise and look after His Highness.' He bent to stroke Marquis who had wandered down the stairs and was now sitting at Nate's feet.

Sherie smiled at the cat fondly. 'He's been out cold on my bed for hours. Let me just feed him and I'll be with you.'

Nate laughed. 'I'll wait while you peel his prawns and hand press the organic llama cheese ...'

Sherie laughed too, relaxing a little. 'No cheese allowed here – cats can't digest it properly.'

'Try telling that to my Mum's cat after it pinched the Christmas stilton – it eats anything!'

Sherie had suggested they get a cab but Nate insisted he'd drive her. 'I won't be drinking much anyway as it's partly my do. You don't have to stay to the end if you get bored. Get a cab whenever you want.'

'I'm sure they'll be lots of interesting people to talk to,' said Sherie politely, praying there would at least be one or two.

The gallery was new and consisted of two large rooms in what had once been a Chinese restaurant in the market place in Margate's Old Town.

A sandwich board outside heralded the imminent opening of its inaugural exhibition: *Down to the Sea Again* – open to the public from 10 am the following day.

Sherie had seen Nate's latest finished painting when it was still on its easel but now she caught her breath again, seeing the beachscape resplendent against a white wall, the evening sun streaming through the large picture windows, highlighting the vibrant colours.

There were four of them exhibiting on a nautical theme and Nate's work stood out as the most arresting by far. Sherie began to wonder where she would hang *Tide Turning* if she bought it. It was quite large and she had a lot of art already. Maybe if she rearranged the walls of her bedroom ...

She looked around at the twenty or so people holding plastic glasses of wine and gave Nate a big encouraging smile, although her heart was sinking. She didn't feel like making small talk with strangers. She took the drink Nate held out to her and spoke brightly. 'Right, I'm going to work my way round and look at everything. You go and mingle. I know you need to network.'

She picked up the list and approached a canvas entitled *Crab and Beach Hut* and pretended to study it minutely even though she had dismissed it as lacking any real presence or conviction, from the doorway.

Nobody seemed to be taking much notice of the paintings. The two women behind her were debating the wisdom of the latest rise in entrance fees to Margate's Dreamland, and a bloke in the corner was engrossed in his phone.

She moved slowly around the room, pleased to see that a smaller work of Nate's – a study of shells – already had a red dot on it to indicate a sale. It was 7.15 p.m. There was another hour and three-quarters to go before Nate could leave. Sherie wondered if she could decently suggest she waited for him in a nearby bar. She had a novel she was longing to finish, in her handbag. But she didn't want to hurt his feelings. There were still two or three paintings to stand in front of. She'd give it another half hour ...

'Sherie this is Carlos.' Sherie turned to see a dark-haired, Mediterranean-looking man of about her age. 'Sherie is a very important art-consultant,' said Nate. Sherie was touched by the pride in his voice.

'Ah – so what can I offer you to consult on here?' Carlos took her hand and kissed it with an exaggerated bow. Sherie smiled tightly and looked at the list in her hand.

'I was just looking at your *White Cliffs*.' She resisted the urge to add that it was vastly overpriced in her opinion as well as being derivative, and instead made polite enquiries as to how long he'd been painting and where he had been exhibited before, punctuating his ensuing monologue with 'really?' and 'how interesting', until he eventually came to the end of a self-promotional spiel which Sherie suspected contained more than a dash of fantasy.

'The Royal Academy. Gosh.' she said drily, noting that Nate was no longer beside her.

'In Scotland,' Carlos added hastily, as if he'd suddenly realised Sherie might be able to disprove him.

'Such an achievement!' Sherie backed smoothly away.

'Sorry,' said Nate when she re-joined him. 'Got called over to speak to her–' He nodded towards a tall woman in a fitted purple dress. 'Something to do with Tourism at Thanet

District Council. Harry, the gallery owner, wanted me to speak to her.'

'No problem. I was just thinking—'

'I should have invited Fay and Len,' said Nate suddenly. 'Or wouldn't this be her thing?'

'I don't know her views on art,' said Sherie honestly. 'But I do know she wouldn't keep them to herself.' She took on Fay's forthright tones. 'Eighteen hundred quid for a bit of white paint on blue paint? Is he having a larf?'

'Well I think that too,' said Nate, lowering his voice.

Sherie nodded. 'And he's not got half your talent.'

'Oh I didn't mean that—' Nate looked embarrassed. 'I just meant it's a lot to expect to get here in a tiny gallery in Margate.'

'Too much,' Sherie was brisk. 'For what it is. Your work on the other hand,' she continued. 'Wouldn't look out of place in the swishiest of galleries. You're good, Nate, you're really good.'

Nate smiled self-consciously. 'Well thank you. Do you think Fay—'

'You must be Nathaniel!' A woman in her late fifties wearing very bright lipstick swept down on them and grasped Nate's hand. 'I absolutely love your work and want to talk to you about doing something very special for me. I've just bought a house in Westgate and the walls are looking terribly bare ...'

Sherie discreetly stepped back, smiling as she watched the woman propel Nate into a corner, clearly enamoured, by the look of the way she was simpering, by more than just his art.

As she neatly avoided Carlos and went out onto the pavement for some air, Sherie reflected on the way it was those with the genuine talent – like Nate – who were always the self-effacing ones, while the Carloses of the world blew the trumpets. She wondered idly if Nate found Fay attractive. Fay already had one youthful lover – she clearly had something about her that appealed to younger men. She wondered what Nate had been about to ask.

Would Fay and Len have come along if they'd been encouraged to? Sherie had no idea what sort of bloke Len was or what he was interested in. She'd heard Fay talk about going to the pub with him and how terrific he was at running her business, but she knew nothing more about him, except that on the couple of occasions she had met him, he seemed very kind ...

Standing outside the gallery, looking across the old square at the stretch of sea at the end of the narrow street opposite, the couples and families wandering around in the warm evening, Sherie was suddenly acutely aware of her aloneness.

She had her friends and her sister, her parents were still alive, but there was nobody to whom she felt she could lay herself bare. Nobody to whom she was more important than any other. She didn't have a husband like Charlotte did, or a permanent lover or even a child, who might love her without condition.

Fay was in the same boat – she had made it clear Cory was short-term and kept at a distance – but Fay seemed to relish her independence.

Fay was supremely self-sufficient. She might be in bed with Cory now, or out for a drink with Len after work but she never seemed to *need* anyone. She couldn't imagine that Fay ever felt lonely watching TV at home on her own. Or sat at her kitchen table, longing to have someone to tell about her day.

Sherie shook herself as self-pity threatened to creep over her. She had Marquis – he could always to be relied upon to curl up in front of a TV drama. And keep to himself the things she whispered into his furry ears.

Sherie straightened up, trying to ignore the anxious flutterings in her stomach. She fixed her smile as Nate appeared back at her side and scrutinised her.

'You all right?' He was looking at her with concern and she thought how kind he was too. If she were in her thirties again, she'd have thought him a real catch ...

'Fine. Channelling my inner Fay,' she added, pulling a wry face at his confusion.

Fay had poured a glass of red wine. She mostly had a rule about not drinking on her own but there was just enough for a glass left in the bottle she'd shared with Cory the night before. And her hands were shaking.

She'd brought the laptop home because there were things she needed to look up in private. The office was like Piccadilly bloody circus with Elaine hovering about and Len in and out. She'd had to shut the page down a dozen times.

She knew even as she was searching, that it would be better if she didn't find out more now. Because there was nothing she could do to change anything. She just had to wait. Until such times when ... If ...

Fay stared at the screen in front of her, quickly scanning the words, and then dragging her eyes away. She put her head in her hands repeating the words she always turned to. 'I will get through – I always get through.'

There was no point looking for any more. But still her hand moved robotically to click on yet another search box. She was like a gambler or crack addict, knowing the results of her investigations could only cause her pain and fear but who could never quite let go. She felt the adrenalin jolt through her as she took a sharp intake of breath at what came next.

Angrily, she slammed the lid of the laptop down. She should have had more self-discipline, she should never have brought it back here.

'It will be OK,' she told herself.

And if it isn't? A tiny persistent voice whispered at the edges of her fevered mind.

Fay squeezed one hand so tightly with the other that it hurt.

Then I don't fucking care …

Chapter 20

R oz pushed the Dyson into the cupboard of the utility room that was bigger than her entire kitchen. She had polished and hoovered as Charlotte had asked her to, but the place had looked pretty immaculate already. Roz crossed to the sink where the long-stemmed white roses she'd collected from Jan at Church Street Florists, on her way over, were waiting to be arranged. Charlotte had a viewing here at nine the next morning and was fairly confident she was going to make a sale.

'They've seen all the photos,' she'd told Roz, 'and it's exactly the location they're after. So if you could air it ...'

Roz had flung open all the windows and now made her way systematically around the house closing them again. She didn't want any sound carrying from what was going to happen next ...

Roz had been going to stop. But the washing machine was on its last legs and the electricity bill had been huge again. They'd increased her direct debit just as the tax was due on her ancient Volvo. If it failed its MOT next time it would have to go. Roz was going to work on the bus to save money on petrol and parking. She could do without a car. But Amy couldn't do without clothes. Especially as her daughter was barely speaking to her since the revelation about her father.

She'd hoped if she was honest with Amy, it would clear the air and they'd get back some of their closeness. But her daughter had listened to the true account of how she'd come to be conceived with increasing disgust. When Roz had finally finished, and answered Amy's questions as truthfully as she dared, her daughter had looked disdainfully at Roz. 'No wonder you kept that hidden,' she said.

'I was thinking of you,' Roz had said, as Amy stalked towards the door. 'I didn't want anything to make our lives complicated.'

She'd failed on that one on all fronts, she thought ruefully now as she locked the window in the master bedroom and closed the door behind her. She'd promised Amy she'd told her everything – what would her daughter say if she knew what else she was concealing? For the first time, it being just the two of them, made Roz feel vulnerable instead of strong and self-contained.

As Roz secured her hair a little more tightly into its bun and smoothed down her skirt, she shuddered at the thought of Amy also discovering how she'd paid the recent bills.

She'd tried everything else. She'd asked Vivienne about more hours at Turner Contemporary but there was no budget for any more staffing right now. Roz had been looking for better-paid jobs but there was nothing in Thanet for a soon-to-be fifty-year-old with no specialist skills. Her years, pre-Amy, as an art director at the London ad agency, seemed a lifetime ago. The job description had probably changed beyond all recognition.

So she'd said yes to 'John' and 'Eddie' and would make a few more hundred pounds while she still could. As soon as the house was under offer, she'd have to think again anyway. Charlotte would take back the key then. It might be a long time before she had another on her books that wasn't over-looked or under scrutiny by the neighbours. The woman next door to the other one she cleaned, didn't miss a trick.

John had been in and out in forty minutes when she'd first got here and had still paid for the full hour. Easy money since he'd spent at least twenty of those minutes standing in the corner while she occasionally hissed 'Bad Boy!' between dusting the chandeliers.

Once Eddie had left she would distribute the flower vases and be on her way. He'd been vague in his messages – despite her asking all the standard questions – but she imagined the usual paraphernalia would do. She put her slipper and cane down by the end of the sofa, put her suit jacket back on and reapplied her lipstick, wishing she could raise as much enthusiasm for this particular pastime as Melody clearly maintained.

He was certainly prompt. The bell rang at exactly a minute past midday. Slipping her heels back on, Roz walked slowly down the hall towards the front door, arranging her features for maximum severity.

She opened the door with unhurried deliberation.

'Yes?' she intoned icily.

Then she shrieked. 'Oh my God!'

She stared in disbelief at the tall figure on the doorstep. This couldn't be happening twice.

'Please don't shut it!' He'd got a foot over the threshold and was wedging the door open, holding out his hand and smiling as if he'd come round for tea. 'I'm the Eddie you're expecting.'

'But it's you!' she said stupidly.

'Yes, it's me,' replied Jamie, as she leant weakly against the hall wall. 'But I thought you might not accept me if I gave you my real name. Can I come in? I'm going to pay. It's a professional engagement – I really do want to talk to you.'

'NO, I couldn't possibly–'

'Wait till I've explained.'

'You're a parent at my daughter's school, a colleague of my friend Charlotte. I can NOT–' Roz hesitated. 'Do whatever it is you want. I am giving it all up anyway,' she added desperately. 'It was only ever temporary. It was for research for a part,' she said wildly. 'That was what I meant to say before.'

He grinned. 'This is also academic.'

'What?'

'We'd better shut this.' He closed the front door and stood in front of her. 'Can we sit down?'

Roz sat opposite him on the sofa. She listened in silence and then stared at him in disbelief. 'You are writing a thesis on the potency of fear?'

'That's right,' said Jamie smoothly. 'And I'm concentrating on investigating the root of the emotional responses which cause people – particularly men – to seek out situations in which they feel threatened or humiliated. So I just wanted to buy some of your time to ask you some questions on why, for example, when you are going to cause discomfort or pain–'

'I absolutely don't believe you,' Roz interrupted hotly. 'You aren't in further education!'

'You're not in a play!'

Roz looked back at him. He seemed amused. She felt mortified. 'No, I am not in a play.' She stood up. 'Would you please leave now?'

'Would you please have lunch with me?'

Jamie was smiling at her charmingly and Roz felt at a loss.

'I've tried everything,' he said. 'I asked Charlotte for your phone number, I went to the gallery, I have been to this house several times and knocked on the door hoping you'd be here. But then I thought it might completely freak you out if you were – er – busy, so in the end I went on the website your friend gave me and searched for Miss Sterling!'

Roz gave a sharp sigh of annoyance. Bloody Melody.

'I was going to say it was for research on the contact form, but I thought if you refused, I'd be stuck. So, I made an appointment.' He offered a shining smile. 'It was the only way I could think of definitely getting to see you again. Without appearing like a stalker,' he added.

'Why would you want to?' she asked churlishly.

'Because I like you and I am seriously interested in why you are doing this and–'

'For money. I don't actually get off on hitting men with sticks if that's what you mean,' she said crossly. 'I am completely embarrassed by it all and still terrified,' she added frankly, 'that you will tell Charlotte.'

'I won't.'

'OK.'

'As long as you come out for dinner with me!'

Roz gave a little jerk of alarm. He looked immediately contrite. 'Hey, I'm joking – I'm not blackmailing you really.' He put his hand on her arm. 'I'm sorry. I didn't mean to frighten you. Don't look so worried.'

Roz shook his hand away, feeling as if she could cry. 'I am worried. If my daughter knew …'

Jamie spoke calmly. 'Nobody will know anything from me. It's a job isn't it. I guess you're providing a service …'

Roz looked at him narrowly. She remembered how Melody had been convinced Jamie was a potential client.

'I try to give the men who come to me, what they want,' she said carefully. 'I don't judge.' She suddenly wanted to make it all crystal clear. 'But I am doing it for financial reasons only – this is not what I am into in real life.'

Jamie smiled. 'Me neither!'

Something in Roz dropped in relief. Jamie went on: 'Look, I won't tell a soul and I don't care why your punters get their rocks off being beaten senseless, but I really would love to get to know you better.'

He looked at her appealingly. 'Let's make a deal. Meet me for a drink and if after one hour you want to go home you do, and I will never bother you again. If not – if you can stand me a little longer – we go for dinner – somewhere casual from which you can easily depart at any time. How does that sound?'

He smiled again. He had a nice, open face, what looked like his own hair, good teeth, even features. If they'd met differently, she might well have been happy to have dinner with him. But it was a long, long time since she'd done anything like that and right now, with all that was going on in her life …

As the silence stretched between them, and her guts knotted with anxiety, his eyes stayed fixed on hers, not laughing now but looking almost concerned.

She recalled Amy telling her about the girlfriends who came and went and wanted to be friends with his daughter. 'Don't you have a partner?' she enquired eventually, playing for time.

'No I don't. I separated from my wife five years ago and I haven't found anyone I want to settle down with since.'

Roz noted the careful wording. Lots of casual sex was presumably OK as long as there was no settling.

'And you?' he asked.

'Charlotte told you I'm single,' she said shortly.

'She still wouldn't give me your phone number,' he smiled.

'She knew I wouldn't like it.'

'And you may have been snapped up since.'

'Hardly.'

'Can I have it now?' He was looking at her appealingly. 'So we can make some arrangements?'

'Let's just make them now.'

'OK – that's tremendous! 7pm?'

She frowned. 'What, tonight?'

He looked touchingly pleased. 'Tonight.'

Chapter 21

All the time she was getting ready, Roz wondered why she hadn't just refused him point blank.

Part of it was still fear that he would tell Charlotte after all – what did they say about keeping your enemies closer? Part of it was that she'd always been rubbish at saying no if someone was really persuasive – why else would she have installed that hugely expensive double glazing it had taken years to pay off. But part of it was – curiosity.

There was something about this supposedly wealthy, school-supporting, fund-raising, playboy surveyor that interested her. A drink couldn't hurt. Perhaps it would take her mind off things. After an hour she would say she had enjoyed his company very much but would have to forgo dinner as she'd promised Amy she wouldn't be late and – a la the advice on excuses she had handed out to Sherie – had an early start in the morning.

They had agreed to meet in The 39 Steps, a popular brewhouse near the seafront, known for its extensive range of gins. Roz had been there once or twice with Sherie, but had chosen it this evening for the unlikelihood of her bumping into anyone else she knew.

It was warm. Roz had twisted her wavy hair into a knot to keep it off her neck and tied a red silk scarf around it.

She'd changed her mind several times about what to wear but had eventually, after taking off the second dress she'd chosen as being too over-the-top for a casual drink, had put on a pair of loose linen trousers with deep pockets that had a reasonably flattering cut and a red embroidered t-shirt. She put on flat sandals she could walk in and strolled from her small terraced house off the Broadway, the half mile down the High Street, enjoying the evening sunshine.

As she walked under the railway bridge and up the other side, past the familiar shops and pubs and estate agencies, she thought about her daughter.

Amy had her friend Claire round and, predictably, had shown little interest in where Roz was going. Claire had turned and smiled but Amy hadn't looked up from whatever they were watching on YouTube, when Roz had said goodbye.

'I won't be late,' Roz had said. Her daughter had nodded, eyes still fixed on the iPad screen. 'Whatever.'

Roz tried to shake off her sadness and worry as she reached Pierremont Park, skirting a group of Italian students on the pavement, and walked on past the gift shop Expressions, Westwood Aquariums and the new pizza place that had opened in what had once been NatWest Bank.

As she crossed the road and strolled on down past Crusties the bakers, where she bought their bread in an effort to support the slowly-dwindling number of independent shops, she recalled when the High Street had boasted all four major banks plus assorted Building Societies. Now only the Nationwide remained.

Roz stopped at the cash machine, peering nervously at the balance on the cash receipt, before heading on towards the Costa Coffee that inhabited the building that had always been Barclays. Fay had written a letter to the *Isle of Thanet News* when that had opened, complaining about blots on landscapes and the curse of the multi-nationals in ruining the character of the traditional seaside towns and squeezing out small businesses. She had insisted all four of them pledge never to set foot inside – they weren't allowed in Iceland either – and frequented only the quirky cafes and bars that were privately owned.

Roz paused for a moment and gazed at the glistening sea visible beyond the despised chain and the long-established Suzanne's – purveyor of colourful shrimping nets and buckets and spades – before taking a deep breath and turning into Charlotte Street towards The 39 Steps.

Jamie was sitting at a table in the corner when she got there. He had a small beer in front of him that looked untouched and he sprang to his feet as she came in, appearing strangely delighted. Roz felt suddenly silly and shy. She hadn't been on a 'date' for years. She wished she'd been firmer and stayed in to wash her hair.

She twisted her bracelet nervously while he fetched her a Silent Pool gin with orange-flower tonic and sat back down opposite her.

She wondered what they would talk about, her mind suddenly devoid of any conversational topics. 'Do you er live in Canterbury?' she asked, although she knew he did, cursing herself for this scintillating opening and wondering if she could perhaps surreptitiously text Sherie and ask her to effect an interruption via an urgent phone call about a flood or earthquake that would necessitate Roz heading for home post-haste.

But she needn't have worried. Jamie talked. As she sipped her drink, he chatted easily about his surveying practice that had grown over the years and now employed six of them including two secretaries, about his love of antique furniture and habit of going to auctions and finding bits he could restore, and his daughter, who had been a promising horse-woman – show-jumping all over the country – but who now was more interested in boys and make-up.

Which was a relief, he explained, on the one hand, because horses cost an absolute fortune and involved lots of dawn starts, but a bit of a shame on the other, as she could have gone far.

'Yes,' said Roz faintly, feeling totally out of her league. Should she match this with Amy's short-lived interest in stick insects? 'Amy mentioned your daughter had a pony.'

Jamie nodded. 'He's quite an old chap now. We've loaned him to a younger girl at the stables where we keep him, but Luci still pops up to see him at weekends.'

'So she lives with her mother? In Broadstairs?'

'Kingsgate. Not far from Charlotte. But she's staying with me tonight. She's going to see something at the Marlowe with a couple of friends – some young singer they all moon over. So she's coming back to me to save Madeleine picking her up – which is always a performance – or her having to get a late train. I'll drop her to school in the morning.'

He sipped at his beer. 'Are you happy with Highcourt?'

'Er yes I think so. Amy seems to be doing OK.' Roz felt awkward, knowing that she didn't really know what it was like these days. Amy was rarely forthcoming and it had been changeover at the Gallery the night of parents' evening. She had allowed herself to be persuaded by Amy that going would be a waste of time anyway and that she may as well wait to see the end of term report which, Amy assured her, would raise no issues.

Jamie nodded. 'I'm thinking of standing to be a governor.'

'Oh. That's very good of you. Charlotte said you ran the PTA.' Roz hoped he wouldn't ask her to join. She hated committees ... She began to formulate a reply that involved her erratic working hours but Jamie was still talking.

'When Luci was little, I was always working and I was overseas for a while. Bahrain. It was a fantastic salary and a great experience, but I missed out on a lot. I suppose I'm trying to make up for it now.'

'Is that why your marriage broke up?' Roz clapped a hand to her mouth. 'Sorry! That was really nosy.'

'Not at all. Maddie would certainly tell you we split up because I was never there. I tend to put it down to the fact that she spent most of the time I was absent, in bed with my tennis partner.' He paused. 'Who she'd always purported to detest.'

'Oh dear.'

'Yes, it was a shame. I miss him.' He smiled and shrugged. 'We'd grown apart. It was as much my fault as hers.'

'What's your excuse?' he went on, smiling. 'How come you're unattached?'

'Oh,' Roz shook her head, self-consciously. 'You know, being a single mother, working ...' She took the last mouthful of her gin. 'Not really had time for relationships.' She stopped, not having the words or inclination to describe her protectiveness of the safe little world she'd tried to create for her and Amy when her daughter was young. A world of just the two of them, that she was always afraid to disrupt, and that was now in danger of being smashed apart ...

Jamie didn't push her. He looked at his watch. 'We have been here one hour and five minutes,' he announced. 'Have I passed muster? Are you hungry?'

Roz smiled. 'I am actually.'

'Good. I've booked a table round the corner.'

They walked the short distance to Posillipo, a traditional Italian restaurant that was one of Roz's favourites.

'Charlotte recommended it,' said Jamie, as they were shown to a table on the terrace facing the sea.

Roz felt a small stab of alarm. 'Did you tell her you were seeing me?'

'No – in case you stood me up.'

Roz took the menu the waiter offered her. 'I wouldn't do that to anyone.'

Jamie was looking at the wine list. 'I asked her about places to eat when I told her I was hopeful. And she told me you worked in the gallery.'

'Ah!'

'She said you liked it here.'

'I do.'

The gin had relaxed her and suddenly it seemed a real treat to be taken out to dinner. She glanced around at the candles and baskets of flowers, listening to the low buzz of conversation as the young waiting staff weaved in and out of the closely packed wooden tables. The air was soft and the lights around the garden and twinkling along the seafront gave the place a holiday feel.

Jamie smiled at her. 'White or red? I can only have a little so you choose ...'

'And now,' he said, when they'd ordered, 'it is time to talk about you.'

Roz felt herself squirm. 'There's really not much to say.'

'I'm sure there is. Do you enjoy working at the Turner? Are you artistic yourself? Do you watch EastEnders, like

177

sugar in your coffee, have sisters, make a habit of going out with strange men who won't take no for an answer ...?'

Roz laughed. 'Yes, and five noes.'

'Ah, I do like a woman who can retain a list.'

He was a good listener and she realised it was a long time since she'd done this – sat and simply talked about herself. Her friends knew most of this stuff already, and at home, conversation – such as it was – tended to centre around Amy's preoccupations, rather than her own.

Jamie seemed genuinely interested in hearing about her job, her interests, the forthcoming party he'd already been invited to by Charlotte, and as the light faded and the lights gleamed on the dark sea beyond, quizzed her on her views on everything from contemporary art to Jeremy Corbyn.

Through garlicky bruschetta, piled high with juicy tomatoes and sweet-smelling basil, they bonded over the disappointments of Brexit and the perils of social media, exchanged favourite books and films, talked about their daughters, the burden of student loans and the difficulties of future employment in an uncertain job market.

Jamie was funny and knowledgeable and listed *White Ladder* as one of his all-time favourite albums. Roz, in fervent agreement, had a second glass of the rich fruity Rioja and relaxed further.

'So what about Amy's father?' Jamie asked easily, when plates of steaming pasta had arrived. 'Is he local?'

Roz hesitated. 'No.'

Jamie twirled some spaghetti around on his fork and said nothing.

'He has never really been in our lives,' she said awkwardly.

Jamie nodded in understanding but still did not speak.

Roz saw her daughter's face screwed up in fury and

suddenly longed to spill out the story. She'd wanted to talk to Charlotte about it – as another mother and her friend who wouldn't condemn her – but Charlotte had seemed distracted when they'd spoken briefly about the cleaning. Roz had suggested a coffee soon and Charlotte had agreed it would be nice but she hadn't offered a time when she'd be free and something in Charlotte's manner had stopped Roz from pushing her.

'I've had a row with Amy about it quite recently,' she said. 'She has suddenly showed an interest.' Roz hesitated. 'She never really wanted to know it all before.'

Jamie looked at her with compassion. Roz swallowed.

'You don't have to tell me,' he said.

But Roz took another mouthful of wine and did.

'My parents assumed it was a one-night stand, when I wouldn't give them details,' she said. 'My mother was fairly appalled. When Amy was very small, she accepted that she just didn't have a daddy. Later, I told her that it had been a very short relationship and he'd gone abroad before I realised I was pregnant. That I'd decided to go it alone and her father never knew. She never asked again. Then when she was ten, someone at school was talking about being adopted and who their real parents might be, and Amy thought it was all rather glamorous. She asked me out of the blue what her father's surname was and I panicked and just made up a name – I said he was called Mark Johnson.'

'And he wasn't?' Jamie had stopped eating and was watching her calmly.

'His name was Marcus. He had a different surname.'

Roz knew that later she would probably be horrified at herself – some small sensible part of her was detached, looking on, watching her telling someone she barely knew, the story she'd always kept hidden. She didn't know if it was the alcohol or Jamie's sympathetic expression or just weariness at always covering up, but some strange compulsion drove her on.

'He was the headmaster of a large school. He had a wife who had health problems.'

She scanned Jamie's face for signs of disapproval but he only nodded.

'She was in a wheelchair. He never made me any promises. He said he could never leave her because she needed him and so did his kids, but that they didn't have any sort of relationship any more and that he needed me.'

'He was much older than me,' she added. 'I adored him.'

'And he didn't want to be involved with his child?' Now Jamie gave a small frown.

'At first he was angry. He used to be obsessed about contraception – though he wanted it to be mine. But I had to stop taking the pill because I'd been on it so long and I was getting headaches. And then I found out I had had endometriosis – the consultant said I'd be very unlikely to conceive naturally. I was still careful at first but we had unprotected sex a few times and nothing happened.

'Oh my god–' she clapped a hand over her mouth again. 'I'm sorry this is way too much information.' She shook her head. She didn't usually drink this much. She was becoming inappropriate …

'I feel honoured that you are confiding in me.' Jamie's voice was gentle.

Roz took a deep breath and went on. 'I honestly didn't ever believe I'd get pregnant. I'd told him I couldn't … And then one day – after more than two years, I did!'

'And he reacted badly?'

180

'He was shocked. Fearful about what I'd do. Worried about his job, his reputation. His wife wasn't doing very well. He wanted me to have a termination – he and my mother both – but I couldn't.' Roz was talking fast now. 'It felt like a gift from God. Not that I am particularly religious,' she added hastily. 'It just felt – well it was a miracle. I couldn't have ...'

'Eat something.' Jamie took a mouthful of spaghetti and chewed slowly. Roz lifted her fork and put it down again.

'So I moved. I gave up my job in London and came back down here where I'd gone to school and my parents still were. They've moved to Surrey since – which is a relief.'

Roz took another sip of wine. 'I'd thought he was a good, decent man who took his responsibilities seriously – I told myself I loved that in him, that he had a moral code. That he wouldn't dump a sick wife. Leave his teenage children ...'

Jamie was impassive.

'But I found out later that his wife wasn't ill in the way he'd told me, that his kids were older than he'd said and had already left home. He just didn't love me enough to rock the boat and why should he? I shouldn't have been having an affair with a married man. In the cold, pregnant light of day, I felt a bit grubby.'

'So he never supported you?'

'I told him where I was and for the first two years he sent me money and the odd letter, then it tailed off.'

Jamie shook his head as if in disbelief. Roz shrugged. 'I never expected it. The money was useful but I saw bringing up Amy as my job.'

'And he's not wanted to find out about his daughter since?' This time, the disapproval was clear.

'I did a bit of investigating much later – when Amy first asked his name – and I found out he'd retired because he had cancer. I think he may have died.' Roz bit her lip. 'I suppose I should find out now. Amy has been searching online. She says she's going to find her half-siblings. I don't know if she will, really. I haven't told her their names – so it's not going to be easy. She's angry with me at the moment but she used to say she didn't care about having a father.' Roz felt suddenly exhausted and sad. 'We used to be so close.'

Jamie's voice was reassuring. 'You will be again. Maddie says Luci is a nightmare at times. But if I ever criticise her mother, Luci gives me what for. Quite rightly,' he added quickly. 'And my sister,' he went on. 'She didn't speak to my mother at all, for years. But she's round there every week now.'

'Where do they live?' asked Roz, faintly, feeling she should show an interest although now she was feeling sick inside.

'Dorset,' he said briefly. 'And has there been nobody since?'

Roz gave a brittle laugh. 'As I said, I haven't really had the time or appetite for a relationship ...'

Jamie leant out and took her hand across the table. It felt warm and comforting. She let her fingers rest against his.

Jamie gave her a smile – his eyes dark and shining in the candlelight. 'I have had a really good time with you tonight, Roz,' he said quietly. 'Can we do it again?'

Roz nodded.

Chapter 22

Fay turned her car engine back on so she could switch on the windscreen wipers. What the hell was she doing? Skulking in her car, staring through the rain at some featureless modern offices on a soulless estate outside Ashford, waiting to tail her friend's husband. Ludicrous!

Fay was aware that a lot of her resistance to this mad plan sprang from her not wanting it to be true. She liked Roger – she'd always thought of him as a straightforward, thoroughly decent bloke. He was nice. Nice to Charlotte – nice to her friends. Fay was going to be rocked to her core if he turned out to be as bad as all the rest. But better she be the one to find out than some so-called-professional slimeball who would smash Charlotte's life apart and then make her pay through the nose for it.

People had thought Dave was nice too. Right up to the end. But he wasn't. He had stopped keeping up even any pretence of being kind and caring long before she found out. Had lost interest in trying. Given up on her, on them. Stopped speaking, or listening or even looking her fully in the face. She found that harder to forgive than anything.

'Maybe he was very upset,' his sister had said, when she'd come round to poke about in what had happened. Fay had fixed her with a look of such venom, that the older woman had shrunk back. Then Fay had got up and held her front door open until her sister-in-law scuttled down the path, snivelling. She never spoke to her again.

Roger wasn't like that. Roger was a good man who loved his wife. But maybe Roger was weak. Charlotte had said there'd been a woman before he'd been bewitched by. Fay knew all about that.

Although she prayed Charlotte was imagining things, she understood the torture Charlotte was going through. It was the not knowing that ate away at you. Once you did know, you could deal with it.

The rain was getting heavier. Fay had squashed Len's car into the only free 'visitor' space and she hoped if Roger was going on one of his rendezvous trips he would hurry up about it, before someone realised she shouldn't be there and moved her on.

Len had looked at her suspiciously when she'd asked to swap vehicles, as if he didn't believe her tale of needing to ferry three friends about in something bigger than her two-seater. 'What are you up to?' he'd asked, as she had dropped the keys to her conspicuous red sports car onto the edge of his desk. She'd grinned. 'Nothing you need to worry about, Leonard. Just keep this show on the road while I'm gone.'

Charlotte had said Roger typically went AWOL from around three, so when he came out, would depend she guessed, on how far away his assignation was. Fay had sat through the two o'clock news and *The Archers* – there were a couple of new characters she didn't recognise but Shula hadn't got any less tedious since she'd last listened – and she was beginning to get bored.

She had a stack of paperwork waiting for her in the office

and two potential new clients to visit. She hoped Charlotte had kicked Sherie's sister Alison's solicitor into touch because that week was getting increasingly busy and she couldn't hold the date for ever.

Fay was about to text Charlotte to see if there was an update, when she spotted two figures coming through the main doors of the modern office block. She cleared the windscreen again, and peered through the rain. Yes, one of them was definitely Roger. As she watched, he raised a hand in farewell and ducked his head before walking rapidly away from the other chap and down the nearest row of cars.

Even though he was unlikely to look across this far, and see her, Fay kept her own head down, squinting up through her fringe as Roger got into his dark Mercedes.

Watching carefully to see which way he turned when he left the car park, Fay delayed before following. In films people were always too dim to notice the same car in their rear-view mirror for miles, but Fay knew she'd be on it if anyone was trailing her.

She kept well back as Roger set off down one of the narrow country roads that surrounded the business park. Len's black Ford was unremarkable but she wasn't taking any chances. Unless he had a girlfriend tucked away somewhere very obscure, she knew which way Roger was likely to be going.

As predicted, Roger's car headed for the big roundabout that led onto the ring road. As one road widened into another and he joined the dual carriageway, Fay accelerated, put a car between them and then matched his speed.

Minutes later, she felt a small rush of adrenalin as they reached the Eureka Leisure Centre and he indicated right to join the M20. Maidstone or further afield? The rain was hammering down now and spray from the lorries made visibility difficult. Fay fumbled for the lights on the unfamiliar dashboard. Overtaking a blue BMW and a white van, she settled behind Roger in the outside lane, leaving a distance between them, assuming he would not be able to get a good view of her in this weather.

'Dick!' she said out loud, as the BMW zipped past her and settled in the gap. She could still see Roger ahead of her. He was driving more quickly now – obviously on a mission with his eye on the clock. He kept going past the sign to Leeds Castle and the services – so no tacky little car park tryst then – and past the junction to the A20 and Maidstone East. If he was going to the town centre he would likely come off at the next one.

They'd had to slow down now, through the road works. Fay kept her eyes fixed on his number plate as they passed a blur of orange jackets and sure enough, saw him begin to move across shortly before junction seven. As soon as she was able to – thwarted by lorries and struggling with the spray – Fay followed suit.

She was determined to get to the bottom of this for Charlotte. As they left the motorway and continued onto the A249 for Maidstone, she'd been forced to drop back and there were now three cars between them, but she could still see him.

The traffic was heavy now and progress was slow – Fay managed to get past one of the cars and then it was easy to keep Roger in her sights. They drove on past the Maidstone Hilton, up the hill and left towards the town, the traffic picking up speed as they went past a pub on the corner and a large modern church towards traffic lights and a sign for the town centre. The lights were green but the driver in front was dithering. 'Go on!'

Fay swore out loud as the lights changed and she was forced to stop as Roger sped on.

Bollocks! The lights were red for an age and Roger was out of sight by the time Fay got moving again. She'd have to take a punt and keep heading for the centre hoping she would remember the way to that crummy hotel. Keeping her fingers crossed that was where Roger was going.

Fay drove on, past the council offices, following the main route and looking out for familiar buildings, hissing with annoying as she came to an area that was pedestrianised. She was pretty sure the hotel was down there somewhere. There was no sign of Roger and nowhere to stop. She turned right, pulling in on a double yellow line and getting up maps on her phone.

'Yes, I'm going!' She wound down her window and addressed a damp-looking traffic warden impatiently. 'But I'll be gone a lot quicker if you can direct me. It's like a bloody maze round here.'

Minutes later, she was skirting round the shopping area and driving up a street behind it. She passed the goods entrance to Primark, and there was an archway with a sign for the Wealdstone Hotel. Customer parking only. Fay drove in and found a space, getting immediately drenched as she got quickly out of the car, scanning the other vehicles. Bingo! Roger's car was in the corner.

She ran across the courtyard as the rain beat down on her shoulders, cursing Roger and all philanderers everywhere.

The reception area had been done up since Fay was last there, and was lighter and brighter. Rubbing the water from her face, Fay went into the bar, longing to see Roger locked in conversation with another suit, papers spread out in front of him. There was a couple in the corner, eating, and a couple of guys at the bar. No sign of anyone else.

She peered into the empty restaurant beyond. A young man smiled at her. 'Are you here for cream tea?'

'Not this time.' *Drowned Rats convention perhaps?*

There was a small lounge off the bar that was empty. The old goat must have booked a room for the afternoon.

Fay walked back into reception and approached a girl with shiny brown hair who was intent on her computer screen.

She looked up as Fay stopped in front of the counter and smiled. Fay spoke briskly. 'I'm here to see Roger Forbes.'

The girl gave a small frown. 'Is he a guest?' she asked politely.

'Yes,' said Fay boldly. 'He asked me to call him in his room when I arrived.'

The girl looked back at her screen. 'Sorry,' she said, her tone cooler. 'We don't have anybody staying with that name.'

Damn. Fay kept her face neutral. Of course he'd book under another one. Bastard. Unless she hammered on every bedroom door until she hit lucky, there was nothing for it but to wait until he reappeared.

'How strange,' she said curtly to the receptionist. 'He must have changed his plans. I'll wait for him in the bar.'

Roger would come back to his car when he'd finished and however long it took, she'd be waiting for him. Fay took up a strategic position with a view of the foyer which presumably he would have to cross to get out again.

'Is there any other back entrance to the car park?' she asked the barman, 'apart from that one that leads into reception?' He looked at her curiously. 'No,' he said. Then he grinned. 'Unless you want to climb down the fire escape.'

Fay gave a tight smile back. She doubted Roger would go to those lengths, especially as he didn't even know she was here.

'Thank you. What's the Wi-Fi code?'

She ordered a coffee and sat down. She would not Google anything, she would answer some of her emails. There were two texts from Charlotte, wanting to know what was going on. Fay replied briefly, saying only that she was on the case. She didn't want to inflame Charlotte further until she had found out what exactly was going on.

The rambling hotel had clearly undergone a facelift since she was last here. Fay picked up a leaflet from the table about the Wealdstone's facilities for meetings of all sizes – including liaisons of just two between the sheets presumably – and the weddings and celebrations they could now host in their two-hundred-capacity banquet room, idly reading a sample menu which made up in clichés what it lacked in imagination. Why did everything these days have to be fucking 'drizzled' with something?

Fay made her first coffee last the best part of an hour and then asked for another. She'd answered all the mail she felt like dealing with, and had taken a call from the care home to learn her mother had rolled out of bed but come to no harm, and was demanding plums.

Made a change from bloody oranges. 'I'll bring them Friday,' Fay told Charlie, the kind care assistant who showed more patience than Fay could imagine. Fay could rarely remember her mother eating fruit when she was at home but now she was working her way through the entire green-grocer's.

Fay was getting restless. She wasn't used to sitting around. She was ignoring Charlotte's third message, not wanting to

189

tell her that Roger was secreted somewhere in this hotel, clearly up to no good.

Fay wildly thought of taking the lift upstairs and yelling his name down each corridor. She looked at her watch. It was well after four. If he hadn't emerged by five, she just might.

The barman had disappeared and a young girl cleared her empty cup and brought the new one. There was only Fay and three blokes with laptops in here now. Her eyes flicked constantly to the foyer, afraid she would miss him, but only a woman with two kids and a huge suitcase had passed in front of her in the last half an hour.

Fay phoned Len, still keeping her gaze on the entrance. As she listened to his updates on today's jobs, two smartly-dressed women in heels crossed the foyer and went out through the double glass doors onto the street. They were followed moments later by a man in his fifties and another woman in a floaty summer dress. Three more women came into the bar. Had Roger been at a business meeting after all?

'Gotta go, Len.' Fay stood up and grabbed her bag. She wandered to the doorway and looked across to where the receptionist was talking on the phone. She could hear the women laughing. Charlotte had said in her last text that she had tried to phone Roger and he was switched off as usual. He mostly still got home by seven, she'd said, on a Wednesday, so he'd need to be out of here before six – earlier probably with all the end-of-day traffic ...

Fay could feel her heart beating faster as if something was about to happen. But one more man came out of the lift and strode across to the entrance and then nothing. The receptionist had finished her phone call and was looking at Fay as if wondering why she was still here. Fay ignored her.

And then suddenly there he was. She heard the lift doors open and his voice before she saw him. Roger was in a shirt and tie, with his suit jacket over one shoulder. He was with a woman. Blonde, fifty-ish, in a skirt and pink top. Fay saw him smile and nod at something she'd said. 'I hope so.' He laughed.

Fay had prepared a story. That she was quoting on a job nearby and had nipped in to use the loo before driving back. But the sight of Roger, relaxed and carefree, walking so close to the woman they were nearly touching, drove all pretences from her mind.

She stepped smartly into the middle of the foyer right into their path. She saw the startled look on his face. Fay pounced, her voice sugary tight.

'Roger! What a surprise! Fancy seeing you here – tucked away in a hotel far from home in the middle of the afternoon. No work today?'

The woman's eyes widened. She looked uneasily from Roger to Fay as he gaped. Fay ploughed on. 'Well? Aren't you going to introduce me to your friend?'

Roger appeared to recover himself. He nodded. 'Yes of course. This is Marion.'

'I thought it might be.'

Roger turned to the woman next to him, who gave an embarrassed half-smile. 'This is Fay – she's a good friend of my wife's.'

'Too right I am,' said Fay loudly. 'And her name's Charlotte.'

The woman nodded as if she knew this already and Fay glared.

Then she turned back to Roger. 'What the fuck is going on?'

Chapter 23

In TV dramas you know it's bad news when the police come in twos. If someone's died, one of them is usually a woman who makes a cup of tea.

There are three people in the hospital room. The consultant, Mr Anand – a quiet, sorrowful looking man – a sympathetically smiling nurse and a student with curly hair. They asked me if he could be there too, to observe, and I nodded. How else would he learn? He looks terrified.

After Mr Anand has told me sadly that my stress lump is malignant, the nurse sends the student to get me a plastic cup of water. Mr Anand is the one to hand me the tissues.

They seem surprised I am on my own, that I haven't told anyone else that I am here. I try to concentrate while they talk through the options but the tears just keep silently falling out of my eyes and streaming down my face.

The nurse takes my hand when Mr Anand goes to speak to someone about arranging what will come next. She talks about support and counselling and presses leaflets into my hand, illustrated with women in headscarves. She speaks about success rates and recovery. She is kind.

Afterwards I find a card in my hand with her phone number on it but I can't remember the details of anything she's said.

I could choose to have chemotherapy to shrink the lump before they remove it. I too could lose my eyebrows and wear a turban. They say I might want to go home and think about it. Discuss the options with my family. I shake my head vigorously. No – I say, cut it out now. Please, please get rid of it …

Chapter 24

'Got it!' Charlotte slapped a celebratory hand against the screen of her iPad. 'At last – Alison is exchanging today. I thought I'd never see the day. It's been such a nightmare.'

Fay dumped her large handbag on a kitchen chair. 'So, 26th July's a goer?'

'It is! She'll be all moved in before the party. And I won't be sorry not to ever have to talk to her buyers again. They're not even going to live there – house in Shoreditch, buying it as a rental – but they've messed me about from the start.'

Charlotte rose from her kitchen table and filled the kettle. '*And* I'm waiting for a formal offer on the North Foreland house – but they're definitely going to buy it – so champagne all round on party night I feel!'

'And is that all going OK? I'm sorry I don't feel I've done very much. I've had–' Fay stopped. 'I don't know – I've been a bit–'

'Snowed-under, yes I know.' Charlotte flicked the switch and got mugs from the cupboard. 'It's all under control – there's nothing to do now except turn up. I'll go down in the afternoon and supervise the balloons and flowers. It was supposed to be Sherie's job but she thinks she might be working earlier now and anyway–' Charlotte laughed '–when it comes to entertaining, you know what a control freak I am. Just make sure you've invited everyone you want. Did I tell you Gaynor and Sam are coming home a day early from their holiday just to be there?'

Fay frowned. 'Do I know them?'

'Yeah, course you do – she owns Green's with Sarah. Never there – sleeping partner. They came round on the night we had the party for the final of *Strictly*? Blonde, slim, glamorous. Still got a flat stomach despite two kids. Remember? There weren't exactly lots of us like that.'

'I remember the party. I ate about a hundred of those little spicy sausages – they were to die for – and I still had a hangover.'

Charlotte grinned. 'It was great, wasn't it? I read the other day that there's a rumour Michael McIntyre is in the next series – oh god I so hope so – will be bloody hilarious. Are you watching *Unforgotten*? They ought to get those two in *Strictly*. I love that Sanjay!'

Fay studied her friend as she made coffee. Charlotte had apparently accepted Fay's account of finding Roger ensconced with two suits and a foot-thick contract having a weekly progress meeting, and two days later, was cheery to the point of manic.

Roger had clearly played his part well, by announcing that he'd bumped into Fay unexpectedly and that he'd be glad when this acquisition was put to bed because he was fed up with all the repetitive and largely-unnecessary gatherings.

Fay had seen the way Charlotte's eyes had briefly narrowed when Fay was telling the tale, but she hadn't cross-examined her and Fay was glad – she was feeling edgy and tired and might well have slipped up. 'Well, in that case he's forgiven,' Charlotte had said shortly, and although she'd barely drawn breath since Fay had arrived, hadn't mentioned it since.

Fay inwardly rolled her eyes. Talk about tangled bloody webs.

'I can't stop,' she said, taking the china mug Charlotte handed her. 'I want to get back before they all knock off. I've just been to check up on some clients in Percy Avenue after some cock-up where three oil paintings got left behind – one of my chaps being dozy again. Apparently the smallest one was worth a fortune but the woman seemed remarkably laid back about it. The new owners gave the agent a ring and he brought them round. Can you imagine if they'd nicked them instead?'

'Aren't you insured for things like that?'

'Well, yes, in theory, but her great uncle's brother's cousin or someone had painted it – one of these irreplaceable heirlooms. I should have taken a photo and asked Sherie what its value would be.' Fay gave a hoot of laughter. 'See if I should have pinched it myself ...'

She delved into her bag and pulled out a packet of cigarettes, holding them out to Charlotte. 'Quick one?' They both moved to the ever-open doorway to Charlotte's patio. Fay noticed Charlotte's hands shake slightly as she bent forwards to take a light. She looked at her hard.

'Are you OK, Hun? Anything you're not saying?'

Charlotte looked steadily back. 'I was wondering the same about you!'

'What I'm wondering is ...' an hour later, Fay took a sharp drag on another fag and looked at the row of lorries to the right of her. 'Is what dear Matthew will do next?'

Beside her, in the late afternoon sunshine, Len took a mouthful from the mug of tea he was holding. 'It might not have been him. There were three of them on the job. Who knows who missed it?'

Fay sniffed. 'I think we do. He's not been with it since he had that kid. We've got our reputation to think of. My father would have given him a warning by now.'

'Your dad,' said Len mildly, 'would have told him to go home and get some sleep ...'

Fay opened her mouth to retort as three of her workforce came out of the building behind her, in their boiler suits. The youngest one, Toby, gave his usual salute. 'Night Guv! Goodnight Ma'am!' Matt and Will both lifted hands in farewell. Matt looked exhausted. Fay hesitated, then gave them a wry smile. 'Behave yourselves!'

'Leave it to me,' said Len, when they'd disappeared. 'I've got an eye on it.'

'I hope so! Since you were the one who said he was shaping up so well and I should give him a pay rise!'

Len's voice was even. 'He was – and he will be – and yes, that was the right thing to do. He's a good lad.'

'Well, we'll see. I hope he realises that with extra money comes extra responsibility and we can't–'

'The baby's had colic.'

'That's not really my problem, is it! If the company loses business because of mistakes, then we're all in the shit.'

Len continued calmly as if she hadn't spoken. 'So they're not getting much sleep. It won't go on for ever, things will settle down.'

'In the meantime, I would have thought, earning a living is still fairly vital. You'd better watch what you send him on.'

'I already am.'

'Didn't stop those paintings being forgotten!' Fay knew she was being crabby and Len's unruffled manner made her more so.

'But you've smoothed it all over and no harm was done.' Len gave her a wide smile. 'Got anything nice planned this evening?'

Fay gave him a crooked smile back. 'I have as it goes. Some uncomplicated sex and dirty rice ...'

It was a recipe she'd learned in Spain that she'd not cooked for Cory before. But knowing the way he'd tucked into her lasagne and then the spicy meatballs, she was confident it would be a hit.

Fay poured herself a glass of red wine and began to assemble the ingredients for this risotto-style ground beef and rice dish she'd eaten so much of when she was Cory's age. It had been her flat mate Emilio who'd called it 'dirty rice'. He made it better than she did.

She smiled at the thought of the beautiful Spaniard with his glossy curls and the thick lashes that put hers to shame. She hadn't heard from him in ages. The last she knew, he and Jorge had moved to Madrid for Jorge's new job and Emilio had said they might be in London for a business trip this summer, but there'd been no word since. He put as little on Facebook as she did, but his email address was on her computer at work. She'd drop him a line, tell him she'd been cooking their dish. Maybe she'd finally tell him he'd been right about Dave too.

Emilio had never said 'I told you so' when she'd written, after such a long silence, to say she and Dave had parted. She hadn't explained and he hadn't commented at all. Just said he missed her. That she should move back to Spain – that they always wanted good teachers ...

But she still remembered the way she'd exploded when Emilio had criticised the man she longed to marry. 'He not right guy for you,' he'd said matter-of-factly, as he chopped tomatoes for passata in their tiny kitchen.

'How would you know? You only met him for five minutes,' she'd said angrily, after Dave had dropped her home after another dreamy after-work session drinking warm rioja and nibbling on salty manchego cheese in one of the traditional old bars around the square near the school.

'It is all I need.' Emilio had been unapologetic. He had laughed instead. 'I am – how you say, my teacher? In Spanish it is psiquico.'

'Psychic,' she'd snapped. 'And you're not – you're just interfering. And wrong.'

'Are you sure you don't fancy him yourself?' She'd asked nastily –unforgivably – when she'd told Emilio that Dave would follow her back to England when his contract ended.

'He is very handsome man,' Emilio had said seriously, his dark brown eyes looking almost sorrowfully into hers. 'But–' he had shrugged and shaken his head. As if there was something indefinably wrong that he couldn't put his finger on ...

What had Emilio seen in Dave back then, that she had missed, Fay wondered as she finely sliced onions and crushed garlic. He had felt like her hero, giving up his job in the sunshine as Director of Studies, coming back here to support her during those awful first months after her father had died and her mother wouldn't stop crying. She hadn't had a single doubt when they'd tied the knot in Ramsgate Registry Office. She'd really thought it would be forever ...

Fay had deliberately left the laptop in the office again and her phone was at the bottom of her handbag. She glanced at the clock as she added the beef mince to the sautéed rice. She wouldn't look at anything but she'd just check to see if there was a text from Cory. She hadn't heard any beeps but she'd been watching the news on the small kitchen TV and had turned the volume up as the pundits discussed the latest round of fallout from Brexit.

Adding the rest of the tomatoes and herbs, Fay left the mixture simmering and prepared to grab a quick shower. She tapped out a message to say the door was on the latch and went upstairs. If he arrived when she was still under the water, so much the better ...

Fay was looking forward to the distraction of seeing Cory. She felt like sex, she wanted someone to talk to about something that wasn't work or being bloody fifty. She wanted to push everything else from her mind and feel his arms around her, needed it in a whole new way she wasn't usually aware of. And tomorrow was Saturday. He wouldn't have to leave early in the morning. She'd bought bacon and sausages.

She smiled again. However much they went at it the night before, Cory always woke up as horny as hell and was starving afterwards.

Ten minutes later, as Fay wrapped her silky kimono around her, hair still damp from the shower, she ran her hands down over her hips and looked at herself critically in the mirror. Charlotte didn't give a shit about being fifty, Sherie behaved as if it were some sort of terminal diagnosis. She didn't know what Roz felt really. Roz was strange at the moment, preoccupied. Fay had wandered into the gallery, when she'd found herself finished for the day and in Margate at half past five, thinking Roz might like to go for a quick drink, but Roz had looked fraught and said she had to get home. Probably something to do with that difficult daughter.

At least Fay didn't have to deal with that.

She looked at herself again – she wasn't doing too badly.

She rarely went to the gym these days but she was always moving – as often as not helping to unload the lorries when stuff came in for storage.

Her arms were reasonably toned still, she wasn't over-weight. Hadn't yet got too jowly although she was careful to keep the lights low when she and Cory were in bed. He'd told her he'd thought her younger than she was when they first met.

She looked at her phone when she got downstairs. He hadn't sent a message but he'd been online only minutes earlier on WhatsApp. She turned the heat to very low under her cooking pot, took a photo of the contents and sent it to him. **#domestic goddess**. She added a smiley face to show she was laid back and then watched the screen waiting for him to reply. Two minutes later, there was a ping. **sweet. leaving here in five.**

Fay felt the irritation rise. Leaving where? Work? Home? A pub? He was supposed to be here half an hour ago.

She topped up her wine glass and breathed deeply. Young people had a more elastic view of time-keeping. It didn't really matter. She looked at the salad ingredients she'd been about to chop and shred into a bowl and pushed them all back into the fridge. Last time he'd hardly touched any – they could just have a bowl of the rice mixture – there was veg in that.

Fay lit a cigarette, feeling restless. She hated waiting about. When another half hour had passed, she sent another message. **Eating on my own, am I?** He replied after a couple of minutes. **Soz. call cab now.**

Fay ground out her fag end and emptied the ashtray into the bin. What happened to leaving in five? And where was he that he needed a cab from? It was nine on a Friday – he might wait ages and she'd had too much to drink to pick him up.

Where are you?

This time the gap was much longer.

stag

Fucking terrific. She was slaving over a hot stove and he was getting hammered in the grottiest dive in Ramsgate.

Her fingers rattled out the answer on a wave of annoyance. **Another time then.**

Cory was already online.

Chill x be there soon

She'd turned the food off and was sitting with her wine, gazing unseeingly at *Newsnight*, when the doorbell rang. Cory lolled in the porchway, grinning dopily. 'Don't be like that,' he said, swaying slightly. 'I'm here now and I want to give you a big cuddle ...'

He lurched towards her and draped his arms across her shoulders. 'You feel nice,' he mumbled into her neck.

Fay removed his hands and stepped back.

'Go home, Cory. I'm not in the mood.'

He gave another inane grin. 'You wanted to see me.'

'I wanted to see you at eight when you said you were coming. Not now, when you're roaring drunk. Go back to your friends in the pub.'

He moved forwards again, hugging her clumsily. 'Don't be all– let me in!'

'No. We'll do it some other time.'

'I didn't mean to be late ...' He giggled. 'I got a bit involved,' he said with difficulty. 'I had one, and I got the flavour ... but I'm here now. And I'm hungry!' He grinned again, looking pleased with himself. 'Let's go and have dinner!'

'I don't want you here like this.' Fay heard her voice, remote and icy.

'Goodnight Cory! Sling your hook.'

She shoved him away from her and pushed the door shut, registering the hurt surprise on his face, seeing him frown. He raised his voice. 'Fay, don't do this–'

'I love you.' Cory began hammering against the oak door as she walked away down the hall. 'Come on Fay!'

He carried on thumping the door for a few moments longer. 'Fuck you then!'

Fay went back into her kitchen and sat down heavily, with her head in her hands. 'Fuck you right back!' she said. Before she began to cry.

Chapter 25

A my had wound herself up into another strop. Roz heard the slam of the front door before her daughter stalked into the kitchen and dropped her school bag loudly on the table. Her voice was loaded. 'I gather you're having trouble with the beautiful white truth again!'

Roz straightened up from unloading the washing machine and looked at Amy, who glared.

'What are you talking about?'

'You didn't tell me you were going out to dinner with Mr Lees-Parker – you said it was someone from work! Why do you keep lying?'

'I didn't tell any lies,' Roz said firmly. 'I said someone I met through work. I met him through Charlotte when I was doing one of her houses for her. Which she pays me for, so that makes it employment.' Feeling that that she was on her back foot, made Roz annoyed. 'And I didn't go into any further details because you said you weren't interested!' she said sharply.

'Well he clearly has a more open relationship with his daughter than you have with me, because Lucinda knew all about it,' Amy carried on regardless. 'What you ate, what you talked about, everything ...'

Roz's heart had started hammering unpleasantly. She took

a deep breath and tried to stay calm. 'Yes, we had a very nice meal and chatted about all sorts of things.' Surely Jamie wouldn't have repeated what she'd told him ...

'Lucinda was quite glad actually because she doesn't like his girlfriend. Who apparently was waiting for him when he got back after seeing you.'

'What?' Roz was trembling now. Jamie had said he wanted to see her again. That he didn't have a partner ...

'But I think it's embarrassing. I don't want you going out with my friend's *dad*.'

'Oh, she's your friend now, is she?' Roz snapped. 'It's up to me who I go out with, Amy. Jamie–'

'Well, as long as you don't mind sharing ...'

Roz swallowed hard, as her daughter continued to stare at her aggressively.

'According to Lucinda there are women in and out of his house all the time.' Amy raised her eyebrows. 'Lucinda found this one on the doorstep and she had to put up with her for an hour before he got home. She said she was crying!'

Roz stared back at her daughter in horror, trying to gather herself. Could this be true? What a bitter irony that would be – her pouring her heart out about a long-ago lover who'd been less than honest and all the time, he had someone waiting for him at home ... She bent down and pulled the rest of the washing from the machine, breathing hard, turning her face away from her daughter's gaze.

'There was nothing for her to be upset about,' she said, trying to keep her voice even. 'It was just a friendly meal, nothing more.' Roz stood up and carried the plastic basket to the door. 'So there's nothing for you to feel at all embarrassed about, either.' She took another deep breath. 'I won't be seeing him again ...'

Roz sat on her bed, pressing her hands against her eyes, trying not to cry. She hated being at war with Amy – she missed their old closeness – and she hated how stupid, disappointed and humiliated this situation with Jamie had made her feel.

He'd sent her a message saying he was really busy at work but he'd be in touch soon. She could text him right now and tell him to forget that, to never contact her again – but that would look as if she cared. If he did get back in touch and suggest another meeting she would ignore it. Or tell him *she* was too busy now. She thought again of his hand – strong and comforting over hers. How could she have got him so wrong?

She wondered wildly if perhaps Lucinda had made the story up – jealous of her father seeing anybody else. But she felt instinctively it was true – there had been another woman waiting for him at home. And he certainly hadn't called yet, had he?

Roz spoke sternly to herself – she hadn't been looking for a relationship. So why did she feel anything about what Jamie did? She'd managed this long without a man, and could do so for a whole lot longer. Nothing lasted anyway – she could hardly remember the passion she'd once felt for Marcus, could she? Except that at once she was flooded with memories. The way her heart would leap when she heard his voice on the phone – the wonderful warmth of lying curled into him in her bed, his chest solid against her back, his arms wrapped around her. 'I am so happy here, like this,' he would say. 'If only ...'

They'd lived on if-onlys. Roz had often wondered what would have happened if she hadn't had Amy, would it have gone on and on? Until he got ill perhaps ...

She saw the set of his chin in Amy's, her daughter's brown eyes were his too. Sometimes Amy looked quizzically up to the right when thinking in a way that was pure Marcus. Roz suddenly felt weary and sad. Of course Amy wanted to find out what she could. It was a marvel it had taken this long.

Amy was lying on her bed, still in her school clothes, watching something on the iPad that was propped up against her knees.

'What?' she said flatly, as Roz stood in the doorway.

Roz spoke calmly. 'Your father's daughters were called Joy and Victoria. They'd be in their late thirties by now. They could have married and changed their names. But it should be possible to track them down as we know the names of their parents.'

'You said you didn't remember.'

'It's come back to me.'

Roz sat on the edge of the bed. 'Can you put that down and look at me?' She took a deep breath. 'I understand you wanting to find your family but I want us to do it together. You have to remember that they knew nothing about me or you and it will be a terrible shock to find they have a half-sister. They may not believe you, they may reject you. If his wife is still alive ...'

Amy shrugged as if she didn't care, but she put the iPad down beside her and rolled over to face her mother. 'Why are you being helpful all of a sudden?'

'Because I've thought about it and I've realised it's not fair to withhold the information. But I want to be involved. I will find out the best way to go about things and we'll both do it together and I will support you.' She swallowed. 'Because I love you.'

'So what's changed?' Amy clearly wasn't ready to soften

yet. 'Why wouldn't you tell me all this in the first place?'

Roz kept her bleakest thoughts to herself. *Because it's time and perhaps I'm not enough on my own after all. If anything happens to me, you might need more family …*

'I was trying to be protective.' Roz put a tentative hand out and stroked Amy's hair, letting her breath out slowly as Amy did not resist. 'I didn't want anyone to be horrible to you.'

By the time Roz had shared everything, it was too late to cook. She went for fish and chips while Amy had a bath. She came back to find her daughter downstairs in a pair of pyjama bottoms and one of Roz's t-shirts, putting cutlery and mayonnaise on the table in their small kitchen. Amy took the packages and began to unwrap them. 'I am so hungry.'

'Me too.' Roz reached into the cupboard for vinegar and salt. 'We haven't had this for ages.'

'What sort of food are we having at the party?'

'Charlotte's been in charge of that …' Roz, grateful for a subject away from dead fathers and womanising dinner dates, chatted on about the sort of canapés her friend had ordered, and the finger buffet for later that Charlotte had not only designed the menu for but, Roz was extremely grateful to recall, paid for as well. 'She really is so generous,' Roz said.

'Yeah I like Charlotte.' Amy picked up a chip and dipped it in mayo. 'It must be cool to have her as a mum.'

'Oh, so I'm not in that category?' Roz grinned as Amy pulled a face.

'No, not really …'

Roz washed their plates while Amy did some French homework, feeling a warmth inside when her daughter asked her to test her as she struggled to conjugate the subjunctives for *pouvoir*. It was a long time since Amy had asked her for anything except money.

'We really must think about your birthday, too,' Roz said lightly. 'Sixteen! Have you any ideas?' Hoping that the gifts on Amy's wish list wouldn't be too extravagant. She had managed to pay off a bit of her credit card but it wouldn't take much to max it out again.

'Some better hair straighteners maybe?' Amy looked hopeful. 'Would GHDs be too expensive?'

Roz smiled brightly. 'I don't know. I'll have a look.'

They sat on the sofa and watched part of a drama about a serial killer with a fetish for women's toes.

'Weirdo,' said Amy. She shifted her weight so that her legs dangled over the arm and leant back against the cushions. Her voice was casually offhand.

'Have you got any photos?'

'One.'

'Can I?'

'Of course.'

Roz went upstairs to her bedroom and opened the bottom drawer of her dressing table, feeling at the back for the square flat box she hadn't opened in a long while. Underneath the letters and cards and old theatre tickets, lay the picture. She looked ridiculously young. He would have been she realised, about the same age as she was now ...

She took it downstairs and handed it to Amy. 'You look a bit like him.'

'No, I look more like you.'

Roz smiled, and picked up the phone lying on the low coffee table. Two texts had come in. One was from Sherie saying she had to go to London now tomorrow and couldn't meet at lunchtime.

The other was from Jamie. **Are you free for dinner on Friday? X**

No worries xxx Roz added a smiley to the reply for her old school friend and pressed send.

Then with a glance at her daughter, who was now leaning back against her mother's shoulder, still holding the photo, Roz re-read the second message and hit delete.

Chapter 26

Sherie let herself into her apartment, bone tired, and kicked off her heels at the bottom of the stairs. 'Hello?'

She slumped with relief at the silence, glad the workmen had gone for the day and she didn't have to make either tea or small talk.

She peered into her sitting room. The furniture was pushed back against the back wall, piled up on itself, covered with a dust sheet. The carpet was rolled back halfway across the floor, the floorboards still up in two places and the fireplace a gaping hole. The marble mantelpiece above was covered in a layer of fine reddish dust. Sherie ran a finger through it. *Worth it when it's finished*, she chanted in her head, already sick of the upheaval, but trying to cheer herself with thoughts of being curled in the warmth in front of flickering flames on a bleak winter afternoon while winds howled, and wishing she didn't feel so bleak herself right now.

She stood on tiptoe to gaze in the dusty mirror on the chimney breast. She seemed to be looking older by the day. Numbers were a funny thing. Forty-five sounded old – it seemed so much more ancient than forty-four – whereas forty-six still seemed full of potential. At forty-six she had still been able to scrub up well, still seen the admiring glances of men around her, the occasional envious ones from other women. She'd felt at odds being forty-seven, but sanguine about forty-eight. Then the panic had set in. She'd felt she'd had to suck every last bit of joy out of every moment of being forty-nine – because soon she really would never be thought of as even vaguely young again ...

Sherie shook her head at herself. She knew most people would see her as obsessive and steeped in vanity. Sherie remembered one of her clients, Margie, throwing a huge party when she was sixty, with champagne and a Jazz band because she was 'still here' after surviving bowel cancer. 'I am delighted to be growing old,' she had said in her speech. 'I hope to embrace seventy and eighty with equal vigour ...'

Sherie shuddered.

She went into the kitchen, seeing the biscuits in the cat's bowl but still no Marquis to greet her. Putting the kettle on, she opened the back door that led onto her private patio and the communal gardens beyond, and called him, using the special kissy, high-pitched baby-squeak form of his name that never failed to alert him. He didn't appear.

Frowning, Sherie made camomile tea and walked outside in her bare feet to sit at the wrought iron table. When she'd first got Marquis, she'd intended to keep him as a house cat, so afraid was she of anything happening to him, but he'd showed such determination to get outside, and displayed such obvious joy in bounding after insects and stray twigs that she'd installed a cat flap and made herself live with the constant low level dread that he would be run over.

Three years on, he did not seem to stray out into Reading Street but stayed within the building's grounds or hopped through the fence to the gardens further along the road. Sherie was relaxed about him now. He liked to go out and roam but he usually appeared moments after she did.

As she sat, watching the bushes for signs of movement, her neighbour came across the lawn with a glass in her hand. Diane Wilson had bare feet too – she was wearing a long stripy summer dress, with an oversized cardigan. As she got nearer, Sherie saw she looked as tired as Sherie felt.

'How are you?' she called out politely.

Diane Wilson shrugged. 'Same old, same old.' She stopped in front of Sherie. The glass contained ice-cubes and mint leaves and what looked like tonic. Mixed, Sherie would hazard from the way Diane was moving, with a hefty dose of spirit.

'I don't suppose you've seen my cat?'

Diane shook her head. 'He was out here this morning. Trying to catch a sparrow.' She took a mouthful of her drink. 'He missed it!'

'Yes fortunately, he doesn't succeed very often,' Sherie smiled. 'When he was younger he used to bring in field mice, but he seems to have calmed down as he's got older.'

Diane nodded slowly as if Sherie had said something erudite. 'I like cats. Sometimes he comes in my kitchen – your Marquis.'

'Does he?' Sherie asked, surprised Diane remembered his name. She felt a small pang. 'What does he do?'

'Nothing really. Sits and watches me. I like that. I give him a little bit of ham ...'

'Oh, please don't give him too much,' Sherie was immediately anxious. 'It's too salty – cats shouldn't ...'

'Only a tiny bit. He tried to take it out of my sandwich.' Diane looked pleased. 'It made me laugh. What can he have instead? Prawns?'

'He really eats enough here–'

'How old are you?'

Sherie hesitated, thrown by the abrupt change of subject and the directness of the question. 'Forty-eight.'

'You're lucky,' the other woman was slurring slightly. 'I'm going to be Fifty-six. Fifty-fucking-six – that's almost getting my fucking pension ...'

'I thought you were younger,' said Sherie honestly, wishing guiltily that she'd been truthful. 'So I'm nearly fifty,' she added, in atonement. 'But they say it's only a number.'

'Yes, that's bullshit isn't it?' Diane swirled her ice about and took another swallow. 'It's not *only* anything – it's lines etched across your face and sagging flesh and becoming utterly invisible ...' She spoke in a sing-song voice that sent a chill through Sherie. 'The ageing process,' she drawled, 'has got nothing to recommend it at all.'

Sherie didn't want to hear any more. She opened her mouth to excuse herself but Diane was still talking. 'They say it brings wisdom but I knew more when I was young, didn't you?'

Sherie gave a small shrug. She had no appetite for a faux-philosophical debate with someone who'd been on the bottle all afternoon.

'I must go in,' she said. 'Nice to see you.'

'And very nice to see you too,' said Diane as Sherie stood up. 'My husband is having an affair and he thinks I don't know,' she added conversationally.

Oh no please. 'I'm sorry about that.' Sherie was aware of how prim she sounded.

Diane gave a derisive snort and waved a dismissive arm in the air as if warding something off. 'He's always doing it. They're usually under forty.'

Sherie stood in her kitchen doing her calming breath

technique. She felt like a gin herself after that little lot. Supposing Diane had accidentally locked Marquis in somewhere? Suppose she had deliberately kept him? She went to the back door and called again, banging a spoon on his dish, a sound that had always been guaranteed to bring her beautiful silver cat running. He still didn't appear. Fear gripped Sherie. Then she heard it.

An unmistakeable mewing was coming from the direction of the hallway. Sherie rushed towards it. There was no sign of Marquis. She called again. Again she heard him cry. Sherie looked all around the sitting room, calling, lifting the dust sheets. Then she heard it again and her alarm deepened. Marquis was under the floorboards.

Nate arrived within moments of her call.

'Don't panic,' he said.

Sherie tried to keep her voice calm. 'He's stopped crying now. He won't answer me.'

'He's relaxed now you're here. Probably having a snooze under there.'

Sherie didn't smile. 'I can't believe they left it like this.'

'They were held up today when they thought there was a gas leak but they've fixed it.'

'Oh my god, oh my god!' Sherie clutched at her throat. 'He might have been poisoned. That's why he's gone quiet. Marquis!'

There was suddenly another mew and Nate put a hand on her arm, his voice reassuring. 'Keep calm. We will get him out.'

He lay down on the floor and put his arm into one of the openings, leaning in as far as he could go, making a small chirrupy noise.

Then he sat up. 'What have you got that he really loves to eat?'

215

Sherie thought of Diane. 'Ham.'

'Go and get some then.'

Sherie returned holding a packet. 'This is naked ham from Waitrose – it's got no nitrates.'

'Of course.' Nate nodded solemnly.

'He goes mad for it.'

'Give me some.' Nate took a sliver of meat from her and dangled it from his thumb and forefinger. Then he was lying flat on his front again, down the hole up to his armpit. 'Come on old boy – come and have this.' There was another cry from the far side of the room – this time it was a long, plaintive wail.

'He's stuck, he's lost ...' Sherie was close to tears.

Nate stood up. 'I'll go and get some tools and take the board up over there.' He put a hand briefly on Sherie's shoulder. 'If necessary, we can take the whole lot up.' He paused at the door. 'But I bet he'll have found his way out by the time I get back.'

He hadn't. Sherie had her own arm down the gap, swinging ham and making encouraging noises, when Nate came back carrying a plastic box. 'He's gone quiet again,' she said, feeling sick. 'When did you last see him?'

'I'm not sure.' Nate was fitting a head onto some sort of power tool. '11ish?'

'This morning?' Sherie tried not to shriek. 'He could have been down here hours. He might be dehydrated. Oh please Nate, hurry. Please get these up ...'

'I'm pretty sure he went out.' Nate examined the nearest floorboard and started rooting about in the box again. 'Cats are clever. He'll work it out in a moment. He's just being curious. He was trying to get up the chimney earlier.'

Sherie saw from his expression he'd realised immediately

it was the wrong thing to say but she'd already exploded. 'Why did you let him back in here, then? Why didn't you shut the door?'

Nate frowned. 'Sherie, be reasonable – the blokes were working – they were in and out all the time. Marquis was fine. I'm pretty sure he went in the garden. He's probably only just gone down here.'

Sherie sat on the floor, hugging her knees and worrying about Marquis being scared of the noise, as Nate used the power tool to lift up the many nails holding the old oak floorboards down. His face was creased in concentration as he loosened one after the other, until he could prise two boards up near to where the cries seemed to be coming from. He lay down again, and stuck his head into the gap and used the torch on his phone. 'Come on, old chap!'

Nate sat up and turned to Sherie. 'I can see two huge eyes shining back at me. Give me that ham!'

He got back in position holding out a hand to her as she passed over another slice of meat. 'Oh! Hang on – he's gone the other way.'

Moments later, there was a shuffling sound and Marquis appeared through the original opening. As Nate shook his head in disbelief, Sherie gave a squeal of joy. 'Oh darling! You look like Miss Havisham.'

She scooped Marquis up into her arms, brushing the cobwebs from his face, holding him close against her chest and kissing his head as he purred like an engine.

She gave Nate a wide smile. 'Thank you so much. I'm so grateful. And I'm sorry I was–'

'You were worried,' he finished for her.

As Marquis began to wriggle out of her arms, she carried him into the hall and put him down, turning back to Nate.

'What can I do? Let me make you a G&T. I've got no real food in – I was just going to have a boiled egg –but I'll take you out to dinner. What would you like?'

'Let me put the boards back first. I'm going to shut this door – can't have him going down there again. Then–' He grinned. 'A gin would be good!'

Cross-legged on Nate's sofa, sipping at the small brandy he'd put down next to her coffee, Sherie felt the most relaxed and hopeful she'd been in days.

She looked fondly at him as he sat across from her in the armchair, his feet up on a raffia storage box. He was so kind and thoughtful.

'You don't want to go out,' he'd said. 'You look exhausted. Let's get a take-away and have it in mine where there's some-where to sit. You can bring him.' He'd nodded at Marquis. 'And it doesn't have to be unhealthy!'

But the cat was stretched out asleep on her bed below, apparently worn out by his adventures. Sherie had changed into a comfortable pair of jogging bottoms and a loose long-sleeved t-shirt while Nate had gone for food. She'd insisted on paying but had left it to him to choose and he'd gone to the Turkish at the top of the High Street and brought back halloumi and houmous, delicious grilled lamb koftes, tangy cacik, warm flat breads and several different salads, laying it all out on his long, low coffee table, while she sank gratefully into his bright patchwork cushions.

Coming in from the kitchen with some lengths of kitchen roll, a couple of forks and two plates, so they could eat on their laps, he'd put a bottle of red wine on the end of the table and smiled down at her. 'You suit sitting there. I'd like to paint you. Just like that. Would you mind–' he hesitated, looking suddenly diffident, 'if I took a photo?'

'Oh, I must look such a mess,' she put a self-conscious hand on the hair she'd piled loosely on top of her head in a clip, remembering her make-up had worn off long ago.

'You look wonderful,' he'd said, snapping her with his phone, as she smiled back embarrassed. 'I won't do anything with it. Except remember the pose ...'

He'd been the perfect host, not letting her help clear up, checking what sort of music she liked. Now he was flicking through channels on his TV. 'Have you got the energy for a film? *One Day* is on – with Anne Hathaway – have you seen it?'

She shook her head.

'Read the book?'

She shook again.

'Neither have I but it's by David Nicholls who wrote *Us* – you haven't read that one? Oh, Sherie you'd love it – about this chap taking his family around Europe to see the art.' Nate leapt to his feet and disappeared into another room, returning with a red paperback. 'It's funny and sad and so ... *real*,' he said. 'Here – borrow it.'

She tucked the book down beside her.

'Let's try the film,' Nate's face was alight. 'It's a love story about a couple called Emma and Dexter and it's under two hours. If you get tired ...'

'It's fine.' She'd declined the wine but the food had lifted her up again. If she watched this she could go straight to bed when she got back downstairs and maybe tonight, she would sleep ...

'Great.' Nate got up and again and switched off lights, leaving only the small lamp on in the corner. 'Let's go.'

Sherie, sipping her brandy, was glad she'd stayed. It was ages since she'd watched a film with anyone else but her mother. Dexter, in the story, was now with *his* mother and Sherie felt a strange tug of emotion at the closeness between the two of them.

'You enjoying it?' Nate asked a bit later. 'Oh dear,' he went on. 'Why do they do that? Whenever they show a woman in a headscarf sitting by a window, you know she's going to die. But it's such a cliché!'

Sherie swallowed. She didn't want Dexter to lose his mother. The angry father had already unsettled her. She was so emotional at the moment.

She tried to focus on the happy ending that seemed to be coming for Emma and Dexter. When the next shock came, she tried to pull the kitchen roll towards her without Nate noticing but he turned and saw her face.

'Oh hey!' Nate sprang up and sat down again beside her, throwing a brotherly arm around her shoulders and pulling her against him. 'I've got a lump in my throat too,' he said. 'After all that–' he added. 'I can't bear it for him.'

Sherie kept the paper towel pressed against her eyes but still the tears soaked through. Nate put the other arm round her too. 'I'm sorry,' he was saying. 'I didn't want to upset you.'

Sherie silently shook her head, trying to breathe deeply, to stop herself actually sobbing. She should make some excuse about her hormones being in uproar but didn't want to embarrass Nate or herself further. 'I'm just a flake,' she managed to say eventually, attempting to laugh and making a funny, strangled snorting noise. 'I wanted a happy ending.'

Nate gave her a squeeze and kissed the side of her forehead. 'It's all any of us want,' he said.

Chapter 27

A Happy Ending, Roz had just had to explain again, was not part of the deal.

She did thrashing – slippers, canes, rulers, or on one particularly bizarre occasion, two lengths of rhubarb encased in an unsuspecting wife's stocking – but nothing ... she hesitated as she tried to think of some suitably euphemistic wording to add to the email ... 'intimate'.

Once again, she had intended to put an end to doing it at all, but she was afraid to turn the money down, knowing she needed to earn as much as she could while it was available and still possible. The queries kept coming in and she still had the keys to the house although Charlotte had said this would probably be the last week for cleaning. She needed to get a financial cushion behind her and she desperately wanted to get the straighteners – at an eye-watering one-hundred and sixty-nine pounds – for Amy's birthday. Her daughter had been so much warmer since their talk about her father – apart from the occasional standard hormonal bad mood and slammed door – she had been so much more like her old self.

Jamie had texted twice more – the last time only this morning – but Roz was still ignoring him, anxious not to do anything to rock the boat. Especially since he evidently had no shortage of female company. She certainly wouldn't want to 'share' as Amy had put it.

He'd asked her if she would be around today – either here at the house or the gallery. He had to come to Ramsgate for a meeting and could perhaps meet her for a coffee? She'd felt a moment's alarm that he might drive past but she reminded herself that he wouldn't know her car. She'd still parked right up the road. Just in case.

Roz put her phone back in her handbag and looked at herself in the long hall mirror. 'Darren' had been very specific about his requirements and she hoped she was going to fulfil his vision of a brutal aunt. She had scraped her hair into a tight bun and had on her latest tweed suit and buttoned-up blouse – another charity shop find – teamed with a pair of stout lace-up shoes.

She picked up the print-out of his email which listed his misdemeanours, and familiarised herself with his preferred terms of chastisement. He'd booked for a full two hours so she'd better spin this first bit out as long as she could or her arm would drop off. A lengthy spell in the corner while he reflected on his wrong-doings was probably the way forward. It would also give her an opportunity to change the water for the flowers.

Roz felt her usual mixture of adrenalin, anticipation and nerves, laced with a slight rising hysteria. She remembered a rainy afternoon last winter with Charlotte, watching old films. Charlotte loved anything with singing and dancing and had got a DVD of *Sweet Charity*, which Roz had never seen before. She had a sudden picture of Shirley MacLaine jumping round the bedroom with that top hat and knew just how she felt. She felt a sudden giggle rise in her throat.

If my friends could see me now ...

Fay was glad Elaine was leaving soon for a dental appointment because the woman was driving her insane.

She'd been in and out with queries all afternoon – even though Fay's notes in most cases were crystal clear – and was now apparently unable to decipher a perfectly legible set of figures in order to raise an invoice for storage.

'Yes?' Fay said sharply as Elaine put her head round the door yet again.

Elaine flapped a piece of paper. 'She's phoned up to complain that she didn't start with us till 28th May and we've charged her for the whole month.'

'Well knock it off then,' said Fay, with exaggerated patience. 'Say you're sorry for the *mistake*' – she put a slight emphasis on the word— 'and just charge her for June.' Fay looked at the clock. 'Don't you want to be getting off?'

She watched through the glass as Elaine took down her jacket from the peg near her desk with irritating slowness, and stooped to unplug the computer. No matter how many times Fay told her not to bother, Elaine still did it every night. She worried about electrical fires.

Fay breathed out as Elaine's back disappeared through the door beyond as three of her blokes came in, talking and laughing.

Fay took one last look at the screen in front of her, shut off her computer with an angry jerk of the mouse, and walked to the outer office. 'Where have you two been?'

Toby continued to grin but the other two were immediately straight-faced.

Will spoke. 'The stud farm job.'

Fay narrowed her eyes. 'I know that. You told Len you'd finished there four hours ago.'

Will nodded. 'Yes, but then she wanted us to move some

of the crates from the main house into the barn conversion. So we were a bit longer.'

'How long?'

Will shrugged. 'Half an hour?'

'Sevenoaks to Broadstairs takes one hour and twenty-two minutes at four in the morning and anything from an hour and a half, to one hour, fifty, at other times. Depending on which route you take.' Fay glared. 'Which way did you go?' she barked, looking straight at Matt.

He frowned. 'The usual way,' he said, doubtfully.

'Which is?'

'M20,' put in Will, apparently unfazed by her interrogation. 'And the traffic was all backed up on the A249,' he added. 'Something going on around Detling. It was slow on the M2 until the Faversham turn-off.'

'Hmmm.' Fay looked at them both hard, knowing her rage was misdirected but unable to unbend. 'Just seems to me that these jobs take longer and longer ...'

How much bloody longer? Roz's arm was aching and she was beginning to get a headache.

Darren had warned her he would be making a lot of noise and he wasn't joking. Not for the first time, was Roz glad the house was detached with large gardens surrounding it, and double glazing. Darren was now practically howling.

She was glad she had insisted on a safe word or she would have stopped long ago. As it was, it was hard to keep going when he was bawling and begging for mercy. It was lucky he hadn't pitched up when she was just starting out – she'd have thrown in the towel the first time he screamed.

But he hadn't shouted 'brussels sprout' yet so she made herself keep going.

'Please stop!' Thwack.

'I'm sorry!' Thwack.

'Please don't hurt me!' Thwack, thwack.

'No more! Stop now!' Thwack, thwack, thwack.

Roz glanced at the clock above the mantelpiece and down at the boy-scout shorts of Darren's bottom bent over the end of the sofa. Christ, she was going to deserve this dosh. Thwack!

Darren gave a truly blood-curdling screech of pain. 'Why are you doing this to me?'

As Roz lifted an arm to carry on regardless, she was aware of someone behind her. She was shot through with fear.

'A question I rather want answering myself,' came a familiar voice with an icy undertone she'd never heard before.

Roz swung round, heart banging furiously. Shit, she'd forgotten to put the chain on.

'Well?'

Roz mouth gaped open as Darren twisted round to stare also. Roz tried to speak but no words came out.

'I'm waiting,' said Charlotte.

Chapter 28

Nate was waiting too.

Sherie was not sure whether to be pleased or not to find him spooning chicken into a bowl for Marquis, when she eventually got in after a wearisome journey home.

Geoffrey had been in expansive mood and had spent three hours on something that could have been dealt with in half an hour and then her final meeting had run on, after the client was late.

By the time she'd got to St Pancras, the train was rammed and had ground to a halt outside Canterbury where it had lingered for forty minutes. Sherie had been looking forward to a long, hot bath and an early night.

She'd felt a bit uncomfortable with Nate since crying all over him. Something had shifted and he was now behaving as if they were closer than they were. Sherie, mindful of the weirdness of Greg – who had sent one final, defiant 'bitch' and then gone quiet – did not want to give him the wrong impression, but was also chiding herself for imagining that Nate – seventeen years her junior – would be interested anyway.

'I thought I'd just check if you were back in case His Highness was peckish,' he said now, looking up from putting the pot of cooked meat back into her fridge. He was wearing jeans and a loose linen shirt. He had a tan and his curls looked particularly blonde as if they'd been bleached by the sun. Sherie pictured him on a surfboard, sending the hearts of teenage girls into overdrive.

'That was very kind of you.'

Nate grinned. 'Rough day? Shall I make you a gin?'

'I think I'll just have a cup of tea.'

'OK.'

'But you have one if you want,' Sherie added hastily. 'Help yourself!' Nate had been hugely helpful while the work was being done. Letting the builders in and keeping an eye on Marquis. It was the least she could do.

'Are you pleased with the fire?' He put ice-cubes into one of her tall glasses.

'Very. Want to see it in action?'

She carried her cup into the sitting room and set it down on the low table next to the sofa. 'We'll be sweltering but I'll show you.'

She crouched down and removed the grate at the bottom of the fire to reveal a gas tap, reaching above her for matches. 'Look at this!'

She sat on the sofa, her back against one arm, legs stretched out long-ways, aching feet propped on the cushions. Nate sat in the big chair. Both watched the gas flames flickering – still blue-tinged – through the mock coals. 'Need to give it a few minutes to warm up before it looks truly authentic,' she said. 'But it ends up like the real thing, if we just wait.'

'I'm in no rush.'

They sat quietly for a moment, both looking at the fire.

There was a chink of ice as Nate had a mouthful of his drink. 'Did you hear them kicking off again last night?' he asked

Sherie raised her eyebrows in query. 'No, I didn't.'

She waited, then smiled. 'Well go on then – spill the gossip.'

'Oh, the usual – she was outside crying. I could hear his voice – sounded like he was trying to placate her. I think he got her to go back inside for a while and then I looked out of the window and saw her standing by the gates. Like she was waiting for a taxi or something. I heard their front door slam. But whether that was her coming back in, or him coming out, who knows. I was watching something by then and had lost interest.'

'I haven't seen her since we spoke on Floorboards Day.'

Nate laughed. 'An adventure never to be forgotten.' He hesitated, then said: 'Actually I've been giving her a wide berth. Since she came on to me.'

'Did she? Really?'

'She was drunk. Asked me to help her change a spotlight in her kitchen she couldn't reach. Then was extremely fulsome in her thank-yous. It was all a bit embarrassing.'

Sherie was surprised to find herself pierced with the same sort of pang she'd felt when Diane had told her Marquis went in her kitchen.

'She's a good-looking woman,' she said uncomfortably.

'Not my type.' He paused. 'I tried to be tactful. I told her I had a strict moral code about married women.'

There was a pause. 'I feel sorry for her,' Sherie said eventually. 'I think her husband is unfaithful.'

'Who knows.' Nate sounded as if he didn't much care. 'Maybe she's driven him to it. I find drunk women quite difficult to deal with.'

Sherie bristled slightly. 'Only women? What about drunk men?'

'Oh, I don't like them either. But it was my frequently-smashed mother who made my teenage years a misery. So that's left me with a particular prejudice I suppose.' Nate shrugged.

'Oh, I'm sorry.' Sherie felt immediately contrite and guilty. She'd had quite a lot to drink that night in the Swan – had he been disgusted? Was him asking her if she wanted a gin, and putting a bottle of red wine in front of her the other night, some sort of test?

'I try not to drink too much,' she said awkwardly.

'And you don't,' Nate said. 'My mother had a bottle of wine a day, every day, and could easily do half a bottle of sherry in one sitting. Then she'd either get argumentative or she'd cry. My brother begged her not to get drunk at his wedding, but she still did. Luckily by the time it had kicked in, he was about to leave and didn't realise.'

'And she's still around?' Sherie asked tentatively, aware that all this had been in the past tense.

'Oh yes. Up in Sheffield, still drinking. Doctor's told her to stop but she doesn't listen.'

There was another pause. 'Anyway,' said Nate with forced cheer, 'what sort of day have you had?'

'Fine. Busy. I'm fairly bushed now. I must have a bath.' She flexed her toes, hoping he would take the hint and leave. 'My feet are killing me.'

'Did I tell you I was a trained reflexologist?'

She stared at him in amazement. 'Are you really?'

'No, but I do a shit-hot foot massage!'

Before she could protest, he had bounded across the room, squashed himself into the end of the sofa and taken one of her feet onto his lap.

She squealed. 'Oh no you can't – I've been walking on them all day – they must be ...'

'Hold on!'

He sprang up again and went to the kitchen, returning with the tube of freesia hand-cream she kept by the sink. Squeezing a conker-sized dollop into his palm he began to smooth it over her weary soles, working his thumbs across her instep.

Sherie started to protest but it was utter bliss. She gave a sigh as he expertly kneaded her tired muscles, pulling gently at her toes, sweeping his fingers round her ankle bone in a way that sent a ripple of pleasure right through her. She felt she should pull away, discomfited by the intimacy, and at the same time wanted to stay there for ever.

'Relax,' he said softly. His hands were warm and strong – working on her second foot now, pressing and stroking, releasing the tension from her soles.

'You *are* good at this,' she murmured, and he swept round her ankle again, looking into her eyes in a way that made that pleasure rocket through her again. Sherie suddenly wished she'd had a gin after all – that her inhibitions would melt away. Where was this going? Sherie was torn between excitement and alarm.

Nate was pulling her towards him. Her heart jumped. 'Sit on the floor – I'll do your shoulders.'

'I'm hot!'

The fire was pushing out too much heat for the July evening but the flames were entrancing now. 'Incredibly real-looking,' said Nate, as she crossed the room to turn it off. 'You'll love that in the winter.'

She felt as if she were ablaze herself. Nate was sitting in the middle of the sofa now. He indicated the space below him. 'Sit here.'

'Oh, I don't know ...'

'I'm good at necks too.'

He was. She hesitated, embarrassed, then sat on the carpet leaning back against him, as his fingers found the knots in her shoulders and upper back. Her heart thumped as gently he moved the straps of her dress down over her shoulders and rubbed more cream into her upper arms, his fingers circling and caressing, filling her with a heat that had nothing to do with the gas supply. Sherie found she was holding her breath, wondering what was going to happen.

He'd stopped massaging now and was stroking her, his fingers trailing across the back of her neck and around and across her throat. Sliding across the tips of her shoulders and down her arms, gently touching her earlobes, and smoothing her hair. Sherie's whole body was touched with tiny fluttering thrills of delight. Her mind was racing.

He leant over her and kissed her softly on her cheeks. 'You are so lovely ...' he murmured. She could feel his breath deepening. Part of her wanted to twist round into him and fall with him to the floor, the sensible rest wanted to scuttle upstairs and shut herself firmly in the bathroom.

He had bent further over and was softly kissing her eyelids, his fingers stroking her face. And then somehow he had slid down and was sitting beside her, turning her into his arms. As his mouth met hers, she could feel herself slipping, melting into him, her own breath coming more quickly. Her mind was still resisting – she really couldn't do this – but her body was moulding into his and his hands were touching, caressing, moving from her collar-bone, gliding with delicious slowness across her décolletage and down to ...

'NO!' She jerked away from him. 'Please don't.'

Nate straightened abruptly too – his hands out in front

of him in a gesture of appeasement. He looked stricken. 'I'm sorry!'

She shook her head, unable to look at him. He took her fingers in his. 'Sherie, I'm sorry if I was too–'

'It's OK. I just can't–'

'We can take it slowly–' He tried to put his arms around her and pull her back to him but she arched away.

'I was just going to give you a hug.' He sounded hurt. She still couldn't meet his eyes.

She got to her feet and pulled the straps of her dress back into place. He stayed where he was, looking upset.

'I want you so much but I won't do anything you're not comfortable with – you're really important to me, Sherie,' he said urgently. 'I don't want to ruin anything.'

She picked up her empty mug. 'Please could you go now? I really need a bath and some time on my own.'

'Sure, but please talk to me first. What happened there? One minute you were–'

She felt her cheeks heat up. 'I know. I'm sorry too. I shouldn't have. I was giving the wrong message and I apologise.'

'The wrong message?' He raised his eyebrows, looking incredulous. His voice was tinged with anger now. 'So you didn't want to do any of that?'

'No, not really.' She saw his expression harden and rushed on. 'Well, yes, I did, but– look I can't explain. I'm sorry I've upset you. It won't happen again.'

He was shaking his head. 'Sherie, I really like you. We get on well, don't we? You've become special to me ...'

She looked away from him again, finding the scene excruciating, longing for him to leave.

'I'm too old for you.'

'Nonsense.'

'I'll be sixty before you're even forty-five.'

'Ah! That's what it's about!' He looked relieved, smiling at her again. 'So what? Right now, you are the most gorgeous forty-nine!'

Sherie again felt a twinge of guilt at knocking a year off for Diane. She'd never told Nate how old she was …

'Fay told me about the party,' he said, as if reading her mind. 'So one day you'll be a pensioner. Shall we cross that bridge when we come to it?'

She stared at him, feeling sick. 'We're not going to have a relationship!'

'Aren't we? I'm sad about that. And out of interest, why not?'

'I've told you.'

Nate gazed at her. 'I don't care about how old you are.'

Sherie made herself look into his eyes and tried to speak firmly although her voice was shaky. 'I'm not looking for a relationship. I like being on my own.'

'Is that why you were on a dating site?'

Sherie felt herself flush. 'I'm not any more,' she said tightly.

Nate sighed. 'When I said I really like you, I was playing it cool.' He smiled at her, as if willing her to smile back.

She held herself rigid, unable to speak.

'The truth is, I've got it bad – I think about you all the time – I look forward to seeing you all day. I've been trying to get up the courage to let you know.' He held out his hands again. 'I can't be any more honest than this – I'm in love with you, Sherie.'

'No!' She shook her head wildly.

Nate's voice was calm. 'Yes, I'm afraid I am.'

She willed her voice not to break. 'Well you wouldn't be if you knew everything.'

'Try me.'

He came closer to her again, looking into her face. 'There's nothing you could tell me that would affect how I feel about you. Will you just let me in, please?'

She turned away from him, feeling as if her heart would fracture. 'I'm tired, Nate. I need you to go now. Please.'

'OK.' He nodded slowly. Pushing his feet back into the battered leather mules he'd discarded earlier. Picking up his glass and carrying it to the kitchen. She waited in the hallway, trying to hold herself together until he'd gone.

He touched her briefly on the shoulder as he went past, opening the front door and turning to regard her sadly. 'Can I see you tomorrow?'

She looked back at his hurt, puzzled expression and hated herself.

'I don't think so.'

Chapter 29

After all the weeks of playing the strict headmistress, Roz felt like a disgraced schoolchild. She could actually feel her knees shaking as she waited for Charlotte to open the front door. Charlotte had told her sharply to post the keys from the second house through her letter box but it seemed cowardly not to ring on the bell.

Roz cringed with fresh horror and shame as she recalled the previous day and Charlotte's expression as Darren scuttled away down the drive while she, Roz, tried desperately to explain, knowing there was nothing she could say that made what she had done all right.

'I trusted you,' Charlotte had said coldly, waiting stiffly while Roz gathered her things and left the house. 'Imagine if the clients had been with me!'

Roz didn't want to think about it. She felt sick to her core. Charlotte had been so kind to her – so generous – and she had repaid her so badly. Roz was clutching flowers which she knew were woefully inadequate. She had risked Charlotte's business and probably lost one of the best friends she'd ever had. At a time, she thought tearfully, when she felt she'd never needed her more.

The door was opening. Roz swallowed hard.

'Hello you,' said Charlotte.

'Yes, I was bloody incandescent,' Charlotte summarised, when she had dispensed coffee and tissues. 'But I have calmed down now. Nobody died.'

She looked serious for a moment then gave a sudden chuckle. 'Though that poor guy looked like he might be about to.'

'I am so sorry,' Roz said again. 'I feel absolutely terrible.'

'You don't look too clever, I must say,' Charlotte said.

Roz wiped her eyes. 'I couldn't sleep. And then when I eventually did, Sherie called at some ungodly hour on her way to yoga.'

'Is she OK?' Charlotte asked, sounding concerned. 'She seemed quite stressed when I phoned about the balloons.'

Roz shook her head. 'I don't know. We haven't spoken for ages. I couldn't really work out why she was calling and I was a bit distracted myself because of all this ...'

'So,' said Charlotte. 'Tell me. For the money, you said. Are things that bad?'

Roz nodded. 'I've tried to economise. But I just don't earn enough.' She put her head in her hands. 'And there are no more hours for me. Oh Charlotte, it's all a mess and I feel so ashamed. I suppose it was Jamie who tipped you off, wasn't it? Probably cross because I've been ignoring his texts ...'

'Of course Jamie didn't tell me,' Charlotte said, when she had given Roz another tissue. 'I was driving a client around a few different houses and I saw your whipping boy going in. I didn't know if you were there – I couldn't see who had opened the door. I thought I'd better come back as soon as I was on my own and check it out–' Charlotte stopped. Then she stared. 'You mean he *knew*? Oh bloody hell, does he–?'

'No, no,' Roz shook her head, sniffing. 'He's not a client! But he found out ...'

She told Charlotte the story. Charlotte was clearly having

trouble keeping a straight face. 'Oh my word,' she said when Roz had finished. 'I wasn't going to drink today, but I think I now need a glass of rosé ...'

Roz didn't dare have any. She had the car with her and still felt wobbly but Charlotte poured herself a generous glass full and got out some pretzels.

'Jamie likes you a lot,' she said, when she was halfway down the drink. 'He must do if he's still keen after going through all that!' She laughed. 'Why are you playing hard to get?'

'He's got a girlfriend.'

Charlotte frowned. 'Not what he told me.'

'Well according to his daughter, there's a string of them. Including one who was in meltdown because he was out with me! I can't be getting involved with that. And anyway I don't want to do anything to upset Amy – we're getting on so much better since I've come clean about her father.'

Charlotte looked at Roz thoughtfully, when she'd finished explaining. 'I always wondered if her dad was married. You are such a dark horse ... What else don't I know about you?'

'Nothing.' Roz shook her head and looked up at the clock above the Aga. 'I must go – I need to buy something for dinner.'

Charlotte topped up her glass. 'Yep, I need to get something out of the freezer. Joe's at football – he always comes home ready to plough his way through the entire fridge.'

She walked with Roz to the front door. 'Despite the circumstances, it's lovely to catch up with you – we haven't had a proper chat for ages. I miss that ...'

As she hugged Roz goodbye, she pressed the set of keys Roz had returned, back into her hand. 'The other house will be officially under offer in the next couple of days, but this one still needs looking after.'

Roz looked at her with tears in her eyes. 'I don't deserve you. But thank you. And I promise, I won't ever–'

Charlotte nodded, interrupting her. 'I know you won't.'

Two hours later, Charlotte looked in exasperation at her husband. 'There must be something she can do.'

Roger sighed. 'Well if there is, I'm not the one to ask. I'm the in-house lawyer – I don't employ anyone. And even if I did, your friend Roz is a lovely woman but what skills can she bring to a wealth management company?'

Charlotte took a mouthful of wine. 'It's just not fair, she *is* lovely and she works hard and she's doing the best she can and she's a single mother and she can't make ends meet. I want to help her ...'

'Well you give her a job then.'

'I have – you know I have – she's doing the cleaning and flowers for me but she needs more ...'

Charlotte wondered wildly about hiring a work space for Roz – from what she had said, there were no end of men willing to pay good money to have the living daylights beaten out of them. Maybe Roz needed to rent a proper room and kit it out accordingly. Perhaps she should start a business with her. Employ this friend Melody to manage it?

But she had felt Roz's discomfort and shame. Melody might thrive on it – and Charlotte, having heard the rates charged in ratio to the energy expended, could see the appeal – but Roz wasn't natural dominatrix material. She was shy and genteel – into obscure plays and fine art ...

'Would she even want to drive to Ashford every day?' Roger asked.

Charlotte shrugged, thinking about what Roz had told her – about the headmaster who'd lied about his wife. She'd had enough alcohol to feel reckless – to want to push at the boundaries of risk. Roger was sitting opposite her at the kitchen table. Joe had eaten vast quantities of moussaka and garlic bread and repaired to the sofa and that ghastly comedian on TV who Charlotte had seen making jokes about dead Grannies and blocked toilets. Every now and again, she heard her son hoot with laughter.

'He can turn that rubbish off now,' continued Roger. 'I want to see the news.'

'Have you been in touch with Hannah?'

'When?'

It was the wrong answer. Charlotte's stomach flipped over.

'Any time,' she said sharply. 'Any bloody time at all since you promised me you'd never be in touch with her again?'

Roger looked immediately both wary and confused. 'Where has this come from?'

'Have you?' She glared.

Roger gazed steadily back at her. 'Yes – once.'

'When?'

'About six months ago.'

Charlotte's stomach twisted again. Was that when he'd first started looking shifty? As if he had something to hide?

Roger went on: 'She got in touch with me through Linked-in.'

'I bet she fucking did.'

'She just said she was saying hi.'

'Yeah right,' said Charlotte hotly. 'She wants you back! I knew there was something going on–'

Roger shook his head vigorously. 'She's married with a baby! She came across me when she was looking for someone else.'

'Bollocks!' Charlotte's voice was scathing.

'Well maybe. But whatever. She sounded very happy and she's not—'

'Where? Where is she?' Charlotte heard the shrill note in her voice and hated him.

'York.'

'Oh.' Charlotte exhaled. 'Why didn't you tell me before?'

Roger sighed too. 'Because I knew it would upset you and there was no point doing that. She's miles away and I wouldn't be interested if she was next door.'

'Really?'

'Really.' He pulled a face. 'We've been through all this a million times. Yes, I was flattered and yes, I got a bit carried away, but it's firmly in the past and I will never, ever, do anything like that again.' Roger took her hand. 'You do know that, don't you?'

Charlotte felt suddenly very tired and filled with emotion.

'I suppose so.'

'Love you.' Roger was still holding her hand. As she wiped away a tear, he gave her a light, playful punch on the arm – an old gesture of affection that made her want to cry more. 'Come on!'

'I still feel like there's something you're not telling me.'

'There is – what I've bought you for the rest of your birthday present. Can't wait to see your face!' He smiled at her.

She gulped and finished her last mouthful of wine. Roger rose and put their empty glasses next to the sink. He looked back at Charlotte as he opened the dishwasher. He hesitated for a moment and then his voice was serious.

'Char – are you OK? I'm worried about you.'

Chapter 30

'**Y**ou look very worried'

The nurse is older than me, with a tired, kind face. She is keen to know what sort of 'support' I have in place – probably because she can see I have been crying. After each stage of the pre-op assessment she attempts to be reassuring. My blood pressure is good and my pulse normal.

She takes swabs from my nostrils and armpits, measures me and stands me on the scales. I have lost weight. Once this would have been a bonus – now I worry that it's a sign that things are even worse than they think.

'I expect you've been finding it hard to eat,' says the nurse. 'But you need to try. It's important to keep your strength up.'

I feel sick all the time – food feels alien in my mouth. The party talk we had about duck rillettes with beetroot cream, made my throat close up.

Another nurse – the nice, specialist breast cancer one called Anita – is going to talk to me now about after-care. She has already given me leaflets to read about Macmillan nurses and the risks of lymphedema and what financial help might be available. I can't bear to look at any of them. There are too many photos of women in headscarves.

It will be OK, says the tired, kind nurse says at the end of her bit. 'You'll feel better when it's done.'

I can't imagine ever feeling better again …

Chapter 31

'Got him!'

Fay slapped her hand on the desk in angry triumph, before raising her head. Len was leaning in the doorway looking at her quizzically as she jabbed at her keyboard some more.

'Is there a problem?'

'Yes, Len, I think there is. And now you are here, you can help solve it.' Fay gave him a tight smile. 'Why was Matthew sent on his own to Dartford?'

'Because there was no need for anyone else to go. We were dropping off fifty-eight boxes of books from storage – he could lift each one on his own – and we're short on bodies.'

'We're going to be shorter still when we've got rid of him.'

Len walked further into the room and stood in front of her desk. 'And why would we want to do that?'

'Because he's taking us for a pair of fools. Nearly four hours to get back from this side of the tunnel? Is he having a laugh? Tried to tell me the traffic was slow. Does he think I was born yesterday? I've got his card here from the van. Do you know why he took that long?'

'I have no idea,' said Len calmly.

'Well you should have – you're his manager.'

Len nodded. 'But not a mind-reader.'

'Get him in here.'

'Talk to me about it first.'

Fay jabbed a finger at her screen. 'There was nothing wrong with the traffic at all – he spent over two hours parked up at the Medway services. It's all here.' She tapped at the glass with a red fingernail. 'And he wasn't even due a statutory bloody break!'

'OK I'll go and speak to him.'

'He's there!' Fay sprang to her feet and crossed the room and poked her head into the room beyond. 'Matthew!'

The young man looked round from where he was taking stuff out of his locker and looked at her uneasily.

'In here a minute, please.'

Fay strode back to her desk and sat down again. The young man stood just inside the door, frowning.

'I've just downloaded the data from your driver card.' Fay told him. 'Far from being stuck in traffic as you tried to tell me you were, the vehicle was actually completely stationery at Farthing Corner. What were you doing there for two hours? Eating your body weight in all-day breakfast? Meeting someone for a shag?'

She heard Len's disapproving intake of breath but she ploughed on.

'Or perhaps it was the same as whatever you were doing when you and Will took all afternoon to drive sixty miles? Got another little job going on the side, have you? You told me heavy traffic that time too.'

'It was heavy,' Matt said hesitantly. 'You can look at the card – we were moving slowly for miles.'

'Don't worry, I intend to. But you weren't moving today, were you?' Fay said with low menace. 'So what were you doing at the services? Two hours is a bloody long slash-stop.'

Matt looked uncomfortable and muttered something.

'What? Say that again!'

'I was asleep. I felt really tired, and my eyes were drooping and so–'

'Asleep?' Fay's voice was scathing. 'At three in the afternoon? Is that what I pay you for? I suppose you're going to tell me *the baby* kept you awake. You're not the first person to have a family you know, Matthew. If you can't hack it–'

'We'll have a chat about the best way we can support you–' Len cut across her diatribe and put a hand on the young man's back and another on his shoulder, turning him and propelling him out of the room. 'Come with me …'

He looked back briefly at Fay. 'I'll deal with this now.'

Fay stared, outraged, as Len went out and shut the door behind him.

Fuming, she turned back to the screen, clicking away from the driver data and onto the page she'd had open before. She brought her hand down hard again, her palm crashing against the desk.

'Fuck it!' She pushed the keyboard away from her in a sharp, furious gesture. 'You sperm-spraying bastard.'

She was still seething when Len returned. 'You undermined me!'

Len crossed the room and lowered himself into the opposite chair with irritatingly measured movements. 'I could say the same,' he observed without rancour. 'You tell me I'm his manager and then you wade in yourself.'

'We're not a bloody charity,' she snapped.

'No. We are a family-run business with – I trust, or I don't want to be part of it – a caring and responsible attitude to our staff.' Len looked at her steadily. 'That little baby was in A&E at 4 a.m. this morning. Matthew is exhausted. He shouldn't be driving at all. I've suggested he has tomorrow off and we see him here again on Monday and if necessary, he can do some office work for a day or two or be in the stores.'

Fay started to speak but Len carried on over her.

'He's a good lad. He came to work after two hours sleep and he feels terrible. But actually he did the right thing. Did you want him to carry on and crash?'

'I wanted him to tell me the truth!' said Fay angrily. 'He should have said something earlier if he was that tired.'

'Yes, because you're so approachable.'

Fay's eyes narrowed. 'I'm a good boss, you know I am.'

'Usually yes.' Len said. 'But right now you're being a cow!'

Fay stared at Len in disbelief. 'How fucking dare you!'

'I dare because you know it's true. The way you were being to him was bordering on bullying – you've been bloody unpleasant ever since he and Lisa had that baby ...'

Fay stood up. 'That is not right!'

'It is.'

Fay glowered at him. 'I asked him where he'd been,' she said, furiously. 'He should have come clean straightaway.'

'Yes,' agreed Len, unmoved. 'I told him to do that next time.'

'There'd better not be one.' Fay said coldly, sitting down again and picking up her glass of water.

'I also told him,' continued Len, looking her in the eye, 'that you were upset about something else, which is why you reacted like that, and that your bark is much worse than your bite. I said that by the time he and Lisa come to your party on Saturday, you will have forgotten all about it.'

Fay glared at him. 'I won't and I am not upset!'

'I know you are. But just because you're hurting, you don't take it out on everybody else.'

Fay shifted in her chair. 'What the fuck are you talking about?'

Len looked back at her, still unruffled. 'I know everything, Fay. And I know how hard it must be. I've not said anything before, because you've been grieving but it's about time you moved on now. Time to walk back out into the sunshine, Kiddo.' He smiled at her. She stared back stony-faced.

Len said more gently: 'I know you didn't kick Dave out. He left you and I know why.'

'How do you—'

'I've always known. It's a small town – people talk. He talked. Before they moved away.' Len pulled a wry face. 'Which was the only sensible thing he did do, because I'd have been very tempted to take him behind the bike sheds and give him a good pasting.'

Fay felt shaky. 'Well, it's a long time ago now. I never think about him.'

'And you're lecturing Matthew about telling the truth?'

'Fuck off, Len.' She swung her chair away from him, got up and switched the coffee machine on.

When she turned round, Len had positioned himself right in front of her and was looking into her face. 'No, I won't,' he said. 'I'm being your friend. I saw it in the history on your computer.'

Fay jumped back from him as if she'd been burned. 'You've been snooping on me?' She was trembling in outrage.

Len shook his head. 'Not deliberately. I wasn't prying – I was looking for a site I'd been on a week or so earlier. It had a remote-control car I want to buy for my grandson. I couldn't remember the name of it but I knew it had been on your computer after I'd been doing the data downloads. But when I saw that on your history–' he hesitated. 'I did look at how many times you had visited that page ...'

Fay was flooded with rage and shame and sorrow. 'How bloody dare you–' she said again, stopping as her voice cracked. She jerked her head towards the door. 'It's time you went home.'

Len put a hand on her arm. She shook him off.

'Your dad didn't think he was good enough for you.'

Fay gave a snort of derision. 'He didn't think anyone was good enough for me. Only child – little princess – all that crap.'

'He thought I was.'

Fay snorted again. 'Oh yeah?' she said, her tone uninterested.

Len was looking away from her, as if remembering. 'Your dad asked me to look after you. He knew which way the wind was blowing. He'd had chest pains. Was going to go to the doctor when he had time, but you know him – always working. He said if anything happened–'

'And you've been very helpful,' Fay said stiffly. 'But I'll thank you not to–'

'He knew I'd be there for you because he knew how I felt about you.'

Fay stared at him, her heart suddenly banging. 'You hardly knew me – I was teaching in Spain.'

Len gave her a small smile. 'You'd been home for Christmas – remember how we all went to the pub?'

'Not really.' Fay shook her head.

'Well we did. Your Mum and Dad and Jim who used to work here. And I was glad you hadn't brought the boyfriend with you that time because I was able to sit next to you. You were funny and beautiful and I wished so much that I was married to you instead ...'

'Loyal of you,' she said tartly.

Len gave a sad sigh. 'Sal and I were too young. We were never well-suited. We get on better now than we ever did. The grandkids have bonded us together ...'

'Right well, you be getting off then.' Fay sounded deliberately bored.

'Fay–' Len put a hand on her arm again. She let it stay but held herself rigidly away from him, her insides a tight knot. 'Don't let it eat you up,' he said quietly. 'It wasn't meant to be but you've still got so much to feel good about. You can talk to me– let it out.'

'There's nothing to say.'

'You need to stop looking.' His voice was gentle. 'Picking constantly at the wound – it's not good for you.'

'I know.' All at once she felt exhausted and overwhelmed with sadness. 'Don't go on.'

'Talk to me.' Len put his arms around her and hugged her to him. 'I'm here for you,' he murmured, as she felt her control splintering. 'And it's OK to cry ...'

Chapter 32

'What is she playing at?' Charlotte looked around at the white-clothed tables dotted around the pavilion's ballroom and gestured to the florist to put the elegant green and cream flower arrangements on the one closest to her.

'I don't know any more than you do.' At the other end of the phone, Roz sounded as harassed as she did. 'I had exactly the same text.'

'I don't understand it,' Charlotte said. 'It's Saturday. She'd already got out of this bit – saying she had to see a client who was in Canterbury for the weekend. What could be so urgent that she can't come at all?'

'It doesn't sound right, does it?' Roz also sounded worried. 'Geoffrey surely wouldn't do that to her on her party night and what sort of 'emergency' for God's sake? I'm going to see if I can get hold of him if she won't answer the phone.'

Charlotte turned the nearest floral display towards her and inspected it critically. 'Fay's gone AWOL too – I've called her twice.'

Jesus, what was wrong with them? They'd been planning this bash for months and now the day had finally dawned, fifty percent of the party-givers had disappeared!

'I've got to wait here for the balloon man,' she told Roz, waving at Dan, the pavilion's manager, and gesturing to the flowers. 'Then I need to get back home because Laura's turning up. See what you can find out.'

Nate appeared as Roz was banging on Sherie's door. He looked relieved to see her. 'She went off in a taxi yesterday morning,' he said, 'and she wasn't dressed up for work – you know how smart she always is and–'

'And where did she say she was going?' said Roz impatiently.

Nate shook his head. 'She didn't. I don't know what's going on but she isn't really talking to me any more.' He stopped and looked at the ground. 'I told her I liked her and she didn't take it very well ...'

Roz frowned. 'What do you mean?'

'I don't know – it upset her. We seemed to be getting close and then–'

'But didn't she ask you to look after Marquis?'

Nate shook his head again. 'No, that's what's really weird. She didn't. But I've still got her key so I went in last night to check him when I hadn't seen her come back and there were no lights on but there was already food there. So–' he looked upset. 'She's asked someone else to do it.'

Roz looked at him in confusion. 'This doesn't make sense. I managed to find a number online for her boss and I called him – I know he was invited to the party so I couldn't understand why he'd make her work. He says she told him that her mother was ill and she couldn't work for a couple of weeks ...'

Roz and Nate both stared at each other.

'Do you think she's had some sort of breakdown?' Nate said tentatively. 'Lately, she's seemed ... fragile ...'

'She'd have called me if it was that bad,' said Roz,

remembering uncomfortably that Sherie *had* called, but that she, Roz, had been half asleep and taken up with her own problems.

'Look, let's exchange numbers and then I'll get back to Charlotte,' she said decisively. 'Charlotte has done work for Sherie's sister. She must have her details ...'

'Please let me know.' As Nate tapped Roz's number into his phone, he looked and sounded desperately worried.

'I will, I promise.' Roz gave his hand a brief squeeze. 'Text me so I've got yours. And if you see anyone coming in to feed Marquis, see what you can find out. And Nate,' she called over her shoulder as she walked away. 'For God's sake make sure that cat's all right.'

Alison looked apprehensive when she saw Fay coming into the room, announced as 'the storage lady' by Oliver, who had flung open the front door of the family's new home, crying 'What do you want?'

'I want,' said Fay, good-humouredly, 'to speak to your mum.'

'She's in a mood,' confided Oliver as he led Fay down a hall filled with packing boxes.

Fay could see why. Alison was surrounded by half-unpacked crates while children's feet stampeded overhead and an old lady sat in the middle of it all, looking pained.

'Pleased with the new house?' Fay enquired, wincing as a piercing scream came from above.

'I will be when it's straight,' said Alison wearily. 'Your men were very good,' she added. 'I'll try to get these boxes empty for you as soon as I can. We said Monday but ...'

'No rush,' Fay waved a dismissive hand. 'Just give us a call when you're ready. I'll cancel collection. That's not what

I'm here for,' she added. 'I was wanting to know about Sherie.'

Alison gave an almost imperceptible warning shake of her head. 'Come and see the garden,' she said.

'It's got a climbing frame!' yelled Oliver. He gave Fay a sudden hug around her middle. 'Do you want to try?'

Fay smiled at him. 'I might just do that. You show me first.'

As Oliver raced ahead of them, through the French doors, Alison looked back at the older woman. 'Want to put the kettle on, Mum?'

'Great space,' said Fay, looking at the lawn and the mature fruit trees. Oliver was already at the top of a vast wooden structure at the end, with a rope ladder dangling from one end.

'That was all here already,' Alison said. 'It's sort of what swung it. No pun intended.'

Fay nodded, then turned to look at the other woman. 'So – your sister?'

Alison sighed. 'I couldn't say anything in there. As far as mum is concerned, Sherie is unexpectedly away working. She made me promise.'

'And where is she really?'

Alison looked down the lawn at the climbing frame. 'I really can't say.'

'You can.' Fay was firm. 'I've got a pretty good idea already. But I need the details.'

'I honestly can't give you any.'

As Oliver whooped from the end of the garden, Fay looked at Alison severely. 'I spotted her at the hospital. When I was there having a mammogram.'

She saw from Alison's face that she'd hit home. 'So,' she went on briskly, 'whatever is going on with Sherie, you need to tell me about it. And you need to tell me right now.' She paused as she felt Alison hesitate. 'Because,' Fay said, 'I can help.'

'Will I do?'

Fay had forgotten that Len was coming round to take her to the party. He'd been so fervent and adamant about it, it had been easier to say yes. By then, she'd just wanted to pack him off home so she could throw away the soggy tissues and process the whole, humiliating scene.

Now looking at him in his suit and tie, she made herself give him a grin. 'My God yes Leonard, you do scrub up well!'

'So do you!' he said.

Fay knew she looked good. The red dress went well with her dark hair and she'd made her eyes up to be dark and smoky with a lipstick that perfectly matched the fabric and shoes. Fay felt better than she'd expected to.

'I want to drive you there,' Len had said. 'We can leave the car down by Bleak House overnight.'

Fay had shaken her head. 'I can walk there in ten minutes.'

'You'll be in heels and there's rain threatened.' Len had taken her hand again and this time she had let him. 'It would make me proud to walk in with you on my arm,' he explained. 'To dance with you. And take care of you so you have a wonderful evening.'

Now he looked disappointed as she explained. She gave his arm a brief hard squeeze. 'You can give me a lift,' she said, 'but then you'll have to go ahead on your own.'

Len raised his eyebrows. 'Can't I wait for you?'

'I don't know how long I'll be. And I need you to go and tell Charlotte I'll be on my way and to hold the fort. I need you to help her if she needs it. Tell her I'll explain when I get there.'

Fay smiled at him – feeling a rush of warmth for this kind man who put up with her so unwaveringly. 'I will see you there and I will dance with you,' she added firmly. 'But this is something I've got to do first.'

Chapter 33

Fay got out of the car and walked into Spencer, the private wing of the QEQM hospital in Margate. Nodding at the receptionist, she went through the double doors to one side and up the stairs to the ward.

There was one nurse at the nurse's station, looking in a filing cabinet. While her back was still turned, Fay began to walk purposefully down the corridor looking at the doors.

A uniformed figure sprang from nowhere. 'Can I help?'

'I'm here to see Sherie Wilkins.'

'And you are?'

The sister, who Fay saw from the name badge was called Helen Stewart, had positioned herself to block Fay's way.

'Her friend,' said Fay shortly.

Helen Stewart surveyed her.

'I know she's here,' said Fay. 'I've just seen her sister. I know she's had the op and–'

The nurse shook her head. 'I'm afraid I can neither confirm nor–'

Fay decided to plead. 'Look please – just tell her that Fay is here and I need to tell her something. That it's very, *very* important?'

Helen Stewart hesitated, but Fay sensed a chink. 'And then tell her if she doesn't let me in, she's in deep shit.'

Helen Stewart raised an eyebrow and appraised Fay a bit more.

Fay beamed.

'Wait here,' the Sister said eventually. 'While I pass on that tempting offer ...'

She returned moments later and gave Fay a small quirky smile.

'Room eight.' She hesitated again. 'Be gentle – she's a bit tearful.'

Sherie was propped up in bed wearing what looked like a silk pyjama top with the top buttons undone. Beneath it, Fay could see the dressing that covered the top of her right breast. She was pale and pink-eyed, her blonde hair twisted on top of her head in a comb. Fay pulled up the chair and sat down beside her, glancing around the en suite room.

'You're in the lap of luxury then? No queuing for the bathroom with the proles ...'

Sherie smiled weakly. 'Yes, Geoffrey has always been good about medical insurance. I've only ever used it to have a wart removed about five years ago. I didn't expect– but I'm so grateful now,' she went on. 'Meant I was done quickly. How did you find out? I made Alison promise–'

'Don't blame her – I'd seen you going into outpatients when I was here myself. And then I bullied it out of her ...'

Sherie shook her head. 'She shouldn't have.' Her eyes filled with tears.

'She should. I told her why it was important I spoke to you. Why I could help.'

'It's kind of you, but there's nothing ...'

'I've been through it myself.'

Sherie sat up straighter, her eyes wide. 'You have?'

'Nine years ago. It's an absolute bastard thing to happen but you get through. I did and so will you.'

'But you've never said ...'

Fay shrugged. 'I told Charlotte once. But I asked her to keep it quiet. Didn't want a fuss. Still felt a bit strange about it all then. But – it's hardly exclusive. Every bugger gets breast cancer these days.'

Sherie was still staring at her.

'I wasn't going to be defined by it,' Fay continued. 'And you won't be either. You'll come out the other side and be all the stronger. We're not victims, are we?'

The tears in Sherie's eyes had spilled over. 'But they've taken the lymph nodes under my arm. They've taken them out with the lump. I'm keeping the breast but they say I need chemotherapy to be safe ...' She began to cry softly. 'I'm going to lose all my hair ...'

Fay got out of the chair and sat on the bed. She grasped Sherie's hand. 'Ditto. But it grows back. Look!' she grasped her own shiny locks. 'Thick eh? And my eyelashes are better than they were before. Hairs on my legs are a bit sparse but it means I save a fortune on waxing ...'

She gripped Sherie's hand more tightly. 'I will get you through this – we all will. It will be OK. Is it oestrogen-led? What are they saying?'

Sherie swallowed, picking up a tissue from the mound beside her and scrubbing at her face.

'The surgeon said if I have the chemo and take the drugs after, the survival rates are high.' She gulped. 'But no guarantees.'

'There never are – but hang onto the statistics. I'm still here and so is a woman I got friendly with who went through it at the same time. Saw her only the other day in Waitrose – looking marvellous!'

'I still can't believe it.'

'No, it takes some getting your head around.'

'Do you remember that time we were all in Charlotte's garden?' Sherie blew her nose. 'She'd had a barbecue and there was just us left. And someone said – it may have been Roz – that one in four of us get breast cancer now so statistically it would probably happen to one of us.'

'Cheery!' said Fay

'And Charlotte said: 'it will probably be me'. And do you know, I thought it would be her too. If it had to be one of us. Because Charlotte smokes, and doesn't care what she eats, and never exercises and I've always looked after myself ...' Sherie began to cry afresh 'Why has it happened to me? I've already missed out on being married, never had children. I've spent hours in the gym, and drinking organic hand-pressed fucking smoothies.' Sherie snorted, half laughing half crying. 'It doesn't seem fair.'

'That's because it isn't.' Fay was matter-of-fact. 'It's not how life works. You know that.' She raised her eyebrows at Sherie. 'Teetotal vegans drop dead with lung and liver cancer, while old fuckers on forty fags and a bottle of whisky go on for ever. Don't wind yourself up with that one.'

'I keep thinking I've done something wrong.' Sherie gave a half sob.

Fay was still holding her hand. 'You've been unlucky. Like I was. I went into an early menopause and was mainlining HRT. That might have caused it. I was overweight for a while too – was it that? Or the fact that I smoke or drink too much red wine? I don't know and I don't care. I got it, and I said I'd do anything I was told to, to get rid of it again. I wasn't interested in why – just what was going to happen to put it right.'

'You shouldn't be smoking still, then.' Sherie sniffed and frowned.

'Of course I shouldn't. Or drinking, probably. But–' Fay stopped. 'I've had some real shit go down in the last ten years,' she said, after a moment. 'I want to enjoy life.'

'But–'

'But, actually, I've already decided I'm having my last fag on my fiftieth. Then I'm quitting. You can't get away with things in the same way when you're older – I know that. Though don't quote me back at myself,' she added reprovingly. 'And don't nag me!' Fay looked at her sternly. 'Or I won't.'

Sherie gave a small smile. 'You sound like my nephew Oliver.'

'I like him,' said Fay. 'Saw him earlier.'

'He *is* honoured!' Sherie smiled some more. 'I love him to bits ... Fay,' she went on uncertainly. 'Did you *never* want children?'

Fay was saved by Helen Stewart bustling into the room. 'Nice to see you looking a bit brighter,' she said to Sherie. 'I just need to check that drain ...'

'Need to make a phone call,' Fay took the opportunity to shoot out into the corridor. Her heart was pounding as she dialled. She'd recognised the desperation in Sherie's eyes. The fear and disbelief and something else. The same emotion that had filled her nine years previously when she'd sat in a small white room and been told that the thickening in her armpit wasn't a gland after all, that the slightly misshapen look to her left breast wasn't in her imagination. That now she really could kiss goodbye to all her hopes and dreams.

She'd expected to feel misery and rage but the feeling that had flooded her and never really gone away, was shame ...

Roz was glad she'd put comfort above style and was wearing flat sandals with her long, colourful dress, as she took the stairs two at a time and almost sprinted along the corridor. Behind her, Charlotte had taken her heels off and was puffing behind her in bare feet.

Fay appeared in front of her, standing in a doorway. 'In here.'

Roz shot past her, gazing aghast at her friend. 'Oh Sherie – why didn't you say?'

'I don't know – I didn't want to believe it – it was like if I said nothing to anyone, it might not be real ...'

'But going through all this on your own–' Roz sat on the edge of the bed and took Sherie's hand. 'When did you tell Alison? Has she been supporting you?'

Sherie shook her head. 'Only the other day when I got the date for the op. So she could feed Marquis.'

Roz frowned. 'Why not Nate? I went to your place and he was checking on him but he had no idea where you were ...'

'Oh. Good. But no, I couldn't ask him. It's all very awkward.'

'Why? He was very concerned. He clearly adores you Sherie – why not let him–'

'You didn't tell him anything, did you?' Sherie looked at her in panic.

'I didn't know myself then. Oh Sherie,' Roz burst out emotionally. 'I wish you'd told us. We could have been looking after you.'

'Well, we will be from now on,' said Charlotte firmly. 'As Fay says – we're going to be right there with you. Now what can we bring you?'

Sherie shook her head. 'I'm going home tomorrow. I can't wait to see Marquis.'

'And you'll have to see Nate – he's going to be watching out for you – he was so worried. I had to take his number and say I'd let him know so ...'

'Nate is so lovely,' Sherie said sadly. 'But how could I let him ... I mean he could have any number of beautiful young things. He doesn't want to be saddled with an older, sick woman. Who's bald!'

'I think he just might, actually,' put in Roz.

'You might not lose your hair anyway,' said Fay. 'You can try the ice-cap – some women do and the hair just thins a bit.'

'I feel like now I'm going to be an invalid for ever ...' Sherie wailed. 'It's all going to take months.'

'And then, when it's over, you'll be the same strong, healthy woman you were before,' said Fay firmly. 'When the scars heal and you've had all the drugs ...'

'And radiotherapy ...'

'That's not a problem. Takes longer to get your top on and off than the treatment does.'

'And then they said tamoxifen.'

'I take a pill every day.'

Roz shook her head in wonder. 'I'd never have guessed ...'

Fay shrugged. 'Why would you?'

'What about work?' Charlotte asked. 'You're going to have to tell Geoffrey.'

'I have. He kept phoning me. I had to answer in the end. He said he thought it all sounded strange even before you double-checked with him. I still felt a bit woozy from the aesthetic and I didn't have the strength not to tell him.' Sherie looked moved. 'He was so good. He says I can have as much time off as I want – he says to not even think about work – to take the next few months off.' Sherie's eyes filled with tears. 'He said he'd still pay me just the same.'

'Well you've been good to him too,' said Charlotte. 'He couldn't run that business without you.'

'No,' Sherie shifted into a more upright position. 'And he wants to do even less in the future. He was thinking about taking someone else on, even before this. And,' Sherie looked at Roz, 'I've suggested you.'

Roz gaped. 'Oh my God, I couldn't.'

'Of course you could! I'd help you from home while we trained you up – but you've got a good instinct – you'll easily get the hang of it.'

'But I can't talk about art like you can,' said Roz, shaking her head.

Sherie smiled. 'Oh, you'll soon pick that up. Just look thoughtful and talk about 'new layers of meaning' and 'a complex internal structure' or 'a fresh visual vocabulary'. That covers most bases.'

She put on a faux-studious voice. 'He shines a searing light on a hitherto neglected corner of contemporary commodity culture,' she snorted. 'That's a good one. Heard it the other day.'

'In other words, just come out with any old bollocks,' put in Fay.

Sherie looked serious again. 'Oh Roz, please say yes. I'd feel so upset at the thought of someone else doing my job but if you were doing it ... And as I said, Geoffrey wants to step back in the next couple of years – he needs two of us – so you'd still have a job when I come back. He'll pay a decent basic and then you get something on each deal.'

'Fantastic,' put in Charlotte. 'Fab for everyone!'

Roz felt the excitement flare through her. Then she remembered.

'But the travelling – you're always flying off somewhere.'

'Only for a day or two at a time.'

'But there's Amy. I know she's nearly sixteen but–'

'Amy can stay with me,' Charlotte said immediately. 'I'd enjoy having another teenager in the house again.' She smiled. 'I loved it when Bex was sixteen. Doing each other's nails – watching crap television. She used to be obsessed with that terrible series about all those super rich brats getting million-pound parties. We used to get popcorn. It's not the same watching it on my own.' Charlotte looked wistful. 'It was a great age ...'

'That's not how you described it at the time,' said Roz, smiling too.

'I'm sure it was,' Charlotte said firmly. 'Anyway – Amy is welcome with us any time. We'd love to have her.' She looked at Roz and spoke more quietly. 'I need someone else to look after ...'

Sherie gave a sudden squeal. 'Are you lot looking at the time? The party's started!'

Charlotte rose unhurriedly from the bed. 'It's OK. I've left Laura and Andrew in charge, and also instructed Roger to help until we get back ...'

'It was more important to be here to see you–' Roz grabbed Sherie's hands again. 'We all love you.'

'Don't – you're going to make me cry again.'

'I still find you a pain in the arse.' Fay grinned and held her hand out in a high five.

Helen Stewart put her head round the door, raising her eyebrows at the sight of all three of them around the bed.

'Don't worry – we're going now,' said Fay.

Helen Stewart looked at Sherie. 'There's someone called Nathanial here to see you. Says he's your brother.'

'He's not,' said Sherie

'I didn't think he was.'

'But she does want to see him,' said Charlotte.

'Send him in!' instructed Fay. 'We've got to get moving anyway.'

'No!' Sherie shook her head.

Helen Stewart looked sternly at the others and spoke reassuringly to Sherie. 'I'll tell him you're not having visitors.'

As the sister withdrew, Fay turned to Roz and Charlotte. 'Stop him leaving. I'll be there in a minute.'

'I must say,' she said conversationally, when the others had hastily hugged Sherie and departed, 'I was surprised that night in the pub, that you'd been dating weirdoes from dating apps when you had a real-life Adonis staring adoringly at you.'

'He didn't seem like a weirdo at the time,' said Sherie stiffly.

'You know what I mean.'

'Nate's just a bit young.'

'Never stopped me.'

'Are you still seeing Cory?'

'No – he was SO young he became a pain.'

Sherie gave Fay a shrewd look. 'Well when it comes to not appreciating what's right there, I could say the same to you about Len.' She looked at Fay as if waiting for her to explode.

'You could!' Fay gave a sudden grin. 'But we're talking about you – so what's the story?'

Embarrassed, Sherie gave her a stilted account of their last evening together. 'I panicked,' she said. 'In case he noticed the lump.'

'Well it's gone now,' said Fay practically. 'And he knows what's going on.'

'I suppose Roz phoned him on the way here?'

'Yes I think so. She felt sorry for him.'

Sherie shook her head. 'I wish she hadn't. It's going to be really embarrassing.'

'What would have happened if you hadn't had a lump to panic about?'

'Well probably ... you know ...'

'Do you like him?'

'Well yes, he's great but ...'

'Find him attractive?'

'Yes.'

Fay put her hands on her hips. 'Then get over yourself!'

Fay leant over and gave Sherie a kiss, putting a hand on her arm for a brief moment. Then she turned on her bright red heels and swept out. 'You look amazing by the way,' Sherie called after her.

She heard Fay shout 'thanks' and then the murmur of voices outside in the corridor.

A few moments later Helen Stewart appeared. 'Is that right your non-brother can come in, after all?'

Sherie nodded. 'I guess so.'

Nate was carrying a small bunch of flowers and a large box of chocolates. 'Best the garage had,' he said, sitting down on the chair.

'Thank you,' Sherie smiled at him self-consciously. 'I don't really eat sweet things but–'

Nate moved the chair right up against the bed and leant out to touch her cheek. 'I think you can now.'

Chapter 34

'Oh wow!' Roz, hurrying towards the ballroom in the pavilion, stopped in the open doorway and stared. Fairy lights twinkled on pillars wrapped round with ribbons, clusters of shiny balloons bobbed in every corner, flowers and candles adorned the tables set around the dance floor. The band's kit was set up on stage for later – now the pure voice of Adele came through the speakers, the music mingling with the buzz of conversation from the bunches of people already filling the room and standing on the terrace. Beyond them the evening sun glinted on the sea rippling into Viking Bay.

The group nearest to them, raised their champagne glasses. 'Hurrah!' called out a woman in a black and silver dress. 'They're here!'

'Get us some drinks!' Charlotte called. 'Roz, you remember Laura?'

'Of course!' Roz and Fay exchanged hugs with the attractive brunette. 'Where are Andrew and Roger?' Charlotte asked, as a young man appeared with a tray. 'God, I need this!' She picked up two glasses of fizz and handed them to Fay and Roz before taking one herself.

Laura smiled as Charlotte took a swig. 'Andrew's over there with someone he used to teach with at Highcourt, Roger's not here yet.'

Charlotte frowned. 'What do you mean? I phoned him bloody hours ago and told him to get his arse here pronto – he knew I had to go to the hospital – where is he?'

Laura shrugged. 'I'm not sure. He had to fetch something.'

'You're lying!' Charlotte looked straight at her. 'And you've always been terrible at it, so I don't know why you even try. Tell me right now where Roger is and why he's not at his wife's fiftieth where he should be ...'

Laura shook her head. 'It's nothing to worry about – he really is getting something. Something nice for you.'

'Hmmm.' Charlotte looked sceptical. 'Why this late in the day?'

'Something went wrong with it.'

'Something's going to go wrong with him if he doesn't get here soon!'

Fay had disappeared. Roz was looking anxious. 'I don't know where Amy's got to either. I know she takes forever to get ready for anything but I'd have thought she'd be here by now.'

'I'm going outside to phone Roger. I won't be able to hear a thing in here.' Charlotte delved in her bag. 'I'll be right back,' she sang, swiftly kissing a couple who had just arrived, and darting past them back towards the doors.

She went out of the ballroom, quickly past the second small bar and up to the outer doors, intending to sit on the wall outside and make her call. As she went out into the warm evening, she saw a familiar figure on the pavement above her, his back turned. She walked softly up behind him, trying to stop her heels clicking on the concrete. Roger was on the phone.

'Thank you again,' he was saying. 'I thought it was odd – thought I must be going potty as I know how efficient you are!' He laughed. 'No, not seen her yet. No, she hasn't got a clue.'

Charlotte held her breath. Was this her present he was talking about? He was sounding very chummy.

'Yes, I'm looking forward to it ...' There was a pause and he chuckled again. Charlotte's heart was banging unpleasantly in her chest. There was something about the way he was sounding so pleased with himself ... She crept closer. 'Yes, see you soon. Thanks Marion – OW!'

Roger jerked forward as Charlotte landed a punch on his shoulder and then shoved him hard.

'You slimy double-dealing bastard!'

'Charlotte!'

'I *knew* it – I knew you were up to something. I *said* you'd been seeing this Marion ...'

Roger looked back at her calmly. 'Yes I have.'

'For you!' he shouted, ducking as Charlotte lunged at him again. 'It's all been for you.'

She glared at him. 'Go on then – surprise me!'

'Come with me!'

Roger grasped her hand and began to stride purposefully back down the slope to the inner entrance of the pavilion.

'What are you doing? I want you to tell me ...' she protested, heels clattering as Roger dragged her back through the party, greeting guests briskly as he went, then abruptly stopping and signalling to one of the staff behind the bar. The young man, with spiky hair and a ring in his nose, came to greet them, nodding cheerily as Roger handed him an envelope and murmured something in his ear.

'I'm on it,' he said, going back behind the bar.

'What is going on?' Charlotte demanded. Laura and Andrew appeared at her side.

'I've got to do it now,' Roger said to Laura. 'Before she knocks me unconscious.'

'I'm going to floor the bloody lot of you, if someone doesn't tell me what this is all about ...'

Roz joined them. 'Charlotte, what's the matter?'

'My husband has been seeing a woman called Marion,' said Charlotte furiously. 'I've just caught him on the phone to her and—'

'She sorted this out for me,' interrupted Roger, as suddenly the volume of the music went up several levels and people around them began to look at each other.

'It had to be you,' Roger said to Charlotte.

'What the fuck?' Charlotte looked at him confused, as the unmistakable sound of Rod Stewart came crooning through the speakers.

'That's what he's singing.'

'I know! Very kind of you to play him for me, but—'

'And we're going to dance to it ...'

Roger grabbed Charlotte's right hand with his left one and put his other arm round her waist. 'I hope, after all this, you can still remember how!'

Before she could object, he had swung her onto the dance floor and begun to foxtrot, grinning widely as he twirled her around and everyone began to clap.

'How?' she gasped, as he swung her again before executing an accomplished left turn. She could see the fierce concentration on his face as he went through the slow, slow, quick, quick, she remembered from her classes when Joe was small, and took her into a promenade.

'Lessons,' he said breathlessly, as they turned again and she saw Fay grinning from the sidelines. 'Months of them'.

'Wednesday afternoons?' she asked, as her favourite

singer's deep sexy tones seemed to caress them and Roger held her tighter.

He nodded as they moved together to the music. 'With Marion – the teacher.'

'I was panicking,' he said when the last soulful notes had died away and their guests had erupted into applause. 'Because I thought she'd given me the wrong music. But it was a few tracks into the CD. I hadn't taken that bit in. We've been practising for weeks – I couldn't let go anything go wrong now.'

Charlotte had a lump in her throat. 'It was lovely of you,' she said. 'I never thought I'd get you dancing. It's wonderful present.'

Roger grinned more. 'This isn't the present – this is just the trailer for it. We're going on a *Strictly* cruise in January!'

'Oh my God!'

'Yes,' Roger nodded, his face alight and excited in a way she'd forgotten. 'My mum's coming to stay with Joe and we're going round the Caribbean!'

Charlotte gasped again. Roger was still talking. 'We have dance classes every day and past stars from *Strictly* are on board.'

'Oh darling, I'm so–'

'Anton's going to be there and that vicar chap you like from the radio.'

'The Reverend Richard Coles?' Charlotte gave a small scream. 'Oh my God wait till I tell the others ...'

'Fay already knows!' Roger laughed. 'She thought I was up to no good too – you know that day I saw her? She bumped into me coming out of the class with Marion and I thought she was going to lynch me. She promised not to tell but I was worried for a day or two.' He laughed again.

Charlotte laughed too. 'I'm sure she didn't think anything of the sort!'

Roger looked at her 'But you did, didn't you?' He put his arms around her. 'Please don't again. I have promised.'

Charlotte looked at him, shamefaced. 'OK.'

'I love you.'

'I know.'

Roger took her hand and led her into a corner by the stage, away from the others. 'And because I love you, we're going to cut down our drinking and have three booze-free days a week.'

Charlotte was startled. 'What? Why are you looking at me like that? You have a beer every night.'

'Yes – a beer – you're drinking a whole bottle of wine some nights. I'm not having a go at you,' he went on rapidly as her mouth opened. 'Maybe I've caused you the stress. But I love you – and I want you to be around. We need to look after our health – we're in our fifties now. We can't get away with it like we could when we were younger. We'll do it together. Three non-booze days a week – ok?'

Charlotte sighed. 'Only you could announce a drying-out programme at a party!' She smiled at him wryly. 'Yes, we will cut down – but not tonight!'

'No – tonight you celebrate. But I'll have a better time now I've said this. I've been wanting to for weeks. Marion does yoga and mindfulness too – I want us to try mindful drinking. You focus on it and really enjoy it – savour every mouthful – but you only have one glass. And not every day.'

Charlotte rolled her eyes. "Sounds a bundle of laughs."

'Charlotte – it's for the kids. You know Bex is worried about you?'

'Of course she isn't!'

'Yes – she phoned me at work. She'd been reading an article about women and heart disease. She said – this sounds like Mum. Smoking, drinking, not doing exercise ...'

'OK, OK! We'll do booze-free days – I don't mind – but I am not sitting in a circle with you and this Marion, chanting.'

Roger hugged her.

There was a pause. Charlotte pulled back and looked at him. 'What's she like, anyway?'

'You'll meet her later – she's coming with her husband about nine. And I've booked us evening classes. She's starting up in Canterbury from September. Every Tuesday evening till Christmas.'

'Jesus! Don't say that word when I'm enjoying myself.' Fay appeared next to them. 'You got over the shock now?'

'Bloody Nora.' Charlotte exhaled loudly. 'What a day for revelations! Roger – get us both a drink for God's sake.'

Roger kissed the side of her head and set off in the direction of the bar.

'You OK?' Charlotte looked at Fay. 'Do I detect a new understanding going on between you and Len? Have you finally succumbed?'

'What are you talking about?' Fay shook her head briskly. Then she took a deep breath. 'I didn't kick Dave out. He left me. He left me because he'd got a much younger woman up the duff and she's been shooting out kids ever since.'

'Christ,' Charlotte breathed.

'I couldn't get pregnant – and then I went into the menopause early and then I had the cancer treatment going on so–' Fay shrugged. 'And by then Dave had long lost interest anyway.'

'Not while you were ill?'

'Yep. Very important to him to spread his seed apparently – if he'd known I was a complete failure in that department he wouldn't have married me.' Fay's voice was hard. 'I quote,' she added matter-of-factly.

'Oh Fay!'

'Don't be nice to me!' Fay swallowed, then gave a brittle smile.

'Anyway – Len found out I couldn't stop looking at the Happy Bloody Family on Facebook. I can't read the posts but their photos are all there ...' She paused. 'And he's been–' Fay looked uncharacteristically moved. 'Bloody brilliant actually.' She shook her head disbelievingly. 'He says he's been in love with me for years!'

'Ah that's wonderful,' Charlotte said, moved herself.

Fay grinned. 'So, I dunno ... we'll see. But we had a terrible row and he said at one point he was going to quit, and I must say the thought of him not being there every day ...' She pulled a wry face. 'He knows how to handle me ...'

Charlotte nodded.

'Anyway,' continued Fay, 'I felt I should tell you the truth now. On this auspicious occasion,' she added in a self-mocking voice. 'Since it's all coming out ...'

'Yes, we've all had our secrets.' Charlotte looked across the room to where Roger was holding two glasses. 'I drink too much.'

'Call that a secret?'

'Seriously – it's got a bit out of hand. After tonight I'm going to be dealing with it. It's got earlier and earlier in the day. I guess I didn't want to admit that since my closest friend moved away and my daughter left, I've spent a lot of time feeling as lonely as fuck. A sort of inside loneliness if you know what I mean.'

'I do.'

'That's why I'm always trying to surround myself with people – why I crave gatherings ...'

'Roger sent these!' Roz arrived, arrived carrying the two glasses of champagne. His work people have just arrived, he said to tell you.'

'So spill yours!' Fay put her free arm around Roz's shoulders.

'My what?'

'Charlotte says we've all been keeping something in the closet.'

Roz looked at Charlotte in surprise. 'Have you told her?'

'No, of course not!'

'What's this?' Fay looked from one to the other. 'I was only joking. So you *have* got something to hide? Now I'm really agog.'

'It's all finished now. But I'll tell you in the morning – at the hangover breakfast.'

Fay raised her eyebrows. 'Do I know about this?'

'Oh yes, I meant to say.' Charlotte raised her glass to them both. 'It's a fry up at mine. 10 a.m. The full works plus a post-mortem. Laura and Andrew and Stanley are staying. Roz is bringing Amy. You can bring Len. The more the merrier!' She stopped and gave a wry smile. 'See what I mean?'

She looked around the room. 'Hey, we mustn't stand here like the three witches. Let's circulate!' She kissed them both and swung off.

Fay went to look for Len. He smiled as she approached him. 'You do look wonderful.'

'You don't clean up badly yourself, Leonard. Are all the mob here now?'

'I think so!'

'I've got a tab going at the bar when the fizz has finished. Tell them all to just say they're with Sternhouse and they can have whatever they want.' She glanced over to where Matt was standing with his wife. 'What's their baby's name?'

Matt smiled at her as she approached but his wife Lisa's face was set.

'How is Poppy?' Fay asked.

It was Lisa who answered. 'She's OK. Mum's looking after her. It's the first time I've left her – she's been so unwell I haven't been able to. But Matt wanted me to come with him.' She looked at Fay, challenge in her eyes, making it clear that left to her, Fay could have stuffed her birthday.

Fay took a deep breath. 'I didn't realise you'd been through all that the night before, Matthew, and I apologise for giving you a hard time. It won't happen again.' She paused. 'We haven't really got our ducks in a row about paternity leave – I'm going to talk to Elaine about it – but I would like you to have next week off to get some rest and spend some time with your family. Full pay – and it won't come out of your holiday allowance.'

Matt's eyes widened as Lisa's defiant expression slumped. He was smiling widely but it seemed as if his wife might cry. Fay realised how tired she looked. She was barely twenty. They were a couple of kids. Fay spoke briskly over Matt's thanks. 'So enjoy your evening. Have whatever drinks you like. There's some food coming round soon.'

'Well done,' murmured Len, falling into step beside her as she walked away. 'That was decent of you.'

Fay shot him a sideways look. 'Don't think I'm going completely soft.'

Chapter 35

Roz sighed with relief as she saw Amy finally come through the double doors into the ballroom.

Her daughter was wearing the new top Roz had bought her, over her favourite torn jeans. Beside her was an attractive teenager with long glossy black hair and a short sparkly dress. As Roz began to move through the knots of guests to join them, she stopped in her tracks as a tall figure came through the entrance behind them. Shit. In all the worry about Sherie, she'd forgotten he'd be here.

Jamie was wearing a pale shirt and carrying a huge armful of flowers. Roz realised she was holding her breath as she watched him say something to the girls and then weave through the bodies to where Charlotte was standing in a large chattering group. As Roz stood rooted, Jamie kissed Charlotte and appeared to be introduced to Laura. He kissed her too. He put the flowers in Charlotte's arms and kissed her again.

He was certainly touchy-feely tonight!

Charlotte jerked her head towards the stage and walked towards it holding the huge bouquet. Jamie seemed to hesitate and then he walked after her. As they passed Fay, Roz saw Fay throw back her head and laugh at something. Len was beside her. Roz saw him put his hand on Fay's back. She swallowed, suddenly feeling unaccountably alone.

'Mum, this is Lucinda,' Amy had appeared at her side and Roz pasted a bright smile on her face as she greeted Jamie's daughter.

'How lovely to meet you.'

'Her dad's here too.'

'Oh really?' Roz could hear her voice, unnaturally high and false. She glanced across the room. She couldn't see Charlotte or Jamie.

'It's very nice of you to come,' she said, turning back to Lucinda. 'What would you like to drink?'

'Cosmopolitans,' said Amy immediately.

Roz pulled a face. 'I don't think so. They won't serve you anyway. You can have a mouthful of this – she handed Amy her champagne flute – and then you get a coke or whatever.' She grabbed the last remaining glass from a passing waiter, and raised her eyebrows at Lucinda. 'Will your father mind if you have a sip?'

Lucinda shook her head. 'Oh no, Dad's cool.'

Yes – Roz had forgotten. She'd felt a strange jolt through her at the sight of his tall frame and brown floppy hair, and had half-wished, as she saw his hands on Charlotte's shoulders, his head bending towards her ...

Lucinda had politely handed the glass back to her. Amy was still guzzling from the first one. 'Enough!' said Roz, retrieving it. 'Go and get something soft.'

Before the two girls could move, Charlotte bore down on the them, hugging them both. 'Bex is over there – she's really looking forward to seeing you,' she told Amy. 'Ask her to get you a mocktail – the virgin mojitos are the business.' She nodded towards Roz's hands. 'Don't want to end up a lush like your mother.' She grinned. 'Two at once – respect!'

278

Roz shook her head, smiling. 'You having a good time?' she asked, as Amy and Lucinda wandered off.

'I am!' said Charlotte. 'Bloody fantastic actually – and it's about time you did.'

'Oh, I'm fine.' Roz sipped at one of the glasses. 'Just still in a bit of shock about Sherie, you know.'

'She'll be OK. We'll make sure she is.' Charlotte took one of the glasses from Roz and poured the last bit of champagne into the other one. 'Come on, I've got something to show you before the band gets up there.'

Roz followed Charlotte across the dance floor, carrying her glass. Her friend looked arresting in a three-quarter length turquoise dress and bold turquoise and silver jewellery, her mass of blonde curls floating behind her as she manoeuvred her way through the throngs, pausing constantly as people stopped to congratulate them.

They eventually reached the stage, where to Roz's surprise, Charlotte pushed open the stage door and beckoned Roz to follow her. They went up some steps and round behind a curtain. 'Quick,' said Charlotte, 'before anyone notices us.' She scuttled off across the back of the stage, behind the band's equipment, heading for more steps opposite. 'Up here!'

Roz went after her, dodging cables and music stands. 'What is this?'

Charlotte had disappeared above her round the curve of the stairway – 'It's the dressing room.'

Roz came into a small room with two chairs and some jackets hanging in a cubby hole. A mirror ran along one wall. On the dressing table below it, were three bouquets in cellophane and green tissue, tied with silver ribbons.

'From Jamie,' said Charlotte. 'He brought us one each.'

'That was kind of him,' Roz said, as she realised, startled, that there was someone else in the room.

'Happy Birthday,' said Jamie.

'Thank you.' Roz stepped forward and picked up one of the arrangements, dipping her face towards the blooms to hide her confusion. 'I love roses and freesias. They're beautiful.'

'And so are you,' Jamie smiled at her. 'You are all looking very lovely tonight.'

Charlotte beamed.

'Right,' she said. 'I'll leave you to it. I have an urgent appointment with another glass of champagne.'

Roz glanced at Jamie, embarrassed. 'What do you mean?'

'Talk!' instructed Charlotte. 'And then make a dinner date or something. Oh,' she added, as Roz cringed, 'do you and Luci want to come to the Hangover Breakfast?'

Roz's heart sank. This was excruciating. She knew Charlotte meant well but she did wish her friend wouldn't interfere. She'd explained she didn't want to be getting any closer to him while he had a girlfriend. She'd only end up being upset. Seeing him again, she was aware how attractive Jamie was, how if she saw him too much, it wouldn't be enough just to be friends ...

She didn't want him there at breakfast but she could hardly complain when it was Charlotte's house.

'I'm sure Jamie isn't short of dinner companions,' she said stiffly. 'I'd better get back to the party too. Thank you for the—'

'Stay!' commanded Charlotte, moving rapidly through the door at the same time, as Jamie said: 'Please just wait a minute ...'

Charlotte had gone. Roz stood looking at Jamie, her arms

still full of flowers. He smiled at her and her stomach gave a little flip.

'I would really love to have dinner with you again,' he said quietly. 'I had a wonderful time and I've been so disappointed that you've been ignoring me ever since. May I ask why?'

'Because your girlfriend was upset that night. The girlfriend you told me you didn't have. Lucinda told Amy she was sitting in your house crying while you were out with me. I don't want to be involved with anything like that.' Roz was aware how stuffy she sounded, and reminded herself how eminently reasonable her argument was. 'I don't know why you didn't just tell the truth,' she added in a harder tone.

'I did,' said Jamie. 'Caro isn't a girlfriend. She's an ex-colleague who I go out to dinner or the theatre with, occasionally. Usually when she's had a row with her boyfriend and wants someone to talk to about it.' He gazed at Roz. 'Which was what had happened that night. He's an utter arsehole – but she can't see it. I made her a coffee and gave her a hug and she went home.'

Roz was silent, filled with a sudden and fierce longing for him to put his arms around *her*. 'But I gather there are lots of other women too,' she said eventually.

Jamie smiled again. 'There have been a few,' he admitted. 'I have, since my marriage broke up, been what I believe they call, playing the field. Or what my daughter refers to as 'putting it about'. She is very moralistic and disapproving as only the young can be.' Roz felt her own mouth straighten into a censorious line. 'But only because,' he went on more seriously. 'I haven't found anyone I want to have anything long-term with – or who wants to do so with me,' he added.

281

'And there haven't been *that* many. My daughter also exaggerates.'

'Sounded like a veritable stampede the way I heard it,' Roz gave a half smile.

'I wish.' Jamie stepped forward and took the flowers gently from her and laid them back down. Then he reached for one of her hands. 'What I do wish is that you would believe me that I am not some ageing Lothario, I'm just a bit of a romantic – I've been waiting to find someone who was absolutely right.'

'Hmm, well, no-one's perfect,' said Roz, feeling self-conscious under his scrutiny.

'Indeed not – but you're looking pretty close from here.'

'You hardly know me.' He was still holding her hand. Roz liked the feel of his warm strong fingers entwined with hers.

'That's what I'm hoping to rectify.' He smelled of shampoo and an earthy, spicy aftershave. His brown eyes were questioning and Roz felt things shift inside her.

'Dinner?' he enquired, eyebrows raised. 'See how we get on?'

She nodded.

He drew her towards him, wrapping his arms around her and holding her in a hug. She felt cared for, safe, small. It was a strange unfamiliar feeling – one she could barely remember. A tiny panicky bit inside wondered if she dared relax into it, and take it for real, but then he stood apart from her, and pushed back her hair and, giving her one more long look, bent to kiss her, and she realised she already had ...

The canapés had been circulated, the buffet laid out, and the band were tuning up. 'I love these,' said Fay, leaning out to a passing waitress and taking another mini Yorkshire pudding, heaped with beef and horseradish. 'I wonder if they've got any of the spicy sausages left.'

'It's great grub.' Beside her Len had given up on the champagne and had a pint of real ale in his hand. 'I hope you're still going to dance with me later?'

'Might well do.' Fay smiled at him, surprised at how right it felt to have him with her like this. Once she would have been irritated if he'd stuck to her all evening – now she felt a little flicker of pleasure each time he returned to check how she was, solicitous about fetching her drinks, enquiring if she was enjoying herself sufficiently. 'Don't need any of that,' she'd said tersely when he'd said he wanted to look after her. But it had been so long since anyone had cared like this ... she realised she quite liked it.

'Who are you hoping for?' she asked now, as she saw his eyes flick towards the door. 'Please don't tell me there's some ghastly strippogram ordered because I tell you now, I shall be most unamused.'

'Someone made the mistake of thinking it would be funny to get one on her forty-fifth,' said Charlotte, descending with a smoked salmon blini in her hand. 'We had to buy the poor bastard a brandy he was so traumatised.'

Fay laughed. 'Un-sexiest thing I've ever seen in my life. I told him not to even think about it!'

Charlotte grinned. 'I've come to say that I think we should do the speech in a minute. Cos the band are ready to go. When Roz reappears let's jump up on stage and say thanks and do the shout-out ...'

'Where *is* Roz?'

'In a clinch I hope.' Charlotte looked pleased with herself. 'I have been playing Cupid.'

'Well keep doing it to yourself too – I'm glad to see you and the old boy loved up again.'

'Yeah – we're OK. Bless him. He just said to me–'

'FAY!'

Fay swung round as a dark-haired man of about her age touched her shoulder. She stared at him with a frown. Then gaped. 'OH my Lord!'

'Yes,' said the man, as Charlotte looked on curiously. 'It is me Emilio.' He kissed her on both cheeks. 'It is so long since I'm seeing you and still you are not change.'

Fay grinned widely. 'You haven't changed a bit,' she corrected. 'And neither have you.' She hugged him hard. 'I cannot believe it. What a surprise. Where is Jorge?'

'He is in the toilet.'

'Oh Lord,' she said again. 'Charlotte, Len – this is my old flat mate from Spain. My dear friend ...'

Emilio took Charlotte's hand and kissed it. 'Ah Len–' Emilio held out his hand to the older man. 'Thank you for the ask.'

'What?' Fay looked from one to the other.

Len smiled. 'I found his email address on your computer ...'

'Quite the secret bloody agent these days!' Fay spontaneously kissed him on the cheek. 'But thank you, thank you. I am so happy.'

'You deserve to be.' Len kissed her back. 'You're special.'

Propped up against the extra pillow Helen Stewart had brought her, Sherie looked at her phone. Nate was still holding her other hand. 'Charlotte says I've got to add Becky as a friend because she's going to Facebook live from the party at 9.30 p.m. She says I've got to watch.'

'Well you'd better then. Have another chocolate.'

Sherie smiled at him fondly. 'You're not going to turn out to be a feeder, are you?'

'Only to Marquis. Though I would like to make you my amazing Thai chicken and lemon grass curry.'

'I would like to try it.'

'And I do a very fine cheese omelette.'

'One of my favourites.' Sherie gripped his hand more tightly. 'I'm so scared.'

'It's going to be OK. Look at Fay – how long ago did you say she had it?'

'Nearly ten years. But Fay is so tough and brave and I'm just not like that.'

'I don't think Fay is really either – she's just built a tough front.'

'She was so good today,' Sherie swallowed. 'We haven't always got on but she was so kind. Reassuring.'

'She's great,' said Nate with feeling. 'Straight. I like her a lot – and your friend Roz seems really nice too–'

'And Charlotte. They're all lovely. I'm so lucky to have them.'

'I'm going to make you feel lucky to have me too.' Nate squeezed her hand.

'I already do.' She leant over and kissed him. Then turned her phone so they could both see. 'Look. It's starting ...'

Charlotte, Fay and Roz stood on the front of the stage. Charlotte had the microphone and had finally managed to get everyone quiet, helped by Roger banging a fork against a glass below, and was waving a champagne flute at the crowd filling the dance floor.

'As you all know,' she said loudly. 'Our lovely friend Sherie should be here with us tonight. Unfortunately, however, she's unwell in hospital. So we're going to raise a toast to her and we want you all to sing.'

'Loudly!' Fay had a mike from somewhere too and she pulled Roz towards her to share it.

'I'm slightly drunk!' Charlotte grinned at her friends below. 'So I'll keep the next bit short!'

'I'll believe that when I see it!' came a shout from below, and Charlotte grinned. 'We all three want to say a big thank you to you all for coming to share our special evening – it means everything to us to have our family and friends here.' She smiled down at Roger and Laura, and Becky and Joe, at the front of the crowd below her. 'And all those we love,' she said waving her arm again to encompass them all. Roz looked across the room to where Jamie, his height making him easy to spot in the throng, was smiling. He blew her a kiss.

'My beautiful Becky is filming us so that Sherie can see us all,' Charlotte nodded down at her daughter who rolled her eyes, 'so we've all got something to say. Love you Sherie – see you soon – we'll have another party just for you!' Below her, Sherie's sister Alison was making her way through the crowd. Charlotte waved at her.

'Hang in there, Kid!' Fay looked directly into Bex's phone and put a thumb up.

'Loads of love and see you tomorrow!' Roz added, blowing kisses at the camera.

'Now,' yelled Charlotte, 'we're going to sing Happy Birthday on this momentous milestone for us all – our joint half-century ... but especially–'

'Let's get on with it!' said Fay. 'Come on you lot ...'

'For Sherie!' shouted Roz.

The room erupted into a raggedy but enthusiastic rendition of Happy Birthday, Len leading the singing with a surprisingly booming voice.

Happy Birthday to you ...
Happy Birthday to you ...

Four miles away in her hospital bed, Sherie watched with tears running down her face. 'It's not even for another three months yet,' she said, smiling as she wiped her eyes. 'I wanted to hang onto forty-nine till the last possible minute.'

'It's only a number.' Nate had squeezed himself onto the bed and had his arm round her.

'I know,' Sherie sighed, pointing to the dressing on her chest. 'And this all rather puts things in perspective.'

Happy Birthday dear Sher-ie ...

'You'll always be beautiful, however old you are,' murmured Nate.

Happy Birthday to you ...

Sherie smiled at the figures on the screen. Charlotte looked fairly plastered but immensely happy, Fay and Roz looked quite joyful too.

Charlotte was still addressing the gathering. 'So, raise your glasses everyone to Sherie, to wish her a rapid recovery and a wonderful sixth decade ...'

'OK don't rub it in,' muttered Sherie, half touched, half embarrassed. Nate chuckled. 'They love you.'

'And to all of us!' put in Fay. 'To Charlotte and Roz!'

'And Fay,' added Roz.

The guests raised glasses again. 'Sherie, Charlotte, Roz and Fay!' came the refrain. The camera panned round the sea of faces, lingering on the cake – a tall, three-block affair with a silver five and a silver zero, artfully arranged on the top.

'Looks like a modern sculpture,' said Sherie approvingly, as the camera came back to the stage.

'A toast to the Big Five-O!' cried Charlotte.

'The Big Five-O,' yelled Roger and Len. And the chant went around the room on a roar of applause.

'*The Big. Five. OOHHH!*'

The end.

Jane's twenty things you find out when you're over Fifty

1. You're suddenly getting admiring looks from eighty-year olds. Men of your age may be gazing at the young totty, but to octogenarians you ARE the young totty. This may be the time to take your first cruise ...

2. You will also be attractive to much younger men. You are now the perfect age to find your inner cougar.

3. You hanker after a vehicle that is low-slung and shiny with a roof that comes off. Aka a mid-life-crisis car. (You may also take longer than you'd think to get in and out of the damn thing.)

4. Saga Holidays are actually very good value and some-times even drive you to the airport!

5. Sixty is *definitely* the new forty.

6. You can no longer leave the house with just a credit card and your phone. Now you need to remember your reading glasses too. And the spare pair in case you lose them.

7. Teenagers use words you've never heard of.

8. Tweezers are a handbag essential.

9. You will ban all photos of you from social media unless they've been filtered in blur.

10. It takes an hour to get ready for a video conference call.

11. If you need to look good, you make appointments for the afternoon. (To allow for the creases in your face to fall out.)

12. A silk pillowcase is worth every penny.

13. You are old enough to be thought wise, still young enough to go out on the town.

14. You can never apply too much body lotion.

15. Or moisturiser.

16. You start looking at dresses with sleeves.

17. You stop declaring you'd never have "work done" and just want to know how much it costs.

18. No sooner have you got the kids off your hands, the elderly parents start kicking off.

19. You have less interest in "things" and more interest in paying others to do things for you. Like cleaning and ironing. Or giving you a foot rub.

20. For all the jokes about being over the hill, you've probably got four decades yet – enjoy them!

Acknowledgements

I'm a great believer in the old adage: "write what you know", until I don't know and have to ask. I am immensely grateful, as always, to those who patiently answered my questions, made suggestions, told me their stories or filled in the detail while I was writing *The Big Five-O*. A huge thank you therefore to: Melissa Todd, Elaine Ronson, Katie Fforde, Tracy Greenwood, Bill Harris, Karen Hellier, Philip Kenyon, Morgen Bailey, Janie Millman, Rob and Karen Smith, Kay Spittlehouse, Helen Stewart, Des Crilley, Paul Clayton, Tom WJ and Teresa Limbrick as well as the helpful staff at Turner Contemporary: Beth, Lizzie, Kyle and Bristy. My deep appreciation also goes to Mr Anil Poddar and Dr Natasha Mithal – and for far more than any medical queries for this book. I have been helped indirectly but profoundly by Linzi Easten, Aneta Idczak and Denise Martin-Harker, whose collective wisdom on all things mind-and-body contributed in no small part to the manuscript being delivered on time without the usual wailing (#yogadoeshelp) and thank you Denise – and Jacqui Wellbrook and Claire and her team from Waterstones Thanet too – for the fun we have with BroadstairsLit. My love, as ever, to other dear friends and family – I won't try to list you all, but you know – who support me in so many ways. And I raise a glass to the great team at Harper Impulse – especially Charlotte Ledger, Claire Fenby and my ever-lovely editor Kate Bradley – and my agent Teresa Chris. I'll have forgotten someone – I always do – so big thanks to you too. Any mistakes are mine. You are all wonderful! Xxx